The Queen
& the
Shadow Witch

LEANNA RAPIER

Sword and Suspense Books LLC

Printed in the United States of America Worldwide Distribution.

ISBN: 979-8-9903541-0-4

Library of Congress Control Number: 2024910716

To my children

CHAPTER 1

Once, when I was young, I believed the world was as big as my imagination. As I matured, I cast aside that belief. Real life is difficult, and there is no place for fantasy. If only I could get that idea through my daughter's head before she has to find out the hard way—the way I had.

"Earth calling Sammie."

"Get your head out of the clouds."

"Stop daydreaming."

Or, more simply put: "Pay attention!"

Seems I spend my day constantly repeating these and similar phrases.

I walk over to my daughter sitting at the dining room table. Her math book is open before her, but it would appear her progress is stalled due to her pencil being engaged in a fierce battle with a pair of scissors. I hold my palm out for the scissors until she places it in my hand.

"You don't need scissors to complete your math assignment, Sammie."

I lean over her to look at her notebook. She has completed all of two problems in the last thirty minutes.

Taking a deep breath, I say with feigned patience, "If you don't understand your assignment, ask for help."

Of course, I know she understands these concepts perfectly well. She's a smart girl, and math has always come easy for her. No, the problem is her mind constantly wandering to her make-believe world. But I'm trying to practice patience. When I named my daughter Samantha Patience, I never considered that the next nine years she would be teaching me how little patience I actually possessed. Setting aside her notebook and picking up her math book, I see she has drawn pictures of large-headed dogs all over it. One of them has wings.

"Sammie!" I drop my patient tone, no longer able to hide my exasperation. "I've told you a hundred times that this math book is *not* to be doodled in. Your brother will use this one day. I can't afford to have you scribble all over it." Anyone who thought homeschooling a bright child would make it easy, doesn't understand Sammie. "She is such an imaginative, smart girl," my friend said just the other day. "She must be a joy to teach." *Right*.

"Those aren't scribbles," Sammie says in her most offended tone. "Those are Cha-Chas."

"What?" Now I'm imagining some kind of weird dance involving large-headed dogs.

"A Cha-Cha is a dog that has magic powers."

Oh brother.

"I'm writing about them in my new book. You wanna read it?" Sammie is on her feet dancing with excitement or possibly a strong urge to pee. "Please!"

"Why don't you write about something more realistic?" I encourage while wondering where my daughter comes up with these silly ideas. No, I don't wonder. *I know*. I just don't want to admit she is a replica of me at that age—wide eyes as if they can't take in the world fast enough, untamed hair in static excitement, and an imagination as big as the sky but as impractical as building a vacation home in the Mariana Trench.

"Cha-Chas *are* real!" Sammie says emphatically.

Now, I know better than to argue with her when she gets like this. She doesn't *really* think they are real, but when her imagination starts spinning, she tries to convince me until I almost believe she convinces herself.

"I'm tired of math. Can I work on my book now?"

"You haven't *done* any math." I sigh. "Look, do these problems"—I circle a few—"and then you can type up your story for thirty minutes." At least it is somewhat educational. "But, make sure you use the correct fingers—no pecking. And use spellcheck."

"Oooo, you just wrote in the book, Mama." Sammie looks at me with mock disapproval.

I roll my eyes like a teenager and walk away. She gets it from me—her wild imagination. However, I was painfully shy as a child, and my mother worried that I was too withdrawn. My fantasy world was my escape from reality, my safe place away from the ridicule of others. Sammie, on the other hand, is about as outgoing and talkative as they come. I'm glad she doesn't suffer from self-consciousness the way I did—and still do at times—but I wish she had at least a little sense of propriety. She will babble on to some stranger about all her weird ideas while they are giving me odd looks, and I'm turning red.

"You're not still writing novels are you?" My dad's words still haunt me even though they were spoken years ago. "There's no real money in that."

I knew in my heart he was right, but I thought I'd be the exception. With a daughter of my own, I want to guide her into developing a real skill set one day. Yet Sammie seems determined to follow in my footsteps in all the wrong areas.

After lunch, I've forgotten about Cha-Chas, and my daughter's completed most of her assignments. Overall, it's been a pretty productive morning and my mood has improved. I've really been putting off grocery shopping for too long, so we head out in order to get back in plenty of time for dinner. Sammie and JJ, of course, insist on bringing their favorite stuffed animals. JJ's is a fuzzy brown dog, and Sammie's was once a white dog, but now it resembles a balding, gray rat. I want to tell her to bring something different, but I already know how that conversation would go, so I hold my tongue and hope she forgets it in the car.

We make it through all the aisles in a semi-orderly fashion without breaking anything, and Sammie and JJ only fight once, which is almost miraculous. I'm thinking that I am home free—just check out, put away groceries, have a quick dinner, Sammie can read to me while I do dishes, then put both kids to bed for a relaxing evening. If I'm really lucky, Michael will call me today—I'm counting down the days till my husband's deployment is up...and the years of his current enlistment. I haven't told him yet, but I want him to leave the Air Force and get a regular nine-to-five job, or at least a job that doesn't require him to be gone for months at a time. Still worrying about Michael, I file my kids and the cart into the checkout line.

"Careful." I caution JJ who is "helping" me unload the cart, standing on his tiptoes as his stubby, five-year-old fingers nearly lose their grip on a glass jar. "Let Mama get the heavy stuff." I silently chide myself for talking in third person. I sound silly.

JJ grabs the bread, squishing it, naturally, before heaving apples onto cheesy puffs I don't remember putting in the cart. JJ's been helping me select food again.

"Do you like my Cha-Cha?" My head snaps up. Sammie has been rattling nonstop to the poor cashier, and I've been ignoring her until now.

"Nice. Is that the name of your...is that a dog?" The cashier lady keeps a patient smile.

"His name is Tony Cheesecracker." Sammie holds the pitiful gray thing up high. "And he's a Cha-Cha. That's a magic dog—"

"Sammie! The cashier is busy working."

"Oh, I don't mind." Her name tag says, *Angie*. "Your daughter is very imaginative." Angie smiles again at Sammie. "I bet you make good grades at school. What grade are you in?"

"I'm nine," Sammie says. "I'm in fourth grade, but I do fifth grade math."

"Don't brag, Sammie." The line is getting long and the man behind us looks impatient.

"I'm homeschooled," Sammie adds. "JJ can't read yet. He's only five."

"Oh, well I'm sure he'll learn," Angie says politely and gives me my total.

"His name's not really JJ—it's Jeremiah, but he couldn't say it when he was a baby. He said JJ. Now everyone calls him JJ." This is typical of Sammie. Giving everyone our life's history whether they want to hear it or not.

"And what is your dog's name?" Angie asks JJ who is hugging his brown stuffed dog.

JJ gives a shy smile and says nothing.

"His dog's name is Peanut Butter and Jelly Sandwich *the Third*." Sammie answers for him at top volume. "He's a Cha-Cha too. Did you know that Cha-Chas can turn invisible?"

"Really?" Angie is still smiling, and the man behind us is still frowning.

My cheeks feel as hot as a stove burner. *Weird homeschoolers*, I'm sure they're both thinking. As soon as Angie hands me my receipt, I command the kids to hold the cart and shuffle them out the door.

We get home. Unload. I reheat chicken taco soup for dinner. JJ sets bowls on the table, breaking one. I sweep it up while ordering Sammie to get the grated cheddar and tortilla chips. We sit down for a not so quiet meal as Sammie says fifty words between every bite.

"Why aren't you eating?" I ask JJ, interrupting Sammie, who is asking me something about mermaids.

JJ shrugs. "Not hungry."

"Are there boy mermaids?" Sammie continues to prattle.

"Yes, mermen. Eat your soup. Both of you."

"So mermen and mer...ladies?"

"Maid means 'girl.' You have mermaids and mermen."

"What are the babies called?"

"I don't know. They're make-believe. Eat and quit talking."

"Can I be done?" JJ says.

"You haven't eaten anything." I notice his face looks flushed. I walk over and feel his forehead. It's warm.

"What about—" Sammie starts to ask.

"Sammie! Eat!" I shout. Then controlling my voice, I tell JJ to get ready for bed.

"I can't eat this!" Sammie flops in her chair and pushes her bowl. "It looks like zombie guts!"

"Because you let the chips get soggy from all your talking." Actually, it does look pretty disgusting. I roll my eyes. "Whatever. If you're done, clean up your place. But nothing else till breakfast."

Sammie takes her bowl to the sink, and I quickly pile the rest of the dishes in the sink before going upstairs to check on JJ. He's in his pajamas and crying.

"What's wrong?"

"I can't find my dog!" he wails.

"Here's a dog." I hand him the first stuffed dog I see on the floor.

"No! Not *that* one. Peanut Butter and Jelly Sandwich the Third!"

"I don't see him. This is a nice stuffed dog."

"That's Picklefoot. He's stinky."

I give him a hesitant sniff. Maybe it's time I threw their stuffed animals in the wash, although that always sends the kids into a fit. "Does it have to be...that one?" I don't want to repeat the thing's silly name.

"Sammie says, when I hug him, Daddy can feel hugs 'cause Daddy gave him to me."

Oh good grief. I feel JJ's head again, and I'm certain now he has a slight fever. "Get in bed, and I'll look for him. You probably left him in the car."

JJ crawls in bed still sniffling, and I run downstairs, worrying about JJ and wondering where I put the thermometer. I dig around in the car but can't find his dog.

"Sammie!" I call when I walk back in from the garage. "Where's JJ's brown dog?"

"I don't know," Sammie says. She sits crossed-legged on the couch writing in a journal that I don't recognize. It looks tattered.

"Well, I need it. He won't sleep without it, thanks to you. Why did you tell him that Daddy can feel his hugs?"

"Because it's true."

"No, it isn't, and you *know* it." I snatch the journal from her hand. "Stop it! Stop with the constant silly make-believe stories. Real life is hard, and you can't live in a daydream."

"Give back my notebook!" Tears spring from Sammie's eyes.

I put the journal on top of the bookcase. "When you find JJ's dog." I storm to the kitchen and dampen a cloth. Heading back upstairs, I place it on JJ's head.

"Where's Peanut Butter—"

"Sammie's getting him. Now rest."

"I miss Daddy." JJ looks at me with serious eyes that remind me so much of Michael's the day before he deployed when he asked me if I was going to be okay. Of course I lied and told him we'd be fine.

"I know. I do too," I say as I run my fingers through his soft hair. What happened to the boy that used to have a contagious laugh? It seemed to have left him the day Michael left us.

JJ yawns. "Do you love me forever and ever?"

"Of course."

"Does Daddy?"

"Yes." I kiss JJ on the cheek. "I'm going to help Sammie look for your dog. Stay in bed."

As soon as I get downstairs, I scan around for Sammie, but don't see her. "Sammie? Did you find—" I notice the journal is not on the shelf. *That girl!* She's not downstairs, so I run up to her room. A quick glance reveals that she isn't there either. I give an angry growl and charge back downstairs. I'm certainly getting my exercise today. My cell rings—it's Michael. I grab it as I head out back. "Sammie!" I yell right before answering the call.

"Hello, Beautiful," Michael says.

"Michael, hang on a minute." Still holding the phone, I step past the potted strawberries and glance under the picnic table where Sammie likes to hide, but there's nothing but an assortment of sidewalk chalk. I hurry back through the house and into the garage thinking maybe Sammie went to look for JJ's stuffed dog in the car. No Sammie. I walk back into the house. "Sammie!" *That girl is going to be in gobs of trouble.*

"Michelle?" Michael's distant voice comes through my phone. I put it back to my ear.

"Michael, JJ's running a fever, and Sammie's acting impossible today. I'm so sorry. I really can't talk right now." My gut twists into a knot. Phone calls from Michael are the precious few moments that keep me hanging on.

Michael sounds disappointed, but he tries to encourage me. "Try to relax this evening," he says before giving his usual "I love you" and hanging up.

I stand in the middle of the living room for a moment. Sammie can be dramatic at times when she's upset, but it isn't like her to run off and ignore me. Rather, she might fly into a fit of dramatic tears and backtalk about how I am so "unfair." The only place I haven't looked is out front. I step out into the cooling evening and dodge the sprinklers that have just come on. She's not there. Did she go to a friend's? She knows better than to walk to a friend's house without telling me, and she is always to check in by text or phone when she gets there. An anxious bubble starts to grow in my stomach. Not a good combination with spicy soup.

I stand in the driveway as the sun lowers on the horizon. It will be dark in less than an hour. I scroll through my phone and text every friend she has, even the ones she doesn't play with often. One by one, they answer that she isn't there. The sun has hidden itself behind the hills, only its orange rays lingering in the sky. Now I am worried. Should I drive the car around the neighborhood? I hate to leave JJ in case he starts crying for me. Should I call the police and report a missing child? Am I overreacting? She's probably pouting somewhere.

I run back into the house. "Sammie! Where. Are. You!" I tackle the stairs two steps at a time and peek in JJ's room. He's asleep. I enter Sammie's room, checking the closet and even under the bed as silly as that seems. Then I see the journal. There. Lying open on Sammie's bed. She *did* take it. Only it isn't Sammie's journal. It's mine.

I pick it up. I have stashes of journals in my closet I've kept since I was nearly as young as Sammie. Throughout my teen years and early adulthood, I filled them with ideas and stories of my fantasy world. I had even tried to publish a couple of novels in my early twenties, but rejection after rejection left me disillusioned. When I found out I was pregnant ten years ago, I decided it was time to set my childhood fantasies aside and be the adult my child would need. My journals have lain untouched, buried in my closet and dust. Now Sammie has one of them...and she's been writing in it.

I start to set it down when the last words on the page arrest my attention.

Mamas so mad and JJ is sick. I have to find Penut Butter and Jelly Sandwich the third. Tony Cheescraker will help me look. Maby he went to Kalpania. I wish I coud go ther—

The ink at the end was smeared. "Sammie..." I choke on a lump in my throat. *I have to find her.* A heavy tear drops from my eye, further blurring the ink on the page. The world begins to spin and my heart thumps wildly. Am I fainting? I've been lightheaded before but have never actually fainted. Panic attack? I don't know what those are like. I've never had one. A flash blinds me, like lightning without thunder.

I'm standing, so I haven't fainted. However, I am no longer in Sammie's room.

CHAPTER 2

Instead of the cool evening sun filtering through Sammie's curtains, I'm blinking back the bright glare of high noon in the middle of a hot street. But it isn't the quiet street in front of my house, pungent with fresh cut grass as the sprinklers turn on for the evening. Neither is it the busy downtown streets, reeking of car fumes and some burger joint. It's a dusty, unpaved road that smells of rotting fruit and horse dung. I'm in a village, smaller than my neighborhood. The dome-shaped houses cause it to resemble mushrooms nestled in a hollow between rolling green hills. On my left, I'm standing three feet from a fruit cart with flies buzzing around it, and to my right a shaggy pony tosses his head and nickers. That explains the smell.

There's a growing circle of villagers congregating around me staring, their astonishment matching my own. I stare back, making a squeaking noise as air escapes my lungs, unable to form a coherent thought much less speak. The pony nuzzles me as though hoping for sugar, and evidently, the only one not in the least disturbed by my sudden appearance.

"Witch!" A hefty lady wearing a drab, old-fashioned dress shakes her broom at me. "Seize her!"

Nobody moves, save a few that actually back away.

"Bind her, Dallet!" The lady pokes her broom at a heavyset, bald man wearing an apron.

Grunting, Dallet grabs me, pulling my arms behind my back. His clothes smell of sweat and fresh baked bread, causing me to envision an onion bagel. A thin, pasty fellow runs up with a rope.

"Wait, stop!" I finally find my voice. "I'm not a witch!" I struggle to free myself, but Dallet keeps a firm hold. The thin man binds me with the rough rope.

"Not a witch, eh?" says the broom lady, brushing aside a strand of gray hair that's slipped free of her tight bun. "Then how did you magically appear in Oodlesville?"

"You're the one holding a broom," I snap. "Wait. Oodlesville? Did you say—?"

"She has a point, Mailene." Dallet chuckles. "Maybe she ain't a witch. Prattles likes her."

I'm guessing "Prattles" is the pony, who is still nudging me and whinnying.

"Aye, she's a witch alright," Mailene says. "She already has you and the pony under her spell. But not me. I know a witch when I see one."

"Did you say this is Oodlesville?" I'm shouting above the growing chaos of gasps and cries of "witch!"

"Burn her," says Mailene.

"What!" Now I do something very silly. I try to pinch myself because that's what you're supposed to do to prove whether you're dreaming. But with my arms tied tightly behind my back, this proves difficult. The rope is chafing my wrists. Would dream rope do that? I shake my head.

"I don't like the smell of a burning," the thin man whines. "Beheading is quicker."

"What do you know, Jenton?" Mailene whacks him with her broom, making him wince. "You have to burn a witch to kill her spirit."

"I don't know that we need to be doing any killing yet," Dallet says. He uses his free hand to mop the sweat from his reddening head that's baking like a roll under the sun. "We don't know for sure she is a witch."

"I'm not a witch. If I was, I could just turn you all into toads."

"This is why we need to kill her quick," Jenton says.

Well that backfired.

The crowd scatters as a heavily armored horse and rider jangle up. The knight wears a full suit of plate armor with a bright magenta plume on his helmet, and the horse, likewise armored, bears a similar plume, only of cyan. A brilliant yellow sun is painted on the knight's chest plate. The horse stops just short of me, tossing his head with a snort as golden medallions jingle on the horse's armor. At their grand entrance, even Prattles backs away. Only Dallet still keeps a firm grip on me.

The armored man dismounts with surprising ease and lifts his faceplate to reveal his eyes. "What seems to be the trouble?"

"Mailene thinks we have ourselves a witch, Sir." Dallet points at Mailene who is shrinking into the crowd, then nudging me forward says, "She appeared out of nowhere."

"No one appears from nowhere." The knight's voice is not threatening.

"I'm not a witch," I repeat for the tenth time, hoping for an ally. "I didn't mean to startle anyone."

"Of course you're not. I, Sir Lightlee, would certainly know a witch if I saw one." He is speaking loudly for the benefit of the crowd. "Be about your business. I'll take care of this." Sir Lightlee takes the ropes from Dallet and unbinds me.

"Th-Thank you," I mumble before feeling a rush from my head as my vision grays.

<center>~~~</center>

I'm lying on something damp, and my arms itch. I sit up slowly.

"Here, drink this," a voice says.

I'm sitting on grass under a tree on the edge of Oodlesville. Sir Lightlee hands me a leather canteen, and I take a sip of lukewarm water. Apparently, I passed out—a ridiculous thing to do.

"Folks around Oodlesville are unaccustomed to strangers." Sir Lightlee's helmet is off. His horse nibbles at the grass. "What is your name, fair stranger?"

"I...um...Michelle. Michelle Sansbury." I stare at him. He is tall with bronze skin, and dark copper-brown hair falls a bit messy over his forehead above gorgeous hazel eyes. His strong chin is graced with a dimple and a five o'clock shadow. I feel myself blushing and stand too hastily to my feet, forcing me to rest my hand on the tree for balance. "*Mrs.* Michelle Sansbury. My husband is overseas."

"Ah, the war," Sir Lightlee says, also standing. "It has taken many of our best men."

Which war? I doubt we are speaking of the same thing. I put my hands to my head. What is going on?

"Come. You are in need of a physician. Let me escort you—"

"I'm fine. Really."

"In that case, I must be on my way."

"Magdalin. You are going to Magdalin, right?"

"Yes." He shows no surprise. "Have you been to the City of Stairs?"

"Not exactly. Actually, I'm not fine. I need..." What am I supposed to say? *I need to go home?* My son is sick, my daughter missing, and I'm stuck in a fantasy. I scratch my arm, prickled with bumps. I'm allergic to grass. If this is all in my head, imaginary grass shouldn't bother me. "The Queen," I finally say. "We are...she is my...cousin."

Sir Lightlee's head drops. He looks up. "Have you not heard? I am afraid our illustrious Queen is dead."

"Dead? How can...?" *This isn't right.* "She's a powerful enchantress. How can she be dead?" If I really am in a fantasy world and haven't completely lost my senses, the Queen might have the power to send me home.

"It was the Shadow Witch that slew her. The people of Oodlesville undoubtedly mistook you for her because they are oodlers."

"Oodlers?"

"Simpletons lacking in imagination. They only know what's been done and do what they know. I doubt any of them have ever encountered a real witch. Everyone has been on edge since the death of the Queen. Yet, if you be her cousin—and I don't doubt this, for you bear a familial resemblance—then you could not have come at a more crucial time." Sir Lightlee's voice becomes hushed. "But we cannot talk here."

"Then you must take me to Magdalin right away." A dream. Hallucination. Whatever this is, it feels real. And until I can prove otherwise, I have to treat it as such. Sir Lightlee tells me to wait for him, and while I do, I rack my brain. Who could best help me? There are books in Magdalin—a great library. I could search them for answers. Although the obvious answer is I'm planted facedown on Sammie's bedroom floor.

Sir Lightlee returns with Prattles fitted with a saddle. "He seems to like you, so I borrowed him for your journey. Are you well enough to mount?"

"Yes." After a moment of struggle, I finally submit to allowing Sir Lightlee to give me a boost. Prattles isn't more than a small, dapple gray horse, but I don't know a thing about riding. I find myself struggling to stay astride Prattles, either sliding off to one side or bouncing to the other. Not having a clue what to do with the reins, I cling desperately to Prattles' mane, who's thankfully content to follow Sir Lightlee's horse, a muscular creature with a glossy red coat and ebony mane. I'll be quite content never to find myself atop such a beast.

As we wind through the green hills dotted with farms and orchards, I try to survey my surroundings as best I can between adjusting my balance on Prattles. A quick glance behind me, and I can see the White Mountains. Far off into the east, I can barely make out the Ruby Cliffs. And though I can't see it yet, I know ahead is Magdalin, the City of Stairs, and to its west, Port Billows and the Unending Sea. South is the Great Mer Bay. I know every feature of this world because I created it. This is Kalpania.

Ironic, I can't help but think. Here I was scolding Sammie for living in a daydream, and now I'm trapped in a make-believe world of my own creation. Only it's richer and more vivid than I ever imagined. If possible, the colors are brighter and the shadows starker than the real world. *But this can't be real.* I tell myself. *Can it?* Suddenly it occurs to me—I entered Kalpania while I was holding my old journal. Could Sammie be here too?

Sir Lightlee interrupts my musings by calling for a break for supper. He waters the horses at a stream while I try not to let him catch me rubbing my bum, trying to restore circulation. When he comes back, he encourages me to rest on the grass, although sitting is the last thing I want to do at the moment, especially on grass. Instead I lean up against a tree, assuring him that I'm fine. He pulls some meat, cheese, and a couple rolls out of a knapsack, and we eat a quiet meal. I half expect our minuscule supper to taste like cotton as it does in my dreams and don't know whether to be pleasantly surprised or dismayed when it tastes quite ordinary. In fact, the cheese is excellent, although the bread is a bit dry.

As I eat, I try not to stare at Sir Lightlee, who's too engrossed in his food to notice. I created him too. Does he know? It wouldn't seem so. Only when I wrote him into my story, he was a young squire, not yet knighted. I foolishly modeled him after my teen crush, Bradley. He was to be the hero of my story—that was until Bradley broke my heart. Sir Lightlee had matured into a man far superior than Bradley, who, last I had seen, looked a bit rough, having taken on some bad habits and worse friends.

Somehow this world grew beyond what I originally created and not entirely how I envisioned. Oodlesville has also evolved since my writing days. The village had been little more than doodles of domed houses with a few simple lines describing it. My imagination had hit a wall, and I lost interest moving onto something else. Perhaps that's why they became oodlers. I decide that when I make it home, the first thing I'm going to do is write a tragic end in my journal for that awful Mailene broom lady. I shake my head. What is wrong with me? I tell myself again that none of this is real, and each time it becomes less convincing.

"You keep doing that? Why?" Sir Lightlee says.

"What?"

"Shaking your head."

"I...have a headache." Not entirely a lie.

"I'm plagued with those frequently myself." Sir Lightlee pulls some dried herbs from his saddlebag. "Swallow this with a little water. It will help."

His hand brushes mine lightly as he passes me the herbs, and despite that he's wearing gloves, my face grows warm. *Don't be stupid.* I tell myself. I'm a married woman crushing on a make-believe man in my make-believe world. When my very real husband is fighting a very real war overseas and anything could happen to him. This is all the more reason I must get Sammie to focus on reality—before she ends up like me, evidently going mad.

"Sir Lightlee," I say. "With the Queen dead, who rules Kalpania?" The Queen, as I had written her, had been a powerful young enchantress and only heir to the throne.

"The King of course," Sir Lightlee says, "but, alas, he has been overseas because of the war for so long, many presume him dead."

How silly of me to think that my fantasy queen would not have started a fantasy family in my absence.

"So leadership has fallen to young Princess Taika. That is until"—Sir Lightlee lowers his voice even though there is no one but the horses to overhear—"she was kidnapped. And with the young Prince Trauen dangerously ill, we cannot afford to have this new turn of events known abroad. It would send the kingdom into panic. As I said before, you came at our time of greatest need."

My jaw tightens. I have no intentions in getting involved in the politics of a fantasy land, but I decide it's best to play along until I can figure out where Sammie is and how to get us back home. "Of course, I'm here to provide whatever assistance I can. But I will need help. I'm looking for a young girl, nine years old, who seems out of place like me. She ..." I try to think of an excuse that would be believable. Thankfully in a make-believe world, a make-believe scenario should work just fine. "She is a young enchantress, and perhaps could help us find the missing princess."

"Excellent," Sir Lightlee says. "I cannot say I have heard of such a girl, but as soon as we arrive in Magdalin, I will send out word to find her. She sounds like the very sort of girl Princess Taika would be fond of, for the princess also is an enchantress, although not yet as powerful as her mother had been."

Our light meal finished, I am ungracefully mounting Prattles when he gives a frightened snort and bolts. I fly back off the saddle and into the shallow creek, where I flail ridiculously in the cold water. A shadow falls across me, which I at first suppose is Sir Lightlee coming to help. Instead, I look into the evil grimace of a sickly gray being, whether man or beast I cannot tell. It reaches a long clawed hand and seizes me by the throat. A cold shiver runs down my spine that makes the stream feel like a warm bath.

Then I do something that I've always despised in heroines. I scream. Until my voice is cut off by the gray fiend's grip.

CHAPTER 3

My heart skips into an erratic rhythm as I choke and gasp for air. My feet slip against the stones in the creek searching for purchase as the gray creature pulls me toward his hideous face. I stare into his pale eyes, which seem like they should belong to a dead fish. Long pointed ears poke their way out of his mop of hair. Coarse and gray, animal-like hair covers his ash-colored skin. The only clothes upon his gnarled body are a loincloth. I kick pitifully and dig my nails into his tough skin.

"The Shadow Witch bids you welcome to her domain," the creature hisses, his breath blasting my face with the stench of rotten eggs. "She invites you to her palace."

Somehow I doubt this invitation comes with an option to decline. The creature's eyes widen and he grunts, his icy grip releasing me back into the stream. The reason is soon evident. Sir Lightlee pulls his sword out of the gray thing's torso then, in one clean stroke, severs his head. The body slumps to the ground, limbs still jerking, and the head tumbles into the creek. I can't seem to will myself to look away as the water darkens with the thick blood swirling and pooling into the shallows. I want to scramble out of the tainted water, but my body rebels against my mind. The blood is black, not dark red, but the deepest black, devoid of all color. Colorless—that's what this creature was—like something that escaped out of a black-and-white horror film.

Sir Lightlee's firm grip pulls me out of the water. I'm shivering, but from the creature's touch, not the water. I put my hand to my neck and pull it back, red staining my fingers. Sir Lightlee wordlessly hands me a handkerchief, a stern frown planted on his face.

"Th-Thank you." I dab my neck. "What was that thing?"

"A shadow elf." Sir Lightlee doesn't elaborate as if that's all the explanation necessary.

"But...what did it want with me?" I remember writing wood elves into my story, but they had been beautiful, lithe beings—nothing like that hideous beast. "I mean, how does the Shadow Witch even know I'm here?"

"Little escapes her notice. Her powers grow every day." Sir Lightlee begins to unsaddle his horse. "She means to have all Kalpania under her dominion. Even now she speaks as if it is already hers. Many resist, but...with Princess Taika missing, I fear it may only be a matter of time before her reality is our reality."

"You think the Shadow Witch is the cause of the missing princess?"

Sir Lightlee's lips tighten and he makes no answer, which is answer enough. Fear grips me, and I cross my arms trying to steady my shaking hands. What if Sammie has encountered one of those creatures? Or worse, the Shadow Witch herself? I want to believe this is all a dream. But what if it's not? What if this *is* another world—another reality? Though to my world Kalpania is fantasy, maybe here my world is the fantasy. Someone could be reading about my life right now— writing *my* story. I shake my head. *Absurd.* Hadn't I squelched my overactive imagination years ago?

Sir Lightlee, having finished caring for his horse, unsaddles Prattles, who, happily nibbling on grass, is not in the least disturbed by questions of reality or the role he plays. He is, after all, only a pony.

"Why are you unsaddling the horses?" It occurs to me that Sir Lightlee intends to go no farther today. "We can't rest here. Not with that..." The shadow elf's body, head and all, have disappeared.

"Do not be concerned," Sir Lightlee says. "That elf was only a scout, traveling alone. It is unlikely we will encounter anymore of the Shadow Witch's minions in these parts. It is unusual for them to venture so near to Magdalin."

"But where did it go?" I'm peering into the darkening shadows as night falls, half expecting to see the thing walking around holding its head.

"Go?" Sir Lightlee's tone registers surprise at my question. "Why, it was nothing already. It dissipated."

"You killed it. It can't simply vanish."

"He was a shadow being, already dead. I only released him from the witch's power." Sir Lightlee rolls out his bedding then does the same for me. "Rest. We will be off early tomorrow morn. I expect to reach Magdalin in time for luncheon and tea." His voice turns annoyingly cheerful.

I lie down, but I think sleep will never come as I worry about Sammie and JJ—and shadow beings wandering in the dark.

~ ~ ~

I awake early, my back stiff. Bones pop and muscles spasm as I sit up. I'm feeling much older than my thirty-six years and desperately wishing for a cup of coffee. I blink stupidly in the early dawn, rubbing my eyes and trying to bring them into focus. Sir Lightlee is already awake and saddling the horses. He is still clad in a full suit of armor. Did he sleep in it? Even his helmet is back on this morning, and, though the weather is comfortable, that seems stuffy and unnecessary. But who am I to judge how a knight ought to display his accoutrements?

"Ah, good morning." Sir Lightlee notices I am up as I stretch my sore limbs. His visor is up, so I can see his eyes, but not much else. "Sore? To be expected if you are unaccustomed to riding. But take cheer, the journey should be easy this morning."

He hands me a hard biscuit and cheese as my on-the-go breakfast. I nibble at it and sip water from the canteen. Worry gnaws at me more than hunger, and I wonder what, if anything, Sammie has had for breakfast. And what of JJ? He will be in tears waking up alone in the house. I clench my teeth till I think they might crack and say a silent prayer for my children.

Sir Lightlee seems oblivious to my distress as I permit him to help me mount Prattles, who nickers far too cheerily for my liking at this early hour. Before mounting his own horse, Sir Lightlee fishes an apple out of his bag. Prattles takes a large bite and the rest goes to Sir Lightlee's horse, who I now learn is named Wyot.

"Do you have another of those?" I ask.

"I always save an apple for the horses," Sir Lightlee answers as he mounts his steed. "But you shall have fruit of great variety once we reach Magdalin."

I frown, unable but to feel resentful that the horses were favored over me. Perhaps Sir Lightlee and Bradley had more in common than I originally thought. It had been a point of contention among us that Bradley often took more care to his dog's needs than my feelings.

The pain of Michael's absence hits full force, and I wish he were here. Sammie follows Michael around like a puppy, and he is far more tolerant of her antics. Often I accused him of leniency, but perhaps none of this would have happened had he been home—or if I had been a more patient mother. Blinking back tears, I push away my guilt. None of that helps the current situation.

We continue riding northwest and soon leave the rolling hills behind, entering flat farmlands dotted with quaint domed farmhouses and barns. Like Oodlesville's, every structure is round, like half-planted golf balls.

Triangular-shaped roofing fits neatly together forming a dome that reaches the ground, broken only for an arched hexagonal doorway. The barns have triangular skylights while most of the homes have triangular window panes fitted together to make a larger hexagonal window.

It is approaching mid-morning, when I finally see the gleaming City of Stairs rising in the horizon like a white and green ziggurat. I audibly gasp. Magdalin is more beautiful than I could have ever conceived and beyond my ability to adequately describe. My early days of writing were two-dimensional compared to this three-dimensional world. If only I had been a more skilled writer, painting a picture in words that would do justice to Kalpania's majesty, my novels would have made it off the floor.

Soon we are before the great, marble-white walls largely overtaken by vines. There are six walls forming the six levels of the city. Posted along our path and upon every corner of the walls, bright cyan banners whip in the morning breeze. Each flag is emblazoned with a yellow sun. Magenta rays stream from the sun giving the illusion of movement as the flag ripples in the wind. The intricately carved gates part for the day, welcoming visitors, while stoic guards frown a stern warning to any who might have unfriendly intentions. Looking up as much as I dare for fear of losing my balance on Prattles, I gaze at the mural of animals and plants carving their way along the wooden gates—a phoenix flying under a sun, below it a sphinx and centaur appear ready to engage in battle, opposite a stag flees a pack of wolves, and towering above them a giant stands with one foot upon a mountain.

The clamor of the city reaches my ears as we enter the first level. Here are the common markets. On this side where we entered, it is mostly farmers selling their produce. I know on the north we'd find raw materials such as cotton and wool. Located in the south are markets for meat, dairy, and eggs. The west, rising above Port Billows and overlooking the Unending Sea, would be the fish markets. Everywhere sellers shout their daily deals as buyers shop with handwoven baskets, and beggars call out for morsels while stray dogs roam for scraps.

At each of the four corners of the city, broad but steep steps rise to the second level. We make our way to the southeast corner and stable our horses in a livery below the stairway before ascending. The city switches to a more sophisticated noise. The second level is comprised of specialized shops from blacksmithing to bakeries. My stomach growls as the yeasty smell of fresh baked bread wafts to my nostrils. This level is dotted with inns and restaurants offering comfortable stays and delicious feasts. The white walls before us are overgrown with flowering vines flowing down from the third level, providing a scenic backdrop to travelers dining at the outdoor tables.

By the time we conquer the steps to the third level, I am rethinking my design for this "City of Stairs," even if it is beautiful. My legs feel like jelly, but it does not diminish the joy of reaching the gardens. Cool and lush, the heavy scent of blossoms hangs in the air as we walk the cobbled pathways, which wander through the great weeping trees and around bubbling fountains fed from the wells below. Though not modern by our world's standards, Magdalin has an elaborate plumbing system. At least that part of my design was well thought out.

Before ascending any farther, I request a break to which Sir Lightlee assents. He leans against a tree while I utter a short sigh of relief as I sit by the cool of the fountain. My day-old blouse is rumpled and smelly. I wonder when I tore a hole in my capris, which are dreadfully stained. Of course, I wore white the day I got whisked into my fantasy land. At least I have on tennis shoes and not something so ridiculous as flip-flops.

The garden is peaceful, but not quiet. Besides the splash of the fountain and twittering of birds, there is the laughter and screams of children at play. A father is helping his young son fly a kite shaped like a phoenix. A mother picnics with her daughters, the blanket spread with homemade goodies. A young couple walks hand in hand confiding in hushed tones. A boy and a girl, neither of which can be older than eight, play an imaginary game between the willows. I smile to force back tears. Sammie and JJ would love it here.

"Aren't you uncomfortable with your helmet on?" I say to divert my reflections, hating that my voice sounds choked.

Sir Lightlee gives a short shake of the head. "I would not wish to impose upon you my unkempt appearance."

I blink my eyes at his vanity. This is also a trait he inherited from Bradley, who kept a comb in his pocket in case a hair got out of place. How great a vanity that he even has the visor down! "Really, you must be roasting in that suit. Look at me—I'm a mess. I won't be at all shocked."

A scream makes me jump and Sir Lightlee whirl. Not the scream of a child at play this time, but the curdling, blood pumping shriek of a child that has seen a nightmare come to life. The boy—the one that had been playing with the girl in the willows—dashes past me falling into the arms of his mother. I don't see the girl, and thinking she must be injured, I leap up, ducking through the willows, before halting so suddenly I almost fall back.

The girl stands staring, a snapped twig in one hand. She turns her head up toward me, and I put a hand to my mouth.

CHAPTER 4

Whether the girl stares at me or nothing at all, I can't tell because her eyes are the same lifeless eyes as the shadow elf. She wears neither a frown nor a smile, her expression less of menace and more of blankness. The colorful homespun apron dress only accentuates the paleness of her flesh. Her long, French-braided hair is a dull gray.

"Are you...are you hurt?" The words fall from my mouth in shock because I'm not sure I believe what I'm seeing.

In one hand she grasps a broken stick. The other hand she holds up to me. Dark blood drips, falling onto a blade of green grass. "I cut it when I broke the branch."

Her voice is monotone, not afraid or angry. The hair on my arms prickles, and I take a step back. *She's just a little girl,* I remind myself.

"Fredric said it was a sword. He's stupid. Branches are branches. So I took it from him, and broke it."

She comes toward me as though to give me the snapped branch. I reflexively push her arm back, suppressing an urge to scream. A chill runs through me. She's cold as ice...like the shadow elf.

Sir Lightlee appears, lifting the girl off the ground. She doesn't fight him off, her non-reaction more disturbing than if she had screamed or cried. A heart wrenching wail breaks behind me. I whirl. A man sobs on his knees. A woman runs up and stops at the sight of the child.

"No...no, no, no," the woman whispers in chant as though to undo the child's gray transformation. "Not Anela. No, Anela come back to us!" She falls down sobbing, putting her arms around her husband, who is bowed to the ground.

"I will take the child to the infirmary," Sir Lightlee says.

The man finally looks up. "Please. Please, help Anela." The man stands. "I will go with you."

"No," Sir Lightlee says with a firmness I think unnecessary.

"They need to be with their chi—" I begin.

"No!" Sir Lightlee turns on me. I imagine his hazel eyes turning dark behind his visor as Bradley's would when he was angry.

Sir Lightlee walks off carrying the daughter with the parents still clinging after him like starving dogs after a bone. Until he puts his hand upon the hilt of his sword and orders them to return home and see to the care of their other children. "Lest the same fate be upon them."

I'm rooted in place as I watch the father and mother, still weeping, gather the rest of their children, and shuffle them away. Fredric, eyes wide with terror, glances behind at his sister as his mom drags him by the hand. My eyes follow the family in shock and pity before I turn and run after Sir Lightlee.

"You should've let them come," I huff as soon as I catch up. I avoid looking into Anela's blank stare.

"The infirmary is for those stricken with shadow illness. None else may enter but those on duty," Sir Lightlee responds. Softening his tone, he adds, "Continue up to the palace. I will meet you there this evening." He pulls a coin of some kind out of his side pouch. "When the guards see this medallion, they will know you to be my guest."

I turn the coin, nearly as big as my palm, in my hand. It bears the image of a sun on one side and a phoenix on the other. For a moment, I don't move. The garden returns to its peaceful state minus the people, who all seem to have disappeared after the incident. Birds return to their song, and the fountains bubble as cheerfully as before. I force myself to shove away thoughts of the strange illness upon Anela and of her grieving family. I have my own family to consider. With determination I clench the medallion in my hand, and head toward the stairs leading to the next level.

<div align="center">~~~</div>

The fourth level of the city is mainly homes. A few are extensive, multilevel rooms tiered like a cake with patios on their roofs and their own mini gardens around them. Others are the size of the average suburban home with a small yard or vegetable garden or a treehouse for the kids. Many are so tiny I can't imagine them having more than a couple of rooms. These modest homes are crowded together with no spaces between them. Yet, they are quaint and beautiful in their own way. They have shared lawns, and like most of the homes, a flat patio roof.

Though all the homes are built of a similar white brick to the city walls, each home has painted doors and window frames of varying color. Common colors like red, purple, yellow. Unique colors like cyan, coral, burgundy, and one Sammie calls wormy green. Other homes, I'm certain, have colors that don't exist in my own world. If we used most any of these colors on our house, our homeowners association would have a fit.

The neighborhood is strangely quiet. Few people are out, and those that are, glance furtively at me and go back into their homes. Word must have gotten around about the garden incident. Although I can't help but wonder if it is my foreign clothes that have them unsettled. People gawked at me even when I was in the crowded lower city, but without Sir Lightlee's presence, it's changed to fearful glances.

When I reach the fifth level, I'm exhausted again. Sir Lightlee promised we'd reach the palace in time for lunch, but now it is past noon. I've worked up a huge appetite, although with all my anxiety, I'm not sure I'd keep anything down, but coffee would be amazing. I see a building that looks like a coffee shop or small restaurant, but upon an examination of their chalkboard menu, they only serve tea and pastries. I roll my eyes, remembering now I didn't drink coffee back when I wrote novels. It took being a sleep deprived mom for me to grow an affinity for the bitter drink.

"Well, that's the first thing I'm going to change," I mumble as I push through the shop door. A mini bell attached to the door announces my entrance. Frowning, I stare at the menu, which is identical to the one posted outside, while the shopkeeper fiddles with her hands. However, I'm not thinking about tea. *This is not real,* my inner monologue chides me. Even if I rewrite my journals, it won't matter—it's fiction. *Or is it?* The lines of reality have blurred.

"C-can I help you?" The young girl's voice shakes. "Did you want some tea?"

"I suppose." I order black tea, deciding it's the closest thing I can get to coffee. I don't have any money, now that I think about it. Does it matter? I made this world; I ought to be able to get a cup of tea. "Especially fake tea," I mutter. "None of this is real." Maybe if I say it out loud, I can keep a grip on my slipping sanity.

"We use the finest tea leaves in Kalpania." The girl hands me a steaming cup of black tea. "That'll be two *neelings.*"

"I...uh ..." I pull out the medallion that Sir Lightlee gave me.

"Oh, you're with Sir Lightlee." The girl's face brightens. "I'll put it on his tab."

It seems Sir Lightlee is the local hero. Taking advantage of this, I order a small cake.

I sit at a table outside the shop, sipping my tea and contemplating what to do next. The fifth level is the last public level, the sixth being the palace. This is the governing level. Most of the buildings are courts of law, institutions of learning, and museums guarding articles of historical or magical value. There is also a hospital. I suppose that must be where Sir Lightlee took Anela.

My eyes are drawn to a tall, domed structure with triangular, stained glass skylights. It sticks out in stark contrast to the square, flat-roofed buildings surrounding it. This would be the Great Library of Magdalin. And this is where I hope to find answers on how to get home. As I set my empty cup down and make my way toward the library, I try not to dwell on my worry for Sammie. One step at a time. For the moment, I have no clue where to begin my search for her, but with luck, I can have a way home for when she's found.

I push my way through the heavy wooden doors of the library and am greeted with the musty smell of ancient knowledge. Books beyond imagination fill shelves that fill rooms, and rooms fill the building. My eyes follow stairs leading up to balconies before winding up to a third and fourth level. I steady myself on a nearby column, feeling an oncoming headache from the smell of old books...or anxiety on where to begin my search. I had imagined a great library, but like everything else in this world, it exceeds my wildest fantasies. If I created a dewdrop, I get a monsoon.

I glance around for help, but the library appears empty. Walking over to the nearest bookshelf, I pray for guidance. Gilded plaques label the shelves: *Agriculture, Livestock, Irrigation.* Clearly, I'm not in the right section.

"I never thought I'd be looking up books on magic," I say to myself.

"Magic is on the fourth level."

I jump and whirl in the most ungraceful manner to face the voice behind me. Or below me rather. At my feet, a withered old man, with a wrinkled bald head and tiny spectacles, smiles up at me. He wears a long burgundy coat—long in relation to his body, he can't be more than three feet tall. His two short arms...wait, *four arms*...hold a book.

"What type of magic would you be looking for?" His nasal voice is absurdly cartoonish.

"I...um ..." I'm trying not to stare and failing. "Do you have a book on traveling between worlds?"

"Ah, yes. I think you mean portal magic." The funny little man crawls vertically up a bookcase and places the book on the top shelf. I see now that under his long coat, he has several short legs ending in horrifying feet of hook-filled suction cups. He is a literal bookworm...or book caterpillar? Still hanging from the top shelf, he twists his head, peering at me, his face now level with mine.

I take a step back.

"Why would you be needing portal magic?" His eyes narrow behind his glasses. "It can be dangerous traveling between worlds if you don't know what to expect."

"I'm not from here," I blurt out before thinking better of it.

"Hmm...thought as much. Why don't you go back the way you came?"

"Obviously," I drawl, "because I don't know how I got here to begin with. Who are you anyway?" It's been a while since I cracked my journals, but I don't remember creating anything like this funny creature before me.

"Obviously," he mimics, "I am the librarian." He crawls down from the shelf. "Fourth floor. Sixteenth bookcase. Eighth shelf," he says as he rounds a bookcase out of sight.

Shaking my head, I proceed up the wide stairway to the second floor balcony then wind my way up to the third landing. The stairs narrow the higher I go. Ascending the final flight, I can barely squeeze my hips between the rails, which eventually force me to turn sideways. Panting, I stand in the middle of the round room. The stained glass windows offer a colorful three-sixty view of the city. Farms lie to the east, and out to the west, sits the palace.

"Sixteenth bookshelf." I cross my arms. The bookshelves stand in three circles and are unnumbered. How do I know which one is the sixteenth? I wander around the inner circle, reading the plaques on the eighth shelf. *Water Magic, Fire Magic, Earth Magic.* I must be in the elements. Skipping ahead, I read, *Garden Magic, Piscean Magic, Equine Magic.* Would alphabetical order be too much to ask? Out of curiosity I flip through a book entitled: *How to Breed a Pegasus.* It seems to be a book of folktales and myths revolving around horse breeding rather than practical information. Sighing, I continue my search: *Ursine Magic, Lycan Magic.* I raise an eyebrow upon reading the gilded lettering of the next shelf: *Cha-Chan Magic.*

"Cha-Chan?" I pull out the first book, *The Mystery of Cha-Chas.* Cracking it open, I read a few lines. *No one knows for certain how long Cha-Chas have lived in Kalpania, but the elusive creatures were first spotted one year ago in the Tangled Woods. Some believe them to be myth; however, claims that they can make themselves invisible may explain why they have gone unnoticed for so long. Rumors report that Cha-Chas resemble dogs, but this is unconfirmed.*

"Sammie," I say and snap the book closed. She'd been writing in my journals, unbeknownst to me until recently. She created Cha-Chas in *my* world. What else has she created? My mind wanders to the book caterpillar. Such a silly creature is just the sort of thing a nine-year-old would create. He has her attitude too.

That's the end of the inner circle—twenty-four bookcases in all.

Skipping the middle, I decide to start from the outer circle. There must be a hundred cases. Feeling hopeless, I wander through them, hoping to find some indication from the titles that I am nearing the location of portal magic when a plaque catches my attention: *Shadow World*. For a moment, I move past it but am drawn back. I run my fingers along the books as I browse the titles before stopping at one—*The Shadow Witch*. The book is no bigger than my back pocket and only half an inch thick.

I sit cross-legged on the floor and turn to the first page. It's blank. Quickly, I flip through the pages—it's all blank. Who creates a blank book? As I stare, words gradually appear on the paper. At first I can't make out the faint lettering that swims before my eyes, but my amazement turns to disbelief as the words materialize, as though written by my own hand, and are brought into focus.

Sammie sat crossed-legged on the couch as she wrote in her notebook. Her stomach growled because she only picked at dinner. She didn't want food; she wanted Daddy. She wanted Mama to be happy again and not yell so much. It wasn't her fault the chips got soggy in her soup. "If only I can live in Kalpania," she thought aloud. In a magical land, all her problems could be fixed.

Mama's heavy footfalls bouncing down the stairs sounded angry. She headed into the garage, slamming the door behind her. A moment later Mama came back in yelling, "Where's JJ's brown dog!"

Why couldn't Mama get their names right? "I don't know," Sammie said.

"Well, I need it. He won't sleep without it, thanks to you. Why did you tell him that Daddy can feel his hugs?"

Sammie hated it when Mama got that tone. "Because it's true." Why was it so hard for grown-ups to understand things any kid would know? Peanut Butter and Jelly Sandwich the Third was a magic Cha-Cha after all.

"No, it isn't, and you know it." Mama snatched the notebook from her hand. "Stop it! Stop with the constant silly make-believe stories. Real life is hard, and you can't live in a daydream."

"Give back my notebook!" Sammie felt warm tears run down her face, and she didn't even try to stop them. Why was Mama yelling at her? It wasn't her fault Peanut Butter and Jelly Sandwich the Third was a troublemaker. He might be invisible or he might have run off.

I stand up dropping the book. What weird trick is this? The book has fallen closed, but I don't pick it up. I don't want to. Still staring at the book in disbelief, I back away. Then I turn and run.

CHAPTER 5

My lungs frantically gulp the fresh air outside the library. *I should go back,* I tell myself, but I can't make my feet turn. The sun is lowering, and soon it will be dinnertime. I shouldn't strain Sir Lightlee's good graces. I promised to meet him this evening, and I'm going to need a place to sleep. Tomorrow, first thing, I will go back to the library and make that ridiculous caterpillar take me directly to the shelf containing books on portal magic. If I have to, I'll use the same tone I take when I demand Sammie clean her room before her every possession finds its way into my time out box for ill-behaved toys.

Setting my feet determinedly on the first steps of the last flight of stairs, I grit my teeth as I begin my ascent. *I will find Sammie,* I chant in my head with each step. *I will get us home. And when I do, I will burn every last journal of this fantasy,* I swear to myself as I take that final step. And, if we ever have the opportunity to purchase a new home, I am going to insist it be a one-story. Life is entirely too short to spend half of it climbing stairs.

Finally on level ground, I face a gate guarded by two stern soldiers with even sterner looking dogs. I don't hate dogs, but I am intensely afraid of them. Even small dogs, and these more resemble ponies, only with square jowls and beady eyes. Neither guard acknowledges my presence as I stare stupidly at their giant brutes whose eyes never leave me. One gives a low growl, and though it never moves a muscle, I take a step back. Sammie and JJ have been begging Michael and me for a puppy, and I am grateful now I never relented. My luck, we'd pick a toy breed that had a recessive gene for gigantism and would grow into a monster.

My fingers slip into my pocket and clumsily pull out Sir Lightlee's medallion. "I..." my voice squeaks. The guards still don't look at me. Clearing my throat and holding the coin up higher, I try again. "Sir Lightlee invited me." One soldier suddenly walks toward me, and I back up again, nearly slipping off the last step.

The soldier takes the medallion from my hand, examines it, and hands it back. He motions me toward the gate the other guard is opening. I move hesitantly between the dogs, but they don't budge. The gate closes behind me, and I find myself alone on a wide cobbled path. It winds through a well-kept lawn dotted with tree-sized bushes trimmed into various creatures—two phoenixes facing each other, a stag, wolf, horse, and a fish that reminds me of a betta, flowers blooming on its fins in a contrasting magenta color.

Almost reverently I keep to the cobblestones, careful not to tread the grass or brush against flowering bushes. After ducking between the phoenixes, I hesitate before white marbled steps. My eyes survey the tall palace—a combination of the square city construction with flat roofed patios and the domes of the countryside topping its highest pinnacles. I know—because I designed it— that inside I will be greeted with yet more stairs. And why in heaven's name did I not think of elevators?

My hand reaches for an ornate knocker on the beautiful mahogany doors, and I'm rewarded with a resounding hollow boom that gives me quite a start. I'd forgotten the door and knockers are enchanted. These doors could only be opened from the inside. Only the Queen (and presumably the Princess) could open them from without. The great doors smoothly glide open, and I'm met by a soldier, uniformed in magenta and cyan with yellow suns embroidered on his puffy sleeves. He eyes me with some confusion, but gives a short bow after glancing at Sir Lightlee's medallion and motions me inside.

I step into a broad entryway and follow the hollow clack of his boots across the marble floor. The room is empty, save for a few wooden benches. We pass between winding stairs with elegant balustrades, leading to many more rooms above. Up ahead, guarded by four armed men, is a door that I know leads to the throne room. Before we reach them, my escort takes a swift left and leads me into a parlor overlooking the Unending Sea. He bids me to wait here and shuts the door, leaving me alone.

Though furnished sparsely, the furniture is delicate and beautiful. I stand hesitantly before an elaborately designed settee that isn't much larger than a wide chair. An intricate rug rests in front of it and beside it a mahogany end table. I am now intensely aware of my filthy capris and dusty sneakers, not wanting to soil anything. This is *my* world! I remind myself, and sit on the settee, which despite its lovely fabric isn't much softer than a bench. Gazing out the hexagonal window before me, I take in the beauty of the Unending Sea as the setting sun metamorphoses the waves into liquid gold.

A maid enters from another door, dressed in skirts of the same uniformed colors as the soldier. Her silvery-white hair is done up in a tidy bun, and bright freckles splash across red cheeks. I stand quickly as she gives a disapproving raised brow at my ruffled appearance. "Follow me, ma'am," she says stiffly and turns back through the same door without checking to see if I indeed follow.

She leads me into a broad dining area but takes a quick right up an enclosed stairway, climbing the steps nimbly despite being at least a couple decades my senior and rather stout. We stop on the second floor and walk past a couple doors when she opens the third to my left. "As Sir Lightlee's guest, please freshen up with whatever provisions necessary," she says in a tone that does not denote suggestion, "and return to the dining area for supper promptly at eight."

I'm in a simply furnished room with a sturdy wooden bed, an unadorned wooden wardrobe, and a side table with a basin of water. Opening the wardrobe reveals two flowing gowns—in the royal colors of course—one magenta and the other cyan. I splash the cold water on my face, and once stripped free of my filthy clothes, I clean myself as best I can before choosing to wear the cyan gown, it being the least flashy of the two. I'm not sure whether to be pleasantly surprised or disturbed by the fact that the gown fits almost perfectly once I've wrestled my way into the thing over an appropriate linen chemise. Finely knitted stockings and leather slippers that lace to the ankles complete my attire.

I'm yanking a comb through my hair while wondering how I will know when it's eight. How did I handle time in my novel? The palace has a great sundial in the courtyard, that much I recall when a strange wail startles me. At first I think I imagine it. But no, I hear it again—softer now, like that of a crying child who has given up on being heard. My maternal instinct kicks in full force as it instantly makes me think of little JJ sick and alone. Stepping out into the hall, I listen to determine the direction of the cry, but it's drowned out by the resounding donging of a not too distant bell that, when complete, leaves behind a deafening hush throughout the palace.

"Ma'am." A sharp voice startles me. It's the unpleasant maid, whose name I never got. "Do not keep

Sir Lightlee waiting. Come." She turns with the obvious expectation that I follow.

I step obediently after her, but my mind is still on the child. Entering the dining hall, I see Sir Lightlee seated to the right of the head of the table, and for the first time, not in a suit of armor, but in a similar outfit as the soldier who greeted me at the door. He stands politely as I approach. He wears the medieval type clothes I gave all my male characters—a short tunic with puffed sleeves and tight pants. Why hadn't I created a more unique attire for my people of Kalpania? It seems strange to think of them as "my people," but I suppose they are in a way. I wish the nameless maid knew this, and I wonder if she gave no name because I failed to give her one.

Sir Lightlee pulls out the chair across from him for me to be seated before returning to his place. I feel self-conscious in my gown, which is lower cut than I would have liked, being a gown made after the fancies of my youth. Bowing my head, I say a brief silent prayer for my food. *And please, God, if you hear me, help me find Sammie and get us back home to JJ*, I tag onto the end of it.

Sir Lightlee is staring at me when I look back up. "Is the food not agreeable?"

"Oh, no. It looks delicious." Truth is, though hungry, I've barely glanced at the food. My mind is filled with too much anxiety. "I was just, you know, saying a prayer."

"Prayer?" Sir Lightlee brushes a dark strand of hair from his brow, revealing a puzzled furrow.

"Yes. To thank the Lord for the food and...give Him my concerns." I answer with intentional vagueness on that last part, not wishing to explain my real situation. I need Sir Lightlee to continue to believe I am here as the Queen's cousin and that my main concern is to help find Princess Taika.

"Ah...I also would thank the Queen for her goodness were she alive. You are fortunate to still have a lord over your country. Do you meditate on a letter? I could provide you with writing utensils."

"Um...not at this time." I distractedly poke at some meat with a three-pronged fork, wondering how Sir Lightlee could have so misunderstood what I meant by prayer. Perhaps he isn't religious. Yet, who am I to judge? Prayer has become scarcely more than a habit formed in my youth. Strange, that the first sincere prayer I've had in years is in a world of make-believe, when for so long my faith has been little more than pretend.

"With the princess missing and the King overseas in the war with Valdisar, we are only left with the young prince." Sir Lightlee pauses for a bite, the absent way he chews revealing his thoughts are on more than food. "Kalpania is in dire need of assistance in this dark time." Sir Lightlee levels a firm gaze on me. "You are the closest thing we have left to a ruler."

"Wha...?" I find it difficult to swallow the meat I've just placed in my mouth—partly because it turns out to be liver. I hate liver. "Look, I'm here to help, but let's just focus on"— *What's the story I told him?*—"finding the young enchantress. You know the one I told you about? Who could help find the princess."

Sir Lightlee gives me a slight frown. "It seems a strange way to go about finding a lost enchantress. By searching for another enchantress whose whereabouts are also unknown."

"Clearly, the princess is not much of an enchantress if she got herself kidnapped!" My make-believe scenario is falling apart as Sir Lightlee is proving to be more intelligent than I expected for a fantasy knight. Seeing his lips form into a stern line, I try to recover his goodwill. "I'm sorry... I didn't mean disrespect. I'm anxious for Princess Taika and..." My mind returns to the wailing child. "Trauen. You said the prince was ill? I heard a child crying when I was upstairs."

Sir Lightlee holds a finger to his lips and glances around. "Not here." There is a seriousness in his hazel eyes that keeps me from asking questions.

He scoots away from the table, and I stand and follow him back up the stairs and past the room where I changed into my gown. We take a left at a hall and continue until it ends at a large window overlooking the sea, its waters now dark as ink under Kalpania's purple moon. Sir Lightlee has taken out a key and is unlocking a door to the right of the window. I tear my eyes away from the moon. Beautiful, but completely ridiculous. My youthful imagination never conceived a logical explanation for the moon's unique appearance.

The door now open, Sir Lightlee leads up a winding staircase to one of the side towers, and we enter a spacious round room. An oil lamp on a table to the right casts long shadows across the room, ending at a bed with a small lump in the middle. Above the bed is a triangular window offering the same view of the moon, like an amethyst jewel dipping into the inky sea and conjuring a shimmering purple stream of moonglade.

Sir Lightlee puts his fingers to his lips and steps softly across the floor. I follow close behind until I have a clear view of the "lump." It's a boy sleeping much like my JJ does, all sideways in bed with covers thrown off. But that's where the likeness ends. Even in the dim light, I see deep shadows around his eyes. The boy's skin is pale; his damp blond hair clings to his forehead. No, not blond. I take a closer look and my throat constricts. His hair is completely white and his skin...

"He's gray," I say in a faint whisper.

"He wouldn't take his medicine," a gravelly voice breaks the stillness.

I jump. The stern maid sits off to my left in a rocker barely big enough for her stocky build.

"None at all?" Sir Lightlee replies in a quieter tone that conveys concern.

"I managed to get a spoonful down," the maid says. She's addressing Sir Lightlee, but her accusing stare directed at me says she doesn't approve of my presence.

Sir Lightlee reaches his hand down and gently lifts an eyelid. The child stirs but does not awake. His eye moves rapidly as though dreaming. "I worry it may not be enough till morning," Sir Lightlee says as he releases the lid.

The child's chest continues to rise and fall peacefully, but I know he is gravely ill. An image of Anela pops into my mind. "He has the shadow sickness."

Sir Lightlee nods absently. Deep furrows write his concern across his forehead more clearly than spoken words.

Compassion overcomes my initial repulsion. I sit on the edge of the bed. The sheets are silken and the covers soft, fit for a prince. I brush Trauen's white strands from his face. His skin is cool, but not ice cold like Anela's. I draw my hand back. "It's not...contagious?"

"It is," Sir Lightlee says, "but not by flesh, but spirit."

Before I can ask the meaning of this riddle, Trauen squirms. The boy sits up rapidly, blinking and whimpering. "Taika, Taika."

"He calls for his sister. It's about the only words he speaks anymore," the stern maid says, tapping her nails lightly on the rocker's arm as she continues to frown at me.

Ignoring the maid's gaze, I ask Sir Lightlee, "Is there some way I can help?"

"Taika, Taaaiika!" The child is wailing.

Still sitting on the bed, I instinctively draw my arms around Trauen, forgetting his gray skin, and pull him to me as if he were my own son. "Shhh, it's okay now. I've come to find your sister." I feel a twinge of guilt at this lie, but the child's wailing returns to short whimpers as he snuggles up to me. His crying is strangely comforting to the passiveness Anela displayed after her transformation.

Sir Lightlee turns and picks up a bowl from a side table and holds it out to me. I take it with a free hand, keeping my other arm tightly around the boy. Inside the bowl is a pasty blue mash.

"Maybe you can get him to take the rest," Sir Lightlee says. "You seem to bring Trauen comfort."

Using the wooden spoon, I scrape the bowl and hold out the spoon to Trauen, but he only turns his head toward my chest. "Hi, Trauen. My name is Michelle. How old are you?"

The boy doesn't move.

"Hmm, I think you must be six."

Trauen shakes his head and holds up five fingers.

"No way! That's the same age as my son, JJ."

The boy sits up, his soft eyes looking at me with some interest. I wonder why his eyes haven't turned gray like Anela's. His eyes are moist with tears and very much alive.

"I bet you're very brave. Maybe you can help me find Taika?"

Trauen's eyes light up. He nods.

"Okay, well I'm going to need your help, so here's what I need you to do. Take the rest of your medicine, so you will be better in the morning."

I hold the spoon and bowl toward him, and he takes it from me and eats it like it's his favorite ice cream.

"Alright, off to bed." I nudge the boy, and he crawls under his covers. I kiss his forehead, immediately noticing his skin is warmer. Some color has returned to his cheeks. I remain at his bedside, humming softly, until his chest rises slowly with the steady breathing of a child fast asleep.

"The medicine seems to work quickly."

"It does. When he takes it." The maid says, still eyeing me but her gaze is less reproving. "Won't do much good for long. That was the last dose."

"You can get more, can't you?"

"Alas," Sir Lightlee says, "it is a mash of a fruit found only deep within the Tangled Woods. The road was cut off by a landslide and what little supply we had left stolen some months ago. The rest was rationed for Trauen since he fell ill shortly after his sister, Princess Taika, disappeared."

A sickening knot forms in my stomach. "But what of Anela and the others who are sick in the infirmary?"

"What of them?" The maid snorts. "They're as good as dead. Trauen still has life."

"But Anela? Her family..." Searching Sir Lightlee's eyes, I know the truth before he speaks.

Sir Lightlee swallows. "There is no cure once the shadow illness has taken full hold."

I struggle to keep my voice low so as not to wake Trauen. "Then why have an infirmary at all? Why give her family hope if there isn't any?"

"Without hope, soon all would perish," Sir Lightlee says as he walks toward the door. "The shadow illness takes root in the heart before the body."

After Sir Lightlee walks out, I stay at the boy's bedside a few moments longer. The circles under his eyes have faded and a look of peace rests upon his face, but tendrils of fear wrap their cords around my heart.

CHAPTER 6

My body jerks, and I leap out of bed so fast that I nearly pass out. The bed gives a low groan as I sit back down and take deep breaths trying to slow my pounding heart. What woke me? A cry. Wailing like that of a frightened child. Images of JJ all alone flash through my mind. *He'll be fine.* I try to reason away my fears. My mother-in-law bombards me with texts multiple times a day. She must realize by now something is wrong. Perhaps she's already stopped by the house and JJ's safe in her care.

A loud knock sounds on my door, causing my pulse to quicken again. I walk over and smooth the ridiculous grandma-ish nightgown before cracking open the door. The stern maid waits with a pile of clothes in her arms topped with boots.

"Attire for your travels." The maid shoves the clothes through the door, forcing herself into the room. "Sir Lightlee awaits for you to breakfast." The maid drops the pile on the bed and wanders across the room picking up my dirty real-world clothes and tennis shoes.

"Travels...? Wait, what are you doing with my things?"

"Burning them. They're not good for much else."

"Just wash them, please."

The maid's ever-present frown turns more downward. "These strange garments of your country are not fit for accompanying a knight of Sir Lightlee's status, Queen's cousin or no." The maid gives a doubtful snort and tromps out of the room holding my old clothes at arm's length.

Putting a hand to my face, I wipe the blur from my tired eyes then stare at the pile of neatly folded clothes on my bed. Finally, I reach out and touch the fabric. It's softer than I expected. A pang in my abdomen alerts me to the realization that I have not relieved myself since last night. There is a bedpan for nighttime emergencies, but I have no intention of using it and give the stern maid more reason to dislike me as it would be part of her duties to dispose of the humiliating contents. Instead, I grab the pile of clothes and accompanying boots and make my way toward the toilet room that I had been directed to after my visit with Trauen last night.

One thing I had noted was, more often than not, books were mute as to the conditions of the restrooms. In particular, fantasy characters seemed to have a superpower of never needing to heed nature's call. I, however, not having this power, am superbly thankful that I had designed Magdalin with an elaborate sewage system. If the ancient Minoans could have flushing toilets, why not my beautiful city?

Not far past the hall that leads to Trauen's room is a back stairwell that leads from the ladies' and children's quarters directly into a fair-sized bathroom. The men's end of the palace opposite has a similar setup. In one corner of the tiled room, is a stone toilet next to a pump. The same piping system that feeds the fountains in the garden also provides the palace with running water. A short stone wall divides the toilet from the tiled tub to which I head after relieving myself. From a small clouded window a patch of morning light streams into the bath as I pump it half full. The water is of course cold, but as the ladies' room is adjoined to the kitchen by a door opposite the stairs, I only need to call to a maid to bring me hot water from the kettle. The men's room, not being near the kitchen, has their own coal stove that they must ignite to heat water if they wish for a warm bath. As the kitchen is almost always warming something, the ladies' room never needs to wait long.

I sink with a sigh into the warm water and close my eyes. A bath was long overdue, but last night I was too exhausted to consider it. Tension seeps out of my body like the dirt from my pores. For a moment, I'm back home. My eyes close tighter as though refusing to acknowledge my surroundings would transport me to my own tub. A cold shadow blocks the sun from the window. Wherever it is that Sir Lightlee intends for us to travel, I sincerely hope it does not rain.

I open my eyes only to stare into the hideous gray face of a shadow elf, his mouth widened into a fanged grin. A clawed hand reaches for me. My mouth opens in a voiceless scream as his ashen hand touches my shoulder, pressing a sharp nail into my skin. A red drop rolls down my arm and drops silently into the bath. My blood mingles into the water, changing it into an inky black abyss. Cold, so cold. I flail desperately, taking in a mouthful of my bath.

Salt? A wave splashes against my face, plunging me into water that goes over my head. Kicking wildly, I surface in a dark ocean. Sea sprays against the jagged rocks ahead.

"Michelle!" A voice calls from the rocks.

Michael? "Help!" I yell before taking in another mouthful of water.

Coughing, I sit up.

The water is ice cold, but I'm in my bath and quite alone. Shaking from cold or perhaps fear, I step out carefully. As the tub drains, I grab a towel from the stack and try to shake the chill radiating down my spine. Falling asleep in a bath is never recommended, especially when your dreams are filled with nightmares. The sunlight streaming from the window reassures me of reality. What reality? I don't know what's real and what isn't anymore. But my breathing is calmer, and I push aside all thoughts of the Shadow Witch and her wretched elves. The palace is the safest place I could be. That is, aside from my home in the "real world."

Once dried from my bath, I drop the towel in a bin. Uncertain of what to do with my nightgown, I also dispose of it in the bin, assuming it would make its way back to the room eventually. I turn to my new clothes. The top is a knee length, hooded tunic with a feminine flare and long tight sleeves. It's made of cotton, dyed dark green. After this, I wiggle into the tight suede leggings still in their natural color and shove my feet into the tall boots, lacing them up with only minor difficulty. This was the traveling garb I decided on for the women in my novels, wanting something that would be more comfortable and practical than a dress. If I remember correctly, modeled after something I saw on the internet.

I walk across the floor testing out the feel of the boots. Everything fits perfectly. Once again, it is beyond belief how real this world seems...is...for there is no longer any doubt in my mind that I've somehow entered a world crafted after my novels. For the briefest of moments, a sense of pride fills my heart. I take to the end of the small room trying to get a good view of myself from a much too short mirror on the opposite wall. All feelings of pride dissipate like smoke in the wind. I look like I'm larping a cliché character from a role-playing video game.

Having forgotten a comb, I fasten my damp hair back in a less than tidy pony tail and make my way through the kitchen to the dining area.

"Aaaeeee!" A squeal of pleasure pierces my ears just before I'm assaulted by a hug that totters me off balance.

"Trauen! Should you be running?" I pry myself free and tousle his hair. Color has returned to the roots of his messy hair though the rest is still snow-white.

"I'm good." The boy's cheeks hold a healthy flush. Taking hold of my hand, he guides me toward the table. "We're going to find Taika today." He lets go of my hand and skips back to his half-eaten meal at the table.

I shoot Sir Lightlee a questioning look. Ever the gentleman, he already stood from his seat when I entered the room, and now he makes his way toward me.

"Where—"

"Truly," he cuts me off sharply, "we make a hasty journey, but..." Sir Lightlee's voice drops to little more than a whisper as he glances back at Trauen, finishing off his breakfast of mash and sausages. "Trauen must not know the true nature."

"Meaning you haven't heard word of"—I appropriately lower my own voice—"his sister's whereabouts?"

"If only. My scouts are scouring the country. For now our immediate concern is to get more glowfruit. We cannot lose the last heir."

"Glow...you mean the medicine?" I begin to comprehend.

"Indeed. One of my men was able to get a small supply being sold off the street. Perhaps from the stolen stash."

"Will that be enough?"

"It must be. If we make swiftly to the Tangled Woods, and if fate be with us, we may obtain more before Trauen is lost to us."

"But he thinks he is going to his sister."

"A necessary lie," Sir Lightlee begins.

A low crackle cuts in. "Must keep the spirit up." The stern maid, ever stoic, sits on a stool near the kitchen door. How had I not seen her? "Depressed spirits quicken the disease," she adds. "As I cannot make such a journey, you will assist Sir Lightlee with the boy. The child's taken a liking to you."

Was that a compliment? Her lips remain planted in an ever present frown that pulls at her freckles. Blinking, I turn to Sir Lightlee. "Wouldn't it be better for the boy to stay here?" I fear my voice betrays the growing bubble of anxiety in my chest. It isn't that my heart doesn't go out for Trauen, but I cannot be sidetracked from finding Sammie.

"The journey will be arduous," Sir Lightlee says, "but it is a risk that must be taken, for it is unlikely I could make the trip back in time. We must take Trauen directly to the source of the fruit.

"Where exactly are we going?" My mind is whirring, trying to come up with a solution.

"The Tangled Woods," the stern maid growls at me. "Eat your food, and mayhap you'll have enough strength in your thin frame to survive those woods." She seems to be sizing me up as though she's expecting my bones to be picked clean by wild beasts.

Thin? I'd been trying to lose my mom bod since JJ was born. Shooting the maid back a snarky frown of my own, I turn from her and address Sir Lightlee sweetly, "Can we make a quick stop at the library first?" I've been struck by an idea. I know every inch of Kalpania, and there was no Tangled Woods or any such fruit as "glowfruit." These are Sammie's additions for sure. What are the chances she's headed toward her own special part of this world? And I think I know a way to find out for sure—if I'm right about that strange book in the library.

<center>~~~</center>

Sammie stared across the sea, mesmerized by the glittering green waters. Half Moon Bay back home was a dirty pond compared to the semi-transparent waters of the Great Mer Bay. Schools of rainbow fish shimmered just below the surface, and a blue pelican swooped low across the waves, opening his great beak and taking in a mouthful of the sea. One lucky fish wiggled free from the bird's grasp and flipped into the water with a wild splash. Sammie giggled as a black sea lion with long white whiskers launched his glistening body out of the sea onto a rock, barking as the pelican flew past.

"Aww, did the poor sea lion get his fish stolen?" Sammie shouted at him.

The sea lion nodded his head as though he understood her question then did a backflip into the waters, spinning gracefully before disappearing in the depths and reemerging with his own fish.

A large, shaggy white dog nudged Sammie's leg from behind.

Sammie turned. "Yes. I know." She scratched the dog behind a long floppy ear. "But every sailor says the bay is closed to ships, and they won't take a little girl if it wasn't." Sammie stuck out her bottom lip and sat with a huff in the sand.

The shaggy dog whined and licked her behind the ear.

"I haven't given up." Sammie took the dog's great head between her hands as the dog licked her on the chin, cheeks, and a great big smack across the lips. Sammie laughed then gave a sigh, doodling in the sand. "I wanted to live in Kalpania sooo bad. Now I just wanna go home. It's no fun with JJ sick. He would love it here."

Sammie flopped onto her back and made a sand angel, not caring what the wet sand did to her blue sundress. The shaggy dog ran in circles around her barking. Sammie sat up, sand plastered all over her skin and clothes. She brushed sandy strands of hair from her face. "No, I don't think so," she told the shaggy dog as he cocked his head to one side. "Mama wouldn't like it here at all. She wouldn't even hear the magic in the sea shells."

Sammie scrambled to her feet. "That's it!"

In response, the dog shook his long shaggy fur, flinging sand in all directions.

Blocking her face from the stinging onslaught, Sammie gave a wide grin then scampered off toward the waves.

52

CHAPTER 7

The waves of the Great Mer Bay wash serenely upon the sand. They don't make a fuss even though the tide's coming in. These are not the forceful waves of the Pacific that smash into the shore, leaving behind unidentifiable shattered shards. No, these gently smooth the sand back, revealing colorful shells that glitter in the early morning sun as it peeks shyly over the distant mountains. I stare to the south over the bay at the hazy shore on the horizon. Even I don't know what lies there. My imagination never conceived of lands beyond the borders I created. Kalpania has grown...or, maybe it was ever immense, waiting for fresh inspiration to explore its expanse. Who would have thought it'd be the wild fancies of a nine-year-old girl, sprouting tangled woods and glowfruit?

We arrived at Fisherman's Haven yesterday evening...or at least what remained of it. The docks were in disrepair, the ships beached, and the town in shambles. No one actually fished in these waters anymore, though they once boasted the best seafood in all Kalpania. Businesses had either closed or been moved to the wharfs along Magdalin. I had seen many a ship sailing the Unending Sea from the palace window, but not one dared to enter Mer Bay. "Merpeople fear the shadow illness," Sir Lightlee explained over dinner at a rundown tavern. "It was leave their waters or war. Those that remain in Fisherman's Haven, do so either because they are stubborn or have no place else to go."

Now, after a restless sleep in a bug infested bed and still sore from two days of riding, I sun on the silky sand waiting for Sir Lightlee to secure us a boat—or rather someone to navigate it. To buy a boat would be easy. The impoverished people that remain here would be happy to sell us a fleet of ships. Finding someone willing to sail into the waters of Mer Bay is another matter entirely.

A laugh draws my attention. Trauen amuses himself with a collection of rainbow shells organized around a misshapen sand castle. A long, skinny shell bridges a moat that Trauen is carefully filling with water from a seashell large enough to use for a dinner plate. A baffled furrow spreads across his brow as the water dissipates into the thirsty sand, and a pensive smile pulls at the corners of my mouth as a longing for my own children tugs at my heart. My hand idly sifts the fine sand, white enough to be mistaken for snow at a distance, if it wasn't that it sparkled with rainbow flecks as though a group of children conducted an enormous glitter craft on the shore. Once a popular tourist location in Kalpania, the Shimmering Shores now host only myself, Trauen, and a noisy bunch of sea lions sunbathing on a rocky outcropping.

I hesitantly open the leather shoulder pouch I'd been given to carry personal items. Inside is *that* book. The one I retrieved from the library just before we left Magdalin. As of yet, I hadn't the courage to open it. It revealed Sammie's thoughts and actions once. Could it do it again? Will I find a clue to where she is? Or would it reveal more than I want to know? The twisting pangs of guilt bore a hollow feeling inside me. I am only hard on Sammie because I don't want her to grow up disillusioned by dreams unfulfilled. Michael's absence is harder on her than I thought. And what had I done? Only squash what childish hope she had left. *You can't live in a daydream.*

I reach into the pouch and pull out the tiny book, handling it as though it were fragile. *The Shadow Witch,* the cover said. Whatever the enchanted book's purpose had been, it is now a window to Sammie. Why or how, I don't know. I take a deep breath and whisper a short, hesitant prayer. It feels ridiculous praying over an enchanted book, but I need answers. Frowning, I open the book to a random page. They are all blank after all. As before, the page swims as the handwriting appears, and I begin scanning even before the words come into full focus. Sammie was here! As I suspected, she is headed to the Tangled Woods...and I know how she is getting there. I pick up a fist-sized round shell near me. *Have I really forgotten the magic?* I hold the shell to my ear. It's faint, but the music is there. I smile.

Closing the book, I watch Trauen. He seems to have lost interest in castle building and has picked up a long, horn-shaped shell. At first he uses the point to dig, then shakes it free of sand and holds it at eye level. Will he figure out its real use? Part of me wants to tell him, but that would take away the magic of discovery. A healthy flush has spread across Trauen's face, and I think he looks even better today than he did yesterday. I wince inwardly as Trauen tries to peep through the tiny hole at the pointy end of the seashell and pray he doesn't gouge his eye. It takes all my strength to restrain the mother-in-me from correcting him. "Let me do it my own way," Sammie's words echo in my mind from last week's failed art lesson. *Have I really been in Kalpania five days?* I was trying to convince her to follow the tutorial, and the end result was frustration on my part and tears on hers. My desire to see my daughter succeed seems in constant conflict with the joy of childhood. How is a parent to know when to let go of a child's hand and let her run even at the risk of falling?

Trauen shakes out more sand from the shell before placing the narrow end to his lips. He is rewarded with a soft "toot." Beaming, Trauen blows more vigorously, playing a simple tune consisting of no more than three notes. Some shells, like the one I held to my ear, hold songs from the past. Others, like the horn-shaped one in Trauen's hand, play the melody within our own heart. The bigger the imagination from within, the greater the composition. I would have expected more from Trauen. Children have imaginations unfettered by practicality. This I knew all too well from Sammie.

"Mrs. Sansbury."

Startled by the voice, I quickly shove the small book back into my side pouch. "Please," I say, standing a little unsteadily and dusting sand from my pants. "Just 'Michelle' is fine."

Armor being impractical for the nature of our journey, Sir Lightlee wears tight leather riding pants, a bright cyan shirt, and a maroon overcoat with too many ornate buttons. A half-cocked beret with a cyan feather protruding from it completes the knight's rather ridiculous outfit that I evidently thought swashbuckling back in my writing days. I would apologize to Sir Lightlee for his attire, but thankfully, he has no idea I wrote him into existence in such an embarrassing manner. It would seem fitting that my ex-boyfriend is reduced to this gaudy display, except it is in no way Sir Lightlee's fault, who is proving to be a kindhearted gentleman and nothing like the real-life jerk that was Bradley.

"Michelle then," Sir Lightlee responds. "You may call me 'Liam.' And you will be pleased to know I have secured us a ship. Just a small fishing boat, mind you, but it will be suitable for our purposes."

Liam? My brow furrows. "You found someone to sail it?"

"Do not fret. Just a couple of men, desperate for any job. Between them and me, we can manage the boat, although, I fear, it won't be the most favorable accommodations for your ladyship and the boy. I do apologize."

"It's fine. Really, don't worry." My mind returns to Sammie. "What about the merpeople? Do you think they will bother us?"

"I'm hopeful such a small vessel will go unnoticed."

"But if they did discover us, they wouldn't hurt a child, would they?" I disguise my concern for Sammie as if for Trauen's welfare—and I *do* care for Trauen, and no longer think of any of the people of Kalpania as anything other than real. Somehow, in some crazy, improbable way, Kalpania *is* real, which means the danger Sammie faces is also real. If Sammie used the music of the seashells to call to the merpeople as I suspect, then my hope is that they are still the kindhearted creatures I wrote them to be. Yet nothing is for certain. Kalpania has taken on a life of its own, evolving as any real world might, only with surprise additions from Sammie's boundless imagination.

"I know not what the merpeople might do, but, be assured, I'd give my life for the prince's safety and yours." Sir Lightlee calls Trauen over, brushing the sand from his ruffled hair. Holding his hand as a protective father might, he leads the way toward Fisherman's Haven.

"Liam," I say as we set foot on the broken stones of the town's main street. "That's your first name?"

Sir Lightlee gives a light nod as he changes direction, leading us down narrow steps that take us through an alley shortcut to the wharf. I give a sheepish head shake. "Liam" is the name of a boy in Sunday School Sammie obsesses over. Looks like I'm not the only one silly enough to write my crush into a story.

A stooped woman with a worn bag slung to her side meanders down the alley picking through the trash. I shudder as we pass. Was she gray or am I being jumpy? She's probably just old. Ahead two men in tattered clothing sit opposite each other, one smoking a pipe and the other with a cap lowered over his eyes, appearing to sleep. Beyond them the alley exits onto the boardwalk, and my heart quickens to match the pace of my feet as I catch up to Sir Lightlee and grasp Trauen's free hand. I try not to look at either of the men as we pass when a tug on my tunic causes me to give a sharp cry. I whirl and face the man with the cap. His gray hand clings to my tunic, but it's not age that's turned his whiskered stubble white. He can't be much more than sixteen.

"Release her." Sir Lightlee has withdrawn his hand from Trauen and pulled a long dagger that more resembles a round spike. It looks stout enough to pierce armor, and the boy, wearing hardly more than rags, drops his hand.

"Help us." His eyes plead. Eyes that are a deep brown, hurting but alive. "Help my father."

I glance at the other man. He's not budged or looked up since the altercation. His pipe hangs from his mouth over an unkempt beard, hoary and matted. His skin is thick and gnarled like an ancient oak.

"I-I'm sorry."

The father looks up at the sound of my voice. His eyes are a hollow abyss. Hopeless. Dead. I tear my eyes from him and back to those of his son, eyes filled with desperation.

Sir Lightlee sheathes his dagger. "I'm sorry. I am no physician." Sir Lightlee retakes Trauen's hand and turns away.

"Wait! What about the medicine?" My voice causes him to pause.

Sir Lightlee's eyes bore into me. "It is of no use to those overtaken by the shadow illness."

"But the boy. It could help—"

"No!" Sir Lightlee drags Trauen down the boardwalk.

For a moment I linger. "I wish I could help," I whisper, but the boy doesn't respond to my words. His eyes stare off blankly, their color fading into darkness as the last glimmer of hope vanishes.

~~~

I stroke Prattles' nose, and the pony pushes his head toward me and rubs it up and down my shirt. I'm not really an animal person, but I'm starting to grow fond of the affectionate equine. Wyot nibbles at my sleeve, evidently jealous, but when I reach out a hand, he tosses his head as if to say he is much too sophisticated for such lowly pleasures. I smile through my tears at Wyot's antics and return to petting Prattles.

After the encounter with the shadow illness, I followed Sir Lightlee and Trauen back to our tavern, one of the few still open businesses along the boardwalk. They went inside for dinner. I was sure anything I attempted to swallow would get stuck, so I went around to the stables.

I bring my head to Prattles and wrap my arms around him in a hug. I feel like a silly little girl sobbing and hugging a pony, but the image of the boy is fixed in my mind. A hand touches my shoulder. I straighten and turn. "Sir Ligh...uh, Liam." I wipe my face with my hands.

Sir Lightlee passes me a handkerchief from his pocket. "It's clean," he says when I hesitate. "Unlike your face, which looks much like Trauen's before I cleaned him up and put him to bed." Sir Lightlee gives me a half-smile.

Looking at my hands, I realize they are grimy from petting Prattles. Blushing, I wipe my face with the handkerchief, then my hands as best I can. "Is that better?" I don't know whether to return the soiled cloth or shove it into my pocket, so I hold it awkwardly.

"I am sorry about the boy," Sir Lightlee says.

"I know we don't have much of a supply of medicine, and we need it for Trauen. It's just..." I clear a lump in my throat. "Like I watched him die." I finish barely above a whisper.
~~~

Sir Lightlee nods. "It's spreading faster. Too fast. Just before I found you in Oodlesville, I was doing my rounds, surveying the villages of Kalpania, especially Fisherman's Haven and Oodlesville. Yet, I saw only one case of shadow illness. I gave him a little medicine and instructed him to make his way to Magdalin's infirmary. I knew it was of no use. The infirmary is full and has long been out of its supply of glowfruit. I hoped only to spark hope. To stall the spread of the illness in this town. I knew I was sending him to his death."

"What is causing it? This sickness. Can't it be stopped?" I'm twisting the handkerchief in my hand as though to wring an answer from it.

"Kalpania is dying."

"What?"

"The Shadow Witch is seeding despair among the people. Rumors and lies cleverly whispered into the ears of the weak spirited, picked up and carried by others until it spreads like a brushfire. The kidnapping of Princess Taika was undoubtedly to fan it into a blaze. I've tried to keep the news from the ears of the people, but from what I've overheard on the wharf today..."

"They know," I finish.

"Yes." Sir Lightlee pulls a couple of carrots from his pouch and feeds them to Wyot and Prattles as if to distract himself.

"How's Trauen? When he saw those sick men, I was afraid of how it might affect him."

"He's well. I gave him some medicine, but he's asking for you. I told him I would fetch you."

"I'll go to him." I walk toward the door, but a question from something Sir Lightlee said earlier gives me pause. "Why especially Fisherman's Haven and Oodlesville? What makes them more susceptible?"

Sir Lightlee faces me. "One is without work and the other without imagination. These two give purpose and vision. Without them breeds despair."

CHAPTER 8

The fishing boat groans in the waves until I fear it will break in pieces. Mer Bay is calm, but the ship, which is little more than a seafaring version of a hooptie, threatens to come apart at the seams. With every roll of the waves, it lists ever more to the left, though Sir Lightlee assures me that it is only a minor list. But I feel as though I'm riding on a drunken whale and have already disposed of my breakfast. The single triangular sail is an impressive patchwork that reminds me of my granny's quilt sampler. The mast is pockmarked, and the rotted nets are shoved atop a couple barrels placed on the right side in an attempt to balance the boat. If duct tape were a thing on Kalpania, I'm certain it would have been put to use.

Trauen bounces from one end of the vessel to the other, pausing only to lean over the short side.

"Trauen!" I call from a crate I cleared of tackle and turned into a seat. "Sit down! You're going to fall out of the boat."

If Trauen heard me, he's ignoring my warning as he continues to hop about the boat like a mad kangaroo, tripping up one of the sailors. He only grunts at the boy and proceeds to adjust the sail while shouting something in boat lingo at the other man fighting the rudder that is perpetually getting stuck.

"I'm amazed we're not going in circles," I remark to Sir Lightlee, who's sitting across from me at the bow of the ship.

"These are capable men." Sir Lightlee doesn't even look up from his lute. He's been softly plucking all morning, having packed the instrument on Wyot's back till now. With the pony and horse stabled back in Fisherman's Haven, the instrument was brought aboard in a leather carrying bag. This morning is the first time I've heard him play, but I'm too anxious to find it anything more than added noise.

At Sir Lightlee's comment, I steal a glance at the two rough men manning the boat. The men's haggard appearances are less than confidence inspiring, but I keep this thought to myself. "When did you learn to play?" This is a silly question. For some reason now forgotten, I had decided my knight-to-be needed to play an instrument.

"As a young squire." Sir Lightlee never breaks his plucking and strumming. I myself know little about music, but that did not seem to hinder the skill of his fingers over the strings. I wrote of a squire, and he grew into a knight. I gave him an instrument, and he plays with the skill of a master. How much control do I really have over this world? I gave them life and gifts, but I think what they do with it is within their power.

"JJ—I mean, Trauen! Sit. Down." I grab the child as he makes a wild leap from a barrel to my crate and forcefully pull him to a sitting position next to me.

If Sir Lightlee noticed I stumbled over Trauen's name, mixing it up with my son's, he doesn't mention it. Trauen is reduced to tears and exaggerated wailing as I tap my leg in guilt and exasperation.

"Trauen? Would you like to hear an amusing song?" Sir Lightlee asks. "I think humor would do our nerves some good." Sir Lightlee levels his hazel eyes on me, and I blush at his subtle rebuke.

Sir Lightlee turns his eyes back to Trauen, who wipes his nose across his sleeve and nods at the knight. Plucking a few notes, Sir Lightlee's voice rings in a handsome baritone:

"There was a man from afar off land
Who liked to dance and sing,
So he joined himself to a marching band
For joy he hoped to bring.

"But his tune was off, and his notes were flat
And his rhythm was worse, you see.
'You dance like a bat, and sing like a cat,'
Everyone did agree.

"In disgrace and shame, he hung his head
And left the marching band
He sang on the streets to earn his bread
But few pitied the man.

"Then an Enemy arose with a fearful roar
Plundering and ravaging all
So the man from afar, went to war
To heed his country's call.

"With courage and unwavering voice
He began to sing and dance
'What monster doth make such a noise?'
The Enemy halted their advance.

"There was a man from afar off land
Who liked to dance and sing,
With a voice no one could withstand
Victory and joy he did bring."

By the time Sir Lightlee reaches the last stanza, he's leaping and dancing himself in the most comical fashion that it puts a reluctant smile on my face. Trauen laughs, clapping his hands and also jumping to his feet in a clumsy dance. But my smile fades as I notice Trauen's hair has turned white at its roots.

The ship abruptly jolts and dips in a wave like one of those aquatic theme park rides I hate so much. I'm flung from the crate and slam into the side of the boat, nearly going over the gunwale. My scream turns into a sputtering cough as salty water drenches me. What's happening? And where's Trauen? I try to spot him without letting go of my death grip on the ship's side. Another wave drenches me. The sailors are shouting obscenities I am certain I never included in any of my writings. Somehow Sir Lightlee has kept his feet, one arm around the mast as the other keeps a white knuckled grip on his lute.

The ship plunges sideways into another wave, and I fear it will capsize. One of the barrels tumbles toward me, crashing to my left before going overboard. Green ropes lasso the bucking ship like a steer at a rodeo, wrapping around the mast and the bow. Salt stings my eyes and blurs my vision. I've lost sight of Sir Lightlee. The boat crashes through the sea at a speed I don't think it was ever designed to take, groaning in complaint. A hand grasps me firmly and pulls me toward the center of the deck, and I cling to the mast where the malodorous sailors huddle, looking even less capable and perhaps a little frightened.

"Liam!" I grip his arm as another swell flings me against him. "Where's Trauen?"

Sir Lightlee points to the right up ahead. Surrounding the boat, merpeople ride atop great orcas, pulling the fishing vessel bound by ropes of kelp. Trauen is held about the waist by a muscular merman that stands rather than sits upon his orca, for I had created the merpeople to have legs rather than the traditional fish-tail.

"He tumbled out of the boat, but they caught him," Sir Lightlee says.

I tear my hands from Sir Lightlee, hoping my face is already too raw from the seawater for him to notice the heat rising to my cheeks.

"I see you saved your lute first." I nod at the leather bag secured to Sir Lightlee's back to which the instrument's been returned. "You let Trauen nearly drown, and me too."

"As it happened, Trauen did not need me to save him, and you were in no immediate danger."

"We will all drown," Yernar, the taller, pinch-faced sailor, grunts, "for trespassing in their waters. They will execute us by pulling us into the deep."

Garren, the stockier, darker one, chimes his agreement with a short expletive.

Sir Lightlee shakes his head, though he makes no contrary argument, which leaves me feeling less than secure in our fate.

The boat slows. We are being pulled toward Mer City. Sharp rocks surrounding the castle-city make a formidable barrier. Any ship daring to pass them, not knowing the precise location to enter, might find its hull ripped apart by rocks hidden below the water's surface, if they even make it that far. The merpeople have improved their fortress since my writing days; great ballista weapons mount the rocks at various points. I point out the new addition to Sir Lightlee.

"Flame arrows," he says. "The great hooks can penetrate the toughest hulls and are lit using a resin that can burn even upon water."

We have safely passed through the rock barrier, and the sea is calmer. The obsidian stone of Mer City reaches into the sky in great spires carved from an island of lava rock. The majority of the castle I know to be submerged. Underwater passageways lead to numerous above water rooms where individual mer-families live and sleep when not frolicking in the waves.

Our fishing vessel, or what remains of it that hasn't broken off into the sea, is drawn into a large cove. The water sparkles blue-green under the bright sun. The black cliffs surrounding the cove are awash in waterfalls of vines abundant with shades of magenta and yellow flowers. The heady floral scent, intensified by salt, fills my nostrils. Garren sneezes violently. I once again lose sight of Trauen as the boat is moored in a deep cave on the far end of the cove beneath the castle rock above.

I shiver but turn down Sir Lightlee's offer of his overcoat. Partly because I'm still angry with him and also because the coat's as soaked as I am. The orcas have been released and several merpeople have boarded the boat. They are more beautiful and terrifying than my inadequate descriptions could pen. Merpeople's faces bear a resemblance to humans but with a flat nose, small ears absent of lobes, and large round cat-like eyes. The three mermaids that stand before us would be intimidating without the long, curved blades. They are both feminine and fierce, standing taller than the average man by several inches.

At the nod of one of the mermaids, Sir Lightlee hands over his sword and scabbard along with the lute. The tallest of the mermaids, whose upper torso glistens in a fine dark brown fur, reaches forth a webbed hand, pulling Sir Lightlee's dagger from behind his coat. Her round eyes narrow as she thoroughly searches him and the sailors. Yernar and Garren's angry frowns are replaced by fearful glances, but they follow Sir Lightlee's example of no resistance. Garren reluctantly relinquishes a thick leather bag. As the mermaid steps back, the long blue-green fur that covers her from the waist down, parts enough to reveal that she stands upon legs and long, flippered feet.

"Stories are true," Garren whispers. "Mermaid tails become legs upon land."

Sir Lightlee frowns in Garren's direction.

"We prefer 'merwomen,' but my name is Latiliel." Latiliel's voice is musical and vibrant. She rifles through the contents of Garren's bag. "You shall remain silent unless spoken to."

Garren snaps his mouth closed, but his eyes follow his bag as Latiliel hands it to one of the other "merwomen."

Perhaps I should not have called them "merpeople" in my book, for they are humanoid, seafaring mammals, closer in nature to an orca or sea lion than the fish-human cross that is typically brought to mind. In the water, their long fur flows freely with a beauty resembling a betta fish, disguising their legs as though they only have a flowing tail. Their upper body fur is smooth and short; save the merwomen have long mane-like fur extending from the back of the neck and covering their bosom. They have nothing like human hair, and their heads are smooth and round and, like their face, covered in the same short seal-like fur as their upper torso.

As they usher us toward the end of the boat, I scan the rocky ledge before us and am relieved to see Trauen standing unharmed next to the muscled merman. Trauen's eyes are wide, and I wave at him. He sees me and smiles, running toward me. None of the merpeople try to stop him. He slips on the slick stone, wincing, but gets right back to his feet.

"I rode a whale!" Trauen shouts, panting, as he stands on the edge of the rock near the boat. His trousers are torn and his hands scraped.

"I saw. Please be careful." I try to reach out to him from the rails of the boat.

The muscled merman reaches us and motions for me to exit the boat. Sensing my hesitation, he grabs me by my arm and heaves me onto the rock. Sir Lightlee and the other men are escorted off the vessel by Latiliel and the merwomen. The merman, still grasping my arm with his long half-webbed fingers, pulls me along the slippery rocks. The barnacles provide some traction but I'd hate to fall upon them. Trauen tags from behind and takes my free hand. The merman leads us deeper into the castle down a dark passage lit on occasion by oil lamps that give my captor's eyes an eerie glow. At least now the rock is dry, but to my dismay, I discover in a backward glance that Sir Lightlee and the sailors are not following, but have been taken elsewhere.

The merman stops at an iron door, unlocking it, and Trauen and I are ushered into a dimly lit room not much bigger than a walk-in closet. The door shuts and the lock's resounding clang pronounces us imprisoned.

CHAPTER 9

I sit on the stone ledge that protrudes from the left wall forming what could be used as a seat or bed in the otherwise barren room. Forcing back tears, I take Trauen in my arms, holding his shivering body close. The white in his hair is lengthening. I examine his scraped hands, relieved to see his blood is still red, but his skin is ashen. Maybe it's the dim light, or maybe it's my fear taking hold.

"I'm cold," Trauen mumbles.

I turn his face toward me. His deep eyes have neither turned gray nor hollow. I set him on my lap and give him a tighter hug.

"Riding a whale is pretty cool." I need to stay positive for Trauen's sake. Fear and hopelessness must not set in.

Trauen nods and smiles. I reflect he probably doesn't know the expression "cool," but he evidently caught my meaning through my faked enthusiasm.

"I can't wait to tell Taika..." Trauen's excitement tapers off at the end. "What if we don't find her?"

"Don't give up. Why don't we pray for her?" My prayer life hasn't exactly become revived since I came to Kalpania. I'm just more desperate.

Trauen stares at me, blinking.

"You know…you don't know what 'prayer' is do you?"

Trauen shakes his head.

Sir Lightlee's confusion at my mention of prayer comes to mind. Does no one in this world pray? Back in my youth, in the days of novel writing, I thought my faith was strong. But I never inserted any of my beliefs into my stories, and maybe because it was all a sham. Over time, prayer and church became little more than religious exercises. It isn't that I've stopped believing in God; I've only stopped believing that He hears me.

"Well…" I try to formulate my thoughts—my beliefs. "Prayer is talking to God. Do you know about God, Trauen?"

Trauen again shakes his head.

"God is the Creator. The One who made all things." I pause and ponder for a moment. *Is He the Creator of this world too?* Until now, I thought I created this world. A world of which I had lost control. Maybe God created it through me. Perhaps this whole adventure is some kind of cosmic joke to show me just how much I am not in control—not of my life, not of Sammie's life.

"Did He make the merpeople?" Trauen asks. "I like the merpeople."

I can't say I'm particularly fond of them at the moment. A loud clack startles me as the door unlocks and opens. I set Trauen down and stand as a tall merwoman enters with an armful of dry garments. She sets them down and exits without saying a word. I direct Trauen to face the opposite corner, which is all the privacy we have to strip free of our wet clothing and don the soft robes. They have a plain shape and tie with a kelp rope about the middle. Not flattering, but warm and dry. The material is a fine multicolored weave, and I realize with a start that I had no idea that the merpeople made garments. Another example of how this world has evolved beyond anything I wrote.

Never having heard the door relock, I pull on it and am rewarded with a heavy groan as it scrapes along the stone floor. The merwoman stands outside. With a silent hand signal she motions us to follow. Trauen and I shuffle after her. Trauen's gown is a little too long, and he trips on it more than once. I am busy trying to keep mine from gaping when we enter an immense, brightly lit room. My eyes follow the great black pillars up to the high stone ceiling. Sunlight streams from openings in the stone through which seagulls fly in and perch on the ledges above.

The room is filled with the shrill yet musical voices of merpeople conversing with one another. It's hard to describe their speech, but it is similar to the communications of orcas and absolutely nothing like human speech. High pitch trills mingle with low pulses, echoing off the high ceiling in captivating harmony. Though I can't understand it, my pounding heart is put at ease, and I think Yernar is wrong about the merpeople's intentions to drown us. They wouldn't have rescued Trauen or given us dry robes if they had evil intentions toward us. I only wish I knew why they had taken our boat, and us, captive.

The merwoman waves us toward a pillar on the right side of the room. Trauen is the first to spot Sir Lightlee and runs toward him. Sir Lightlee picks him up in a hug before setting him down on the stone floor. Yernar and Garren stand off to one side gaping at the noisy scene about us. In the center of the great room, mermen and merwomen lie about a great pool leading into the lower, watery depths of the castle. Though the merpeople don't breathe underwater, they can hold their breath easily for two to three hours. Trauen laughs and points as an orca pokes his nose above the pool to receive a treat from one of the merwomen before diving back below.

Sir Lightlee and the sailors are covered with identical robes to mine, and as I walk toward them, I can't help but notice Garren's hairy chest peeking through his robe. This leads to me excessively double checking mine to make sure I'm decent. A few of the merpeople around us wear robes for warmth when not in the water, but either because of their fur or a lack of a human sense of modesty, give little care to whether the robe is opened or closed.

"What now?" I ask Sir Lightlee when I'm close enough for him to hear my whisper. I'm not sure why I'm whispering. The merpeople seem to have no interest in guarding us, but then where would we go?

Sir Lightlee finishes giving Trauen his medicine before answering. "We wait."

When I realize that Sir Lightlee has nothing more to say, my earlier anger is renewed against him. "That's it? You save your lute when Trauen and I are in danger, and now have nothing more to say than 'we wait'? For what? The merpeople to decide whether or not to drown us? What type of knight are you?"

When I finally break my flurry of questions long enough to take a breath, Sir Lightlee opens his mouth, then shakes his head looking away.

Garren clears his throat. "Speakin' of merpeople." He gives a nod to our right.

Coming toward us is Latiliel, her now dry blue-green fur whirling around her legs gracefully. She returns to Sir Lightlee his lute and the bag to Garren, who practically snatches it from her. Wheeling gracefully, Latiliel commands us to follow with a motion of her hand. Yernar looks as though he's about to bolt and take his chances. Sir Lightlee puts a hand on his shoulder, then picks up Trauen, and follows Latiliel. Grunting in resignation, Yernar follows. Garren strides after, clutching his bag, and I stumble in the rear, still struggling with the robe, but with my curiosity peaked as to the contents in Garren's bag.

Latiliel leads us past the right side of the pool to the front of the great room occupied by a long stone table. The table is low and without chairs, so we sit on the hard ground. Prepared before us is an assortment of food: clams, shrimp, a warm soup consisting of seaweed, and an enormous grilled fish. As I recall from my old journals, the merpeople are mainly carnivorous and satisfied to eat their meat raw, but also will roast food above water for special occasions. This causes me to be hopeful they mean well toward us.

Yernar and Garren seem to have forgotten all fear of the merpeople and are greedily gulping down huge bites of fish. Sir Lightlee remains silent and thoughtful, and I consider apologizing to him for my outburst. At least he thought to keep Trauen's medicine on him. Trauen's color is returning to him, but his eyes look listless. Perhaps he is just tired. I encourage him to sip the soup, fearing he may catch cold...or worse. Lifting the bowl to my mouth, I take a sip. Salty, but not bad.

Latiliel returns with the muscled merman that took Trauen and me from the ship, and also another merwoman. The merman's fur, which appeared dark gray in the dim halls, now shimmers in the sunlight, a deep iridescent blue that only accentuates his impressive bulk. The other merwoman standing beside Latiliel is a creamy white, the long furs about her legs and the mane across her chest a golden red. They stand at the opposite side of the table, and Latiliel announces: "Her Majesty, Queen Nateliah, Guardian of the Sea, and her royal husband, Mordecai, Captain of the Queen's Guard."

A queen! I gave no leadership to the merpeople, wanting them only to be kindhearted and playful sea-people. The distant laughter by the pool and the generous meal shows they still possess these initial traits, but they are like children grown up. Fierce and independent, they abandoned the path I set for them, writing their own story. Facing the present danger in their world, they rose to the occasion and established order amidst the chaos.

Sir Lightlee stands and gives a short bow. The rest of us follow his example. I'm careful not to disturb Trauen, who has fallen asleep on the floor.

Latiliel continues, "Her Majesty, in remembrance of the late Queen of Kalpania, wishes no harm to you and graciously will send forth you and your ship back to your lands. But she warns that you must not again trespass upon these seas until the plague of the shadow illness is cleansed."

"Forgive us—" Sir Lightlee begins.

"You can't...we can't," I interrupt, "Your Majesty. We have to get to the Tangled—"

"Silence!" Latiliel's voice takes on the sound of a dissonant chord.

Something stirs in Queen Nateliah's arms, which are crossed over her chest. A faint bleating sound is followed by the Queen's soft humming. She holds a nursing merchild to her breasts. Mordecai frowns at me. Queen Nateliah trills something to Latiliel in their language.

"Normally, our queen would not speak in your coarse language," Latiliel says, "but she wishes to speak words with you." The disdain toward me is evident in both Latiliel's tone and expression. "Alone."

Latiliel motions for the men at our table to follow her.

"May Sir Lightlee stay?" I point toward him. "Please." I know I'm speaking out of turn again, but I'd rather not be left alone.

Latiliel seems about to silence me again, but Mordecai thrums something to her, then to me in human tongue, "The child may also remain." His voice is like the bass notes of a cello. He nods toward Trauen, still passed out on the ground.

Latiliel departs with Yernar and Garren in tow looking as though they were headed for gallows. Mordecai and Queen Nateliah converse for a moment with each other. Then the queen says, "State your name and purpose for trespassing into our waters." Her voice is higher than Latiliel's, but regal, like a fine tuned instrument.

"My name is Michelle Sansbury, and I'm trying to find my daughter, Sammie. I think she's in the Tangled Woods..." Too late, I realize I forgot to use my cover story.

Sir Lightlee's brow furrows as he looks my way. I avoid his gaze.

"Um...Trauen also needs the medicine made from the glowfruit found in the woods. If he doesn't get it..." My voice fades. I shouldn't let them know Trauen has the shadow illness. Who knows how they will react. I'm making a mess of this whole thing.

"We know the child is ill." Queen Nateliah takes on the note of a concerned mother. She looks down at her own child sleeping in her arms. Not as though she were afraid for him, but as if she is considering how she would feel were Trauen her own. Now she turns toward Sir Lightlee. "We know your faithfulness. We know you seek Princess Taika. She is hiding in the Tangled Woods, and the fate of Kalpania hangs in the balance should she be found."

"I feared the worst. That she was taken by the Shadow Witch," Sir Lightlee says.

"She is not, but the Shadow Witch seeks her. She must not be found." Queen Nateliah speaks a moment with her husband. "We can provide a small amount of glowfruit extract for the prince. It is concentrated. Only a few drops a day is necessary."

"Yet will eventually run out." Sir Lightlee speaks in a tone more desperate than I have heard from him before. "The plague spreads, and Kalpania is on the verge of panic. The princess—"

"Is on a mission that may be the only hope of saving our world," the queen says.

"Then we need to get to the Tangled Woods and help her," I say.

"You mean find your daughter." Sir Lightlee gives me a disgruntled look. "Is your daughter even an enchantress? I don't suppose you ever meant to find the princess."

"I have to get my daughter home."

"Your friend, good knight," Mordecai cuts in, his words are inhumanly low and as harsh as a bass string gone flat. "Is no friend to Kalpania."

His gaze levels on me, and I involuntarily flinch. "I care about Trauen, I wouldn't—"

"You would let us all fall into shadow," Queen Nateliah says.

"You don't know me!" I blink my eyes, holding back the angry tears, feeling like a child being reprimanded. What weird nightmare have I fallen into being scolded by people I created? I want to scream at them. They won't stop me from getting Sammie home safely, and when I do, I will write them all out of existence. Trauen stirs, mumbling in his sleep. A lump forms in my throat. No, I wouldn't—couldn't do that. I may have abandoned my stories, but I still care about them. And somehow they have become real.

The queen stares through me as though she knows my mind. The merpeople are intelligent and possess a magic over the seas, but they are not telepathic. What does the queen think she knows about me? Why is she determined to keep me from following Sammie?

Queen Nateliah looks down tenderly at her infant, stroking it with her webbed fingers. She turns to her husband and he nods. Like many married couples they seem to know what each other are thinking, and I long for Michael by my side. I feel alone and even Sir Lightlee is no longer an ally thanks to my lies. *Oh God, get me out of this nightmare.*

"Your daughter is Princess Taika," the queen finally says to me.

"No, she...what?"

"She called for our help, and we brought her to the other side of the sea to the Tangled Woods. She must complete her mission."

"Sammie can't be. We're not from this world."

Sir Lightlee is staring at me in a way that is discomfiting. I wonder what is going through his head. He is as surprised by this news as me. He turns to the queen. "The Shadow Witch will never stop until she finds the princess."

"All the more reason that I need to get to the Tangled Woods," I say. "She's a nine-year-old child, alone."

"It's the reason we must send you away," Queen Nateliah answers. "You would take the princess from us. But she is not alone."

Unbidden tears form in my eyes, and I quickly blink them away and take a calming breath. Before I can ask any more questions about Sammie or who might be with her, Queen Nateliah passes her sleeping infant to her husband, who holds the child delicately for all his strength. The queen walks to my side and places her webbed fingers on my shoulder, leading me away toward the pool.

I glance back at Sir Lightlee, who stares after me with a pensive frown but remains with Mordecai and Trauen.

"The King will not return," Queen Nateliah says, "for the Queen never made him a part of her reign."

"What?" I say, puzzled over this sudden new topic.

Queen Nateliah releases my shoulder and ascends the stone steps that wind around the backside of the pool. The water echoes as it laps against the black stones in the quiet of the cavernous room—the merpeople have hushed their laughter in their queen's presence. She motions for me to follow, and I keep one hand on the stone wall, fearful of slipping off the open side of the steps and into the inky blue pool below. The stone steps appear to have been roughly chipped for more stable footing, but I still freeze and cling against the wall when an orca leaps within the pool, showering me with saltwater.

Queen Nateliah takes my arm, guiding me up the last few steps and out onto a balcony overlooking the sea to the west where the sun lowers itself into the bay.

"Listen," the queen says.

I hear nothing other than the roar of the sea crashing against the jagged rocks below and the evening cry of the gulls.

Queen Nateliah hums an eerie pulsing call. Is it the waves that are silenced or has my hearing been extended beyond them? A moaning cry glides across the water from some distant place beyond my sight. Weeping? I think I hear someone call my name, but before I can distinguish the voice, I am deafened again by the crashing sea. The queen's large eyes gaze into mine.

"What was that?" I ask.

"What the Shadow Witch does to others. Drowns their voices, so she can't hear them. She contrived a war with Valdisar to rid Kalpania of leadership."

I look away and clutch my robe to my chest. "I'm sorry..."

For what? Not taking a book seriously? Is she saying the King is dead? There's nothing I can do about it now. "Look, I don't understand. What does this have to do with my daughter?"

Queen Nateliah turns, pausing at the top of the steps, and whispers, "Everything."

CHAPTER 10

Sammie shivered and drew her arms around her knees. The canopy of broad leaves provided some protection against the rain, but a large drop plopped on her head and slid down her hair, tickling her ear. Sammie adjusted the robe so it covered her head. The robe was soft, and the merpeople told her it was woven from seagull feathers. It wasn't waterproof, but it would take more than a few drops to soak it.

Where was Tony? Sammie was in a partly hollowed out place in The Branches of the Tangled Woods. When Sammie first saw the woods, she couldn't have been more thrilled. They were just as she imagined them— no, even better. The Tangled Woods grew in a massive canyon. Sammie simply stepped off the clifftop onto a huge branch. Many of the branches were as wide as a grownup was tall, so Sammie didn't fear falling. She ran along them. Some winding higher and others lower—twisting, knotting, meandering around the enormous tree trunks. Other branches grew into each other, making even wider paths. Even the one time when Sammie did slip on the moss, a lower branch caught her. The woods grew so thick you couldn't even see the bottom, so she could almost forget she was high off the ground.

This was where the Cha-Chas lived, and Sammie would find them. Undoubtedly, Peanut Butter and Jelly Sandwich the Third had come back here. Sammie was sure that as soon as she told him that JJ was sick, he would come home right away. Mischievous as he was, Peanut Butter loved JJ and would help him get better. Maybe when he sends one of JJ's hugs to Daddy, he would send a message for him to come home. Then Mama would be happy again. They would be a family, and go to the beach or maybe the redwood forest. It wasn't as cool as Kalpania, but it would be fun because they would be together.

The sun had set, but the forest ceiling of tightly woven branches and leaves blocked Sammie's view of the stars. Sammie hadn't minded during the day. It kept her cool. But Sammie hated the dark. She hummed softly to herself, trying to be brave, trying not to cry. If only she could glimpse the stars. In the morning, she would climb to The Leaves—breathe the fresh air, and watch the sun rise. The Leaves was where the flying and climbing creatures all lived—birds and the giant butterflies, chattering squirrels and lazy sloths. The branches were thin there, and Sammie would have to be careful, but it would be worth it to see the sky.

Sammie tried not to think about The Roots at the bottom of the canyon. There the giant, gnarled roots of the trees tore in and out of the ground, making deep caves and sucking greedily from the swampy pools. It was a dark place, even in the day. A place where Sammie buried her worst fears because Mama told her to think happy thoughts at bedtime. So Sammie tucked them all neatly away in The Roots where they couldn't hurt her...unless she accidentally found herself there. If she slipped. If she fell far enough...

"Count the stars: One, two, three
Beacons shine for you and me
Gentle light from above
Reminding us of God's love
He knows the name of every one
But yours is kept by His Son."

Sammie sang the words to the simple tune that Mama had taught her when she was just a little girl still afraid of nightmares. It had been so long since she sang those words she was surprised she still remembered them. As Sammie hummed through the melody again, it seemed as though a star was floating through The Branches toward her. The warm, soft glow grew nearer and brighter; then Sammie laughed. It was a unilope. The dainty deer-like animal trotted across the wide branch toward her, its one long horn protruding from its forehead, glowing softly. Unilopes weren't dangerous, unless of course you made them very angry.

"Hello." Sammie held out a clump of moss.

The unilope approached her hesitantly then nibbled the moss. Sammie giggled as its warm tongue tickled her fingers. The unilope sniffed her hair and nibbled it too.

"No, no, silly." Sammie laughed. "Ouch!"

The unilope jerked its head around.

"I didn't mean to startle you. But you were pulling my hair."

It shook its head and its horn grew brighter. So did two eyes floating over the branch above them.

"Oh." Sammie could tell by the long, black bushy tail swishing from side to side that it was a purple-spotted jaguar, though she could not make out anything else in the dim light.

The unilope snorted. Its horn flashed brightly to blind the jaguar, and Sammie got a good look at its long claws gripping the tree bark and its shiny white teeth as it gave a low yowl. Then the unilope put out its light and bolted. But did the jaguar follow? Sammie tried to hush her breathing. Purple-spotted jaguars liked to eat unilopes. But did it like the taste of a young girl? She wished for the notebook that had been left on her bed, so she could swiftly write that purple-spotted jaguars do not care to eat children.

The soft padding of paws landing on her branch caused Sammie's heart to skip. Sammie pressed her back against the wall of the hollow and wondered how long she could hold her breath.

~~~

The words fade before my eyes. I flip through the pages, closing the book and reopening it. Nothing. Frustrated, I slam it on the worn wooden table that looks to have suffered far worse abuse. My daughter's in danger, and the Shadow Witch is taunting me with a cliffhanger. I imagine her cackling in some dark room watching me through a crystal ball. Tears burn my eyes as I picture Sammie alone and frightened, and guilt tightens my chest as I reflect on Sammie's wish for us to be a family again. Why hadn't I taken the kids out more in Michael's absence? "We can't interrupt our school schedule. We have to stay on track," were the words I told myself. I was concerned about their academics, but what about Sammie and JJ's emotional health? My discontent with Michael's military career and constant deployments affected my children more than I realized. And Sammie picked up on the unhappiness I tried to hide.

"Can I be of help?" Sir Lightlee appears at my side, his voice cooler toward me, as it has been since the merpeople escorted our ship back to Fisherman's Haven. His hazel eyes seem darker. Maybe it's the dim tavern light.

"Trauen asleep?" I avoid answering his question, and avert my eyes from his gaze.
~~~

Sir Lightlee nods, and I wait for him to either turn away or sit, but he continues to stand as motionless as the palace guards I met at the top steps of Magdalin. That seems like forever ago, and I wonder if Magdalin is still the bright City of Stairs, or if it, like Fisherman's Haven, has given itself over to shadow. We spent only one night in Mer City and are back in the little fishing village the day after we left. The transformation from fading hope to complete despair in so short a time is chilling.

"Sit," I finally say, adding "please" to soften the irritation in my voice.

To my surprise, for I expected him to make an excuse to retire, Sir Lightlee sits stiffly across from me and waves the bartender over for ale. It's the first time I've seen him drink. His usual cheerfulness has faded since the revelation of my real purpose. I thought him angry at me for lying, but I wonder now if he has not also given into the despair around us. The tavern owner, who must also act as bartender and waiter in his own establishment, is the only person left besides us in this forlorn place that has not been taken by the shadow illness.

For a long time neither of us say anything. The rain outside pings off of something made of metal, and I absentmindedly wonder what it is.

"You worried about Magdalin?" I whisper, fingering my mug of tea. I'm beginning to get used to doing without coffee.

"Magdalin, Trauen, all of Kalpania. Yes." His stare feels accusatory.

"It's not true, you know," I say more sharply than I mean to. "What the mer-queen said about me."

"That you are here for your daughter and not to help Kalpania."

"No...that's true. I meant the part of me allowing Kalpania to fall into shadow. Of course I don't want that to happen. And I don't mean to take your princess either. Queen Nat—whatever her name is—she's mistaken about Sammie being Princess Taika."

Sir Lightlee's lips press together into something of a smirk as he leans back and folds his arms. "Queen *Nateliah* is renowned for her insight. Some say it is even more of a foresight. She cut off her people from the rest of Kalpania long before the rest of us knew we were even in danger." Sir Lightlee leans forward. "*Your* daughter *is* Princess Taika. Ask him." Sir Lightlee lifts his chin toward the tavern owner.

"What would he know?"

"*Ask him.*"

"Fine," I say, pushing my weight against the table as I stand and spilling part of my tea. On second thought, I'm sick of tea and could use a really strong cup of black coffee. No sugar, no milk—just bitter dark water to match my mood. The tavern owner smiles as I walk over to him. I hesitate, running a hand across the rough wood of the counter.

"Johann? Right? So the shadow illness didn't get you?" *What a stupid thing to say.*

Johann's still smiling, though I think it's a sort of sad smile. "The shadow illness takes those that have no hope."

What hope could you possibly have? I want to ask, instead, "Did you see a young girl here a few days ago?" There are probably a few young girls in this town. I need to be more specific. "She's nine, about this tall—"

"You're asking about the princess," he interrupts.

"No. My daughter." *A miniature version of me, stubborn, with wild flights of fancy, and no practical skills for surviving the real world.* "She might have been with someone." *Who is Tony?* The idea of Sammie with a boy might have unsettled me except I'm more anxious that he return in time to protect her from the jaguar.

"The child I met was with a shaggy white dog."

Of course.

"She wanted a boat to take her across Mer Bay. And though I told her it was impossible with the way the merpeople been against us. She said, 'Everything's impossible if you don't try.' She was a mighty persistent little thing. Friendly. Brought a smile to everyone. I think she found her way."

That sounds like Sammie.

"But I'd expect no less from the princess," Johann adds. "Her smile kept this town from despair, if only for a few more days. I'm sorry you had to see it die."

"Have you met the princess before? What makes you think this girl was Princess Taika?" I turn and frown at Sir Lightlee, who is smirking even more than before as he eavesdrops on our conversation.

"I never seen her before," Johann answers, "but a princess is something that you recognize by her spirit. She wasn't going to stop for nothing to help her sick brother."

"Glowfruit?" I ask. It and the Tangled Woods is Sammie's creation. Is that why she was determined to go there? Some mislead idea that her magic fruit would cure JJ's fever?

Johann shrugs and laughs. "Something about a 'peanut butter and jelly sandwich.' I've owned this tavern for twenty years. Can't say I even know what that is. But I'd add it to my menu if it'd stay the plague. She promised to return and show me how to make one. That's what keeps me. I'll be here when she returns."

~~~

"If I have to, I'll go by myself," I say with conviction. "You can go back to Magdalin and rot, but I'm going to save my daughter."

I'd never thought of myself as a courageous person. When I was young, all my adventures were in my head. When I finally overcame my fear enough to share them with the world, the slightest criticism cowed me into retreat. I may have given up on my dreams, but I am fully prepared to die for Sammie. I didn't close my eyes
~~~

once last night, impatiently waiting for morning—and with a plan.

"As I said"—Sir Lightlee cinches the saddle on Wyot and takes on a tone of one about to lecture a child—"the road along the bay was made impassable due to last month's earthquake, and the landslide remains uncleared—likely for good. With the merpeople guarding the sea, the Tangled Woods is unreachable. Unless you are proposing we hike over the White Mountains—a venture that could take months and most likely result in our deaths."

"We could take the mountain pass, and—"

"If death by giants is preferable to you."

"If we do nothing, Sammie could be killed or taken by the Shadow Witch, Trauen by his illness..." I take a deep breath, trying to compose myself and hating my traitorous tears. "Maybe if we work together we can save them *and* Kalpania. Otherwise, we might as well surrender to the Shadow Witch."

Sir Lightlee strokes Wyot's nose, not looking at me. "So now you care about Kalpania?"

"I never *didn't* care. I just..." What am I supposed to say? I hadn't thought his world was real?

"Abandoned us." Sir Lightlee pulls out a sugar cube, and Wyot nibbles it out of his hand. Prattles nickers, nudging Sir Lightlee.

"Can I give it to him?" Trauen tugs Sir Lightlee's arm. I'd forgotten he was there; he'd been so quiet.

Sir Lightlee places the sugar cube in Trauen's palm. The boy's eyes dance with delight as only a child can over a pony eating out of his hand. I can't help but smile, even through my tears. Sir Lightlee smiles too— the first I'd seen all morning. I puzzle over his accusation. Sure I lied about my purpose here, but that hardly qualifies as abandonment.

"Trauen needs his medicine, and Sammie needs me." I whisper hoarsely. "I...we just need your help."

Sir Lightlee leads the horses out of the stable before answering. "We'd have to let the horses go once we reach the pass. There are only two ways we can hope to make it past the giants: stealth or speed. With the way you and Trauen ride, speed is out of the question."

I wipe the tears from my face. "Liam, I know you're doing this for Trauen, but...thank you."

Sir Lightlee looks me in the eye. "I do it for Trauen *and Princess Taika.*" He still believes Sammie is the princess.

Sir Lightlee helps me on Prattles and sets Trauen behind me. Today he wears a full set of armor, though his helmet is hooked on the back of Wyot's saddle alongside his lute. The armor had been left in the care of the tavern owner along with the horses when we boarded our ship. He once told me he rides with his armor because it gives the people a symbol of strength in the absence of a queen and king. As we ride toward the end of Fisherman's Haven and pass the expressionless faces of the people, I wonder if there are any left in Kalpania to appreciate the symbol.

"Liam," I say, pointing at the road ahead. The people of Fisherman's Haven have gathered at the edge of town. A few even stand in the road.

"They intend to not let us leave," Sir Lightlee says.

I grip Prattles' reins tighter. Until now those overtaken by the shadow illness expressed apathy, not aggression. Unwanted thoughts of the shadow elf invade my mind—his chilling touch and putrid breath. "Hold on tight." I clasp Trauen's wrist with my free hand as his arms tighten around me.

As we draw closer, the people mob around our horses, forcing us to slow our pace or run them over. Sir Lightlee doesn't seem any more inclined than me to do the latter; even if they are under the witch's power, they were once people of Kalpania with families and homes. I try not to look in their lifeless eyes as their ashen hands and arms grasp at us. Trauen whimpers. A strong hand claws at my arm, and a shiver runs through my body, giving me a brain freeze like I gobbled ice cream too fast. Prattles gives a short lunge, and I tear my arm free, losing a button off my sleeve. The steadfast pony snorts and pushes through the crowd as resilient as a warhorse.

Wyot tosses his head and trumpets, half rearing. The medallions jangle on the horse's armor, flashing in the sunlight. Sir Lightlee pulls out his sword and goads Wyot into a short charge. Several people are knocked over. "Do not force me to send you into oblivion," Sir Lightlee shouts. "Let us pass!"

I breathe easier as the crowd starts to back off. They may be under the Shadow Witch's influence, but they seem unwilling to die for her. A tall man scrambles off the ground, holding his arm. Black blood oozes between his ashen fingers. My stomach sinks as I recognize him. *Yernar.*

We've made it out of the town, and a light breeze picks up, blowing away the stench of rotting flesh. I gulp mouthfuls of salty sea air. The Great Mer Bay sparkles in the distance, surreal and peaceful. We turn our horses on the dirt road that winds toward the hills when something whizzes past my head and glances off Wyot's armor with a metallic chink. Sir Lightlee spurs his horse in front of me as several more *thwumps* sound around us.

A dark arrow is embedded deeply into a nearby tree. The ridge ahead is lined with gray men.

Sir Lightlee clenches his sword, his eyes solemn. "You were wrong. I fight for Trauen and Princess Taika..." He looks directly at me. "And for my Queen."

CHAPTER 11

My heart feels like it is trying to push its way out of my chest. A dozen armed men block the road ahead.

"Shadow elves!" Sir Lightlee shouts. "Go left and don't stop." He spurs Wyot, and they race up the hill as more arrows rain.

I urge Prattles into a gallop off the road and into a field. My riding hasn't greatly improved, and it's all I can do to cling to him and hope he doesn't stumble. Prattles once again impresses me. He's as surefooted as if he'd been bred from a mountain goat. Trauen giggles at our swift ride. My stomach lurches in sharp rebellion at Prattles' choppy gate.

Swift movement from our right catches my eye. A tall, gray creature is keeping pace with our horse. *A shadow elf!* If the vile being was once a wood elf before it came under the witch's power, it is no wonder it can run so swift. Prattles seems to sense the danger and stretches his neck as he picks up speed, but it's not enough to lose the elf. Trauen's grip tightens around me as I fight to stay in the saddle.

A clawed hand reaches out. There's a tug, and Trauen gives a sharp cry. My body slams into the weeds, and for a moment I'm too stunned to move. I lift my head, coughing and spitting out dirt. My head is pounding and bright flashes obscure my vision. I wipe my eyes. The ringing in my ears clear as Trauen's yells are cut short. Stumbling too quickly to my feet, my knees nearly buckle. My vision comes into focus. Trauen's hands claw against the shadow elf's arm that's wrapped around his neck.

I glance around for a stick, or anything I can use as a weapon. "Let him go." My voice is a pitiful screech.

"The book," the elf says in a voice like the grinding of a hacksaw. The wood elves had musical voices.

"Book?" I repeat stupidly. *What book?*

The shadow elf only points with a pale finger. His long, curved nail is black.

I look down at the pouch slung to my side by the strap across my chest. Inside is the book of the Shadow Witch. "Let go of Trauen, and I'll give it to you." Maybe that's the book he wants; I don't really care. It's the only book I have. I guess the Shadow Witch wants her book back.

Dragging Trauen with him, the shadow elf stalks toward me. I back away. I'm not really in a position to bargain, but he'll have to let go of Trauen to chase me down. That would allow the prince to escape.

The shadow elf stops a few feet short of me. He shows no inclination to release Trauen. "The book. Read it."

Backing away a little farther, I open my pouch while not taking my eyes off the elf. I want to be far enough away that he won't be able to snatch the book from me without letting go of Trauen. "Okay. I have the book," I say as I pull it from the pouch. "Let Trauen go, and I'll toss it to you."

"Read," he repeats. His arm tightens around Trauen's neck, whose feet are kicking above ground.

"You're choking him. Put him down!" I open the book to show him I'm complying.

The shadow elf sets Trauen back down. His breath wheezes, but he can breathe.

I look down at the open book, praying it cooperates. I can't read blank pages.

~~~

Sammie walked along the wide branch with Tony on one side and Spottie on the other. Sammie didn't know the purple-spotted jaguar's real name, so she nicknamed her "Spottie." It wasn't a very girly name, but Sammie had thought Spottie was a boy until Tony Cheesecracker came back and told her otherwise.

Spottie suddenly leaped up a branch and pounced at a huge butterfly. She missed and the butterfly landed on Sammie's head. Sammie stood perfectly still not wanting to frighten the butterfly away. "No, Spottie." Sammie said firmly.

Spottie swished her tail in irritation, eyeing the butterfly perched on Sammie's head. Its huge wings spread out, making Sammie look like she had a big yellow hat.

"Everyone should have a butterfly hat, don't you think?" Sammie put a hand on her hip and batted her eyes in a grown up lady impression. "How do I look?" she asked Tony. "Tony?" Where had he gone now? Cha-Chas sure could be frustrating sometimes.

Tony became visible again just below Spottie. The shaggy dog leaped at the swishing tail. Spottie growled and landed on top of Tony, and the two tumbled off the branch and onto another one below.

Sammie ran over with the butterfly still on her head and looked down. Tony had gone invisible again, but Spottie was still on his back. It looked like she was perched in thin air riding an invisible bucking bull.

"You two stop roughhousing this instant!" Sammie mimicked her Mama's voice exactly the way she would have gotten on to her and JJ. "Why, I'm becoming my mother." Sammie giggled. It was something she once heard Mama say.

Last night, when the purple-spotted jaguar had been creeping her way, Sammie had suddenly remembered
~~~

the dried fish the merpeople had given her. Sammie hadn't liked it at all, but Spottie loved it and had been following her ever since. When Tony finally came back from wherever he had been, the two had soon become playmates.

"Tony, we need to go," Sammie drawled out her "o" in exasperation. "Are we almost there?" They were headed toward the Cha-Chas' home somewhere in The Branches in the middle of the Tangled Woods where the glowfruit grew. Peanut Butter and Jelly Sandwich the Third was going to be in so much trouble when Sammie found him. Why don't Cha-Chas ever listen?

Sammie carefully shooed the butterfly off her head. He was making her hot. The air was stickier than Mama's bathroom after a shower, and Sammie wiped the sweat from her eyes with her sleeve and glanced around. She was beginning to feel worried, like someone was watching her. She hadn't seen any sign of the Shadow Witch or her minions, but she knew the worst of the shadow creatures lived in The Roots, and Sammie wanted to find Peanut Butter before they found her.

~~~

I lift my eyes from the book at the bray of a horse and thunder of hooves. A familiar man leaps from Wyot with surprising grace for his stocky bulk and lands in the grass, immediately dropping to one knee. He steadies a weapon resembling a long rifle. Even as the shadow elf turns, the man looses a spear from the gun that punctures the elf's chest—a perfect shot far above Trauen, but it still causes me to suck in a breath. The shadow elf's rasping cry is like fingernails on a chalkboard, and I involuntarily cover my ears. Trauen, freed from the elf's grasp, runs toward me, and I uncover my ears to wrap my arms around the shaking child.

The shadow elf drops to his knees holding the spear with both hands. Black blood stains the green grass
~~~

below him. The man walks grimly toward the shadow being. I gasp as I recognize him. *Garren!* He pulls a short curved blade from his side. Trauen glances up, and I cover his eyes as Garren frees the creature of his head, silencing the hissing cry. The shadow elf's body crumples to the ground. I think the man looks impatient as he stares at the elf until, like smoke in the wind, the body dissipates and no trace remains except the dark blood on the spear and grass below.

Garren collects his spear, cleaning it off in the damp grass. He looks at me and says, "Have to sanitize it properly before I use it to spear fish for supper."

Supper is the last thing on my mind, and my stomach turns at the thought.

Wyot is stamping impatiently in the grass. Red blood runs down his foreleg from a gash in his upper leg. Prattles trots over whinnying and nudges Wyot, who tosses his proud head and rolls his eyes anxiously. Yet, he soon calms, and I think he's glad of the pony's company.

"Where's Sir Lightlee?" Horrible images form in my mind.

In answer, Trauen pulls free from me and runs across the grass. Sir Lightlee is hobbling over, holding that mysterious leather bag of Garren's in one hand and his sword in the other. Trauen is pointing at something—an arrow embedded in Sir Lightlee's inner thigh.

"Eh, I told you to stay put," Garren says, taking his bag.

Sir Lightlee placcs an arm around Garren, who helps him over to a fallen log. Sir Lightlee leans against it, sitting on the grass. In a strange reversal of roles, Garren is suddenly giving all the orders. He demands that I fetch some honey from our knapsack, and sends Trauen to look for a root bulb that acts as a narcotic, while he himself is helping Sir Lightlee remove armor.

When I come back with the honey, I'm given the task of starting a fire, for which I am woefully unskilled. I grab flint and steel from Sir Lightlee's saddlebag, dig myself a fire pit, and build a teepee of the driest twigs I can find. Considering I've never made a campfire before, I'm doing pretty well, copying what I've seen done in movies. I'm thankful the grass around is still damp from last night's storm. I'd hate to cause a grass fire. I shouldn't have worried. Trauen is back with his bulbous weeds, and I still haven't been able to get the wood to catch.

Garren has Sir Lightlee's armor off, which has more pieces than I could've imagined. He sends Trauen and me to break off dry wood from a dead shrub tree. After discarding the damp wood I'd collected from the ground, Garren shows me how to kindle the dry wood. His instructions come with that impatient sound I recognize all too clearly as being my own when Sammie doesn't grasp a concept in school as quickly as I think she should.

The fire finally kindled, Garren makes a poultice of warm honey and leaves from the bulbs. Garren rips away Sir Lightlee's hosen around his injured leg. After inspecting it for a moment, he opens his leather bag, which has a neat arrangement of various tools. He pulls out two quills that are cut flat on the ends rather than shaved to a point. Sir Lightlee grunts as Garren separates the flesh enclosed around the arrow.

Small amounts of blood don't bother me; I've treated enough minor scrapes and gashes on Sammie and JJ, but Sir Lightlee's pained face and sight of the embedded arrow are giving me a lightheaded feeling.

"What are you doing?" Trauen asks, watching Garren's activity with rapt fascination. Trauen isn't squeamish about blood.

"Don't bother the man," I say, blinking away the haze that's overtaken my vision.

Garren ignores my reprimand and answers Trauen. "The arrow's got two barbs. Now if I were to yank it out, it'd rip up the flesh, and Sir Lightlee's leg would be in a terrible mess. But if I get the hollow ends of the quills set nicely over the barbs, I can pull"—Garren pauses in concentration—"and the arrow is out nice and clean like." Garren shows the extracted arrowhead to Trauen.

Garren carefully cleans the wound and makes sure nothing is left behind, and then uses the honey poultice on it before bandaging it tightly with a clean cloth from his bag. I've heated some water by now from our canteen in a copper cup and given Sir Lightlee a tea made up of the bulbous root, which he sips gratefully and a little color returns to his pale face. He is not so much the dashing knight dressed only in his rather dirty undergarments. I think he looks much older. The rising sun highlights a few silver hairs.

When I think Sir Lightlee has fallen asleep, his beret shielding his eyes from the late-morning sun, I ask Garren how he learned to treat such wounds.

"I studied under a skilled physician in Magdalin before returnin' home to offer whatever assistance I could to my neighbors."

Garren isn't the crude sailor I took him to be. He is younger than I originally thought. His red-brown skin, though blasted by sun and salt water, still has a youthful glow to it. He can't be past twenty-five, but anxiety etches lines around his eyes, and no wonder with everyone he knows in Fisherman's Haven taken by the illness, unless others like Johann, the tavern keeper, escaped.

And what causes some to be more resistant to the shadow illness? Johann clings to the promise of a child to make a peanut butter and jelly sandwich. Sir Lightlee fights for a dying country so desperately, he's fallen under the delusion that not only is my daughter the princess, but I am somehow the new queen. And what *is* my part in this story I've been drawn into? I'm powerless to save this world I created, whose people are no longer fiction. My gaze flickers to Garren.

"I saw Yernar..." I hesitate, wondering if he already knows.

Garren's eyes tell me he does. "He was my cousin."

I note Garren speaks of Yernar in past tense. The consensus seems to be that those overtaken by the shadow illness are already dead. My eyes wander to Trauen spinning in circles in the field until he falls down with dizziness. What would Sir Lightlee do if we woke one morning and Trauen were completely gray? Abandon him? Or release him from his living death like the shadow elf? I wrap my arms around me at the thought, even though the sun is warm.

The stomping of hooves draws my attention to Prattles and Wyot. Prattles is grazing, but Wyot seems restless, though the blood on his leg has clotted. "Aren't you going to treat Wyot?" I ask.

"Not till Sir Lightlee is awake to keep him calm," Garren answers. "That horse could kill."

"I'm awake." Sir Lightlee rouses himself. "Just dozed a minute."

"Liam," I say. "Your chest." I glimpse angry red flesh through a gap in Sir Lightlee's linen shirt as he begins to stand. "Garren, he's injured."

Sir Lightlee grabs Garren's arm. "'Tis nothing. An old wound, not yet healed." Sir Lightlee ties the laces at his collar.

"Still, I should look at it," Garren answers, but Sir Lightlee shakes his head.

Against Garren's protests, Sir Lightlee limps his way over to Wyot. The horse snorts, and Sir Lightlee speaks to him in low tones as Garren cautiously treats the gash on his foreleg. A few times I think the horse might bolt, but Sir Lightlee's baritone works like magic.

"The horse's injury is nothing too serious, less so than your leg," Garren says. "It could've been much worse had it hit a major artery. Your luck never ceases to amaze me. It neither hit bone nor went in terribly deep."

"It looked pretty bad to me." Not sure why I felt a need to add my two cents. I tried *not* to look at it.

"It's just a flesh wound," Sir Lightlee says. "Time's not turning backward, and a long road lies ahead."

"Flesh wound." Garren huffs as he cleans his instruments, meticulously placing them in his bag. "I've seen 'flesh wounds' lead to a quick death from blood loss. Or worse, a longer death from infection. Ye've no business being on that leg."

Sir Lightlee consents to rest while Garren collects his armor and ties it up in an awkward bundle on Wyot at Sir Lightlee's insistence that the horse take the lighter load. If he must ride, as Garren most certainly says he must, then Sir Lightlee says Prattles can bear him for the time being.

Trauen skips ahead leaping over puddles in the road as I walk beside Garren leading Wyot. Sir Lightlee's rigid back soon slumps, and I'm not sure if he is hunched in pain or asleep. He's doing nothing with the reins, but the pony faithfully follows Wyot. Trauen jumps in the next two puddles with a gleeful grin at the mud splashing up his legs.

"Trauen! You'll make your stockings damp and catch a cold." I grab his hand, forcing him to walk at my side and finally ask one of the questions that have been buzzing in my mind. "What happened back there with the shadow elves?"

"I took out a good few before being dismounted." Sir Lightlee suddenly stirs. "Garren arrived not a moment too soon. Right after I was shot in the leg."

"Shouldn't your armor protect your legs all the way around?" I say.

"Ah, but then it'd not be suitable for riding. The inner leg is normally against the horse."

This information only reveals my ignorance. How did I write of knights when I didn't know the basics of armor? "I'm amazed you can get all that armor on."

"Not by myself. Johann helped me back at the tavern. In the past I traveled with a squire..." Sir Lightlee's voice trails off.

I don't ask what happened to his squire. No reason to bring up a painful memory of what is obvious. "So the shadow elves are dead? You and Garren got them all?"

"Hardly," Garren grunts. "They suddenly turned and ran as though they did what they'd come to do." Garren looks at me pointedly. "What did that elf want with you?"

The book. "Strangely, he wanted me to read."

"Read?" Sir Lightlee, who looked as though dozing again, sits up straight and halts Prattles.

I'd never told Sir Lightlee about the book. Really, I never thought he needed to know, but now it feels like another secret I'd kept from him. Shamefacedly, I pull the book out of my pouch. The title, *The Shadow Witch*, glints brightly in the sunlight. I think I see a rebuking glint in Sir Lightlee's eyes.

CHAPTER 12

I tuck Trauen in the rough woolen blanket after giving him his medicine and hold his hand while softly singing a song I used to sing for Sammie until he falls asleep. We are holed up for the night in a cave large enough to fit our small party without us feeling like we are on top of each other. One might even stand up in the center of the cave if they were not too tall; Sir Lightlee had to stoop. He and Garren made their beds toward the opening of the cave, allowing Trauen and me to sleep toward the back away from the draft. The horses are tethered just outside.

Against the left wall is an assortment of stashed supplies: a kettle, skillet, tinder for a fire, and a tin of tea leaves. The cave, I'm told, is sometimes used by roaming shepherds. We borrowed the stored woolen blankets—one for Garren and an extra for Trauen. The night is chillier than the previous with a hint of autumn in the air. I wrap my own blanket around me as anxiety wraps my mind.

Sammie and JJ are of course my primary thoughts. Every time I look at Trauen my guilt rises over leaving JJ. He knows how to use my cell, and yet no amount of assuring myself that he is with my in-laws makes me feel any better. Back home they all must be out of their minds with worry. Has Michael been contacted? How will I ever explain this? *Sorry to worry you, Michael. I went on a little trip into fantasyland, lost our daughter, and am riding across a disease ridden country with a knight that looks just like my ex-boyfriend.*

My fingers run across my pouch as I make sure the clasp is secured. Sir Lightlee has warned me not to read anymore in the Shadow Witch's book, so I can't even check on Sammie. "Be assured, there is never only one of a magic book of this sort," he told me when I showed it to him and Garren. The Shadow Witch wants me to read. The book reveals what I am seeking, and so also reveals it to the Shadow Witch. At least, that is Sir Lightlee's theory. It seems to me that if the Shadow Witch is seeking Sammie, her own book would show her, but Sir Lightlee insisted that the spellcaster's book can only show what's revealed in its companion—the book I now possess. Knowledge Sir Lightlee gained in Magic 101, which is apparently a required course for young squires.

I lay staring at the rocky ceiling. I'm exhausted to the bone after three days of walking, but too achy for sleep to come easily. Sir Lightlee had ridden Prattles on account of his injured leg while Wyot got the lighter load of the knight's armor to give the gash on his foreleg time to heal. Trauen rode on Wyot whenever walking became too much for him, but altogether our journey had become painstakingly slow. At least I'll be in excellent shape when I get home—if I get home.

I roll over and try to find a more comfortable position. Garren snores reverberate within the cave. Trauen is undisturbed, but if the good doctor keeps this up, I will never sleep. Michael's snores are like a kitten compared to these lion-chested roars. Sir Lightlee sits up and pokes Garren with the butt of his dagger, and Garren rolls to his side and quiets.

"He has healthy lungs," I say for lack of anything else

to say when Sir Lightlee looks my way.

"Indeed," Sir Lightlee says in a humorless tone. He grunts as he scoots into a more upright posture.

"Is your leg—"

"I'll manage," Sir Lightlee interrupts, his lips are taut, and he seems pale in the dim light.

I hope his injury hasn't become infected and reassure myself that Garren's skills are sufficient. Sir Lightlee tightens the cloth coif around his head and tucks in a strand of stray hair. The coif, I've discovered upon inquiry, protects the hair from getting caught in the helmet. I suppose he's wearing it now as a sort of nightcap.

"I really am sorry." I'm not sure why I'm apologizing, but there's been an uncomfortable tension between us ever since we left Mer City. "I don't know how to explain this in a way that makes sense, but I need to get Sammie home. I shouldn't have misled you, but I need help."

"We will get the princess home." Sir Lightlee rises, testing his weight on his injured leg while stooping to keep from hitting his head on rock. "I'm afraid you are the one who is misled."

"I don't know what you mean..."

"I thought the princess was the last chance for Kalpania to reclaim her glory, but it's not a princess but a queen we need."

I roll my eyes, sighing. "I'm not...look, I lied about being the Queen's cousin."

"I know." Sir Lightlee's eyes never leave me as he shrugs on his coat. "I should have realized from the beginning. I know who you are, yet you have forgotten."

Sir Lightlee hobbles out the cave with his lute, and I eventually doze off to the soft fingerpicking and gentle baritone of a knight singing to his horse. *What an odd man,* I think as I drift into strange dreams.

Darkness and a cold weight presses around me. I kick until my head rises above the waves, but my cry for help is drowned with a mouthful of acrid water. I'm dashed against sharp rocks, and my hands cling to their jagged edges as the receding waves threaten to suck me back into their depths. I whimper, fighting against the panic that's taken hold of me. Barnacles cut into my bare feet, but my hands slip on the algae-covered rocks as I search for a way up their stoic sides. Brine mingled with the putrid odor of dead fish and rotting seaweed assaults my nose as my face is pressed against the crag. A woeful call rides as one with the ebb and flow of the billows and my ears strain to make out the words above the roar of the sea. "Michelle!" My name, someone is calling my name. *Michael?* I look up; he scrambles down the wet reef. He lies across a rock above me, and his fingers strain to grasp mine, dark circles under his pain-filled eyes. I loosen my grip to reach back, but the tide pulls me into the black waters. "Mi—"

"Mommy!" I rise suddenly, groping in the dark. *Sammie, where are you?* I try to call out but I can't make my voice cooperate. I touch a cold body. Garren is dead with a dark arrow protruding from his chest. *This is your fault,* Sir Lightlee's accusing stare says, but he's pointing at someone else. I turn to see Trauen still asleep and try to shake him awake. He rolls over and opens his eyes. They are empty black marbles, and his skin ashen and hair white as snow. He looks at me, blinking dully, but it isn't Trauen. It is JJ. My lips part in a silent scream.

~~~

When I sit up, my head hits the low ceiling. "Ow," I moan, scooting away from the edge of the cave to which I've rolled in my sleep. I move to the more open part of the cave. I'm alone until Garren peeks in and asks if I'm okay. "Yes," I say, then, when he leaves, mumble half out loud, "Just nightmares of this nightmare I'm stranded in." I shove on my boots then try to untangle my hair with a comb. Ignoring the urge to open *that* book, I place the comb back in my pouch before slinging it across my chest and stepping out of the cave.
~~~

"Good morning," Sir Lightlee greets me cheerily. He wears his traveling garb, his armor packed today on Prattles. Wyot is saddled, decked out in his usual armor.

"You're going to ride Wyot?" I ask Sir Lightlee, but I glance around looking for Trauen.

"Garren insists, but I only will if my lady rides first," Sir Lightlee answers.

Sir Lightlee is always polite, but "my lady" is new and I don't care for it.

Garren gives a huff. "Oblige him, or we'll never get on with our journey."

I finally spot Trauen. He springs from the grass where he was crouched like a cat and gives a roar. I pretend to be startled, which puts a big smile on his face.

"So you're going with us?" I thought perhaps Garren would head toward Magdalin this morning as we've reached the crossroad.

"A good physician never leaves his patient," Garren says. "'Specially stubborn ones.'"

I'm happy for this with how moody Sir Lightlee has been lately. I like Garren. He reminds me of my younger brother—dependable and no nonsense, but a good nature. I try to remember if I wrote anyone like him into my stories.

"Will Wyot be okay holding me?"

"Garren says his leg is healing nicely, barely more than a scratch." Sir Lightlee holds out a hand to help me mount.

"Yeah, but yours isn't," I argue. "Really you should be the one riding."

"I'm healing well also, Garren says," Sir Lightlee answers. "I'll take my turn after you."

Garren's lips are drawn tight in silent protest at Sir Lightlee's ill-advised chivalry and abuse of his words. They evidently already hashed this out between them while I was still sleeping.

I move to Wyot's side and, ignoring Sir Lightlee's

hand, secure a foothold in the stirrup and pull myself up. Wyot is tall, but I'm getting better at mounting horses, though I'm nervous sitting on a beast of this size. Thankfully, I don't have to worry about the reins as Sir Lightlee leads him. Garren holds Prattles' halter, chatting with Trauen about bugs he's finding along the way.

Even Sir Lightlee is joining in and, despite his limp, seems back to his optimistic self. He whistles a short tune, and where is the gray I thought I saw in his hair the other day?

We journey back over the same country I traveled at the beginning of my misfortunes. Perhaps it's only the overcast skies once again threatening rain, but the rolling hills that seemed so vibrant green when I arrived in Kalpania are muted. The domed farmhouses and barns that dot the landscape look almost abandoned. There are no movements of farmhands, no shepherds whistling to their dogs, and no one harvesting the fully ripened fields. A lone cow meanders through someone's crop, her udders distended painfully and no one to relieve her distress.

The scene only worsens when we top the ridge and view Oodlesville in the valley below. At first glance the quaint village of domed houses remains unchanged, until one notices that the normal activities that should accompany a town at a little before noon are absent. No children kick a ball across the street, no farmers with their carts trying to sell off their last vegetables before the warm noon sun, no street sweeper cleaning up the trash that litters the dusty road, and, in fact, no one at all seems to be about.

Sir Lightlee, having taken his turn atop Wyot, slides off the horse and sighs, the tired look of yesterday drawn back across his face. "It is as I feared."

We enter the town, walking the horses, and still no sign of anyone. An old dog with its tail tucked between its legs wanders between the buildings looking for scraps. The door to a shop stands half open, but inside it's dark. It's deathly still save for the hollow tinkle of wind chimes in front of the shop. Trauen has grown quiet and reaches for my hand. Garren frowns and heads toward the shop door.

Garren pushes the door open with a grunt as something seems to be blocking it from the inside. He walks out as quickly as he walked in, his deep brown face suddenly losing some of its rich color. He motions for Sir Lightlee, who hurries despite his limp. Sir Lightlee curses, something I've never heard him do, and both men disappear inside. I can't imagine what horror would cause such a reaction in a doctor and a knight, neither men unused to wounds and war.

"Stay with Prattles," I tell Trauen before hurrying toward the shop myself. I don't want to see, but I have to know. This is my world and my people. Despite steeling myself, I'm not prepared for what I see. For I enter in time to see Garren covering a headless body with a tablecloth, just as Sir Lightlee proclaims he found the head. In a twisted turn of events, it was the thin man who wanted to behead me—Jenton.

I stumble out the door, feeling sick at the smell of rotting flesh and the sight of Jenton's fixed grimace before Sir Lightlee likewise covered the head with a cloth. Outside Trauen is petting Prattles, and a rotund, bald man stands beside him.

"Quickly!" he proclaims in a hoarse whisper, and motions for me to follow. It's Dallet, the baker. I'm surprised I remember his name, but my sudden arrival in Oodlesville is imprinted in my memory.

Sir Lightlee, blade half drawn, and Garren close at his heels rush out the door past me. Sir Lightlee sheaths his blade when he sees who it is. He begins to speak, but Dallet shakes his head and again motions for us to follow. I grab Trauen's hand as Dallet leads us between the shop and another domed structure that I think is a restaurant or bar, and into the back door of his bakery.

"Bring in the horses too. Quickly now!" Dallet commands and no one argues.

It'd be a funny thing to see two horses crammed into a narrow kitchen if it isn't for the gruesome scene I just witnessed and the sense of urgency about Dallet.

As soon as we're all inside, Dallet bars the door. Wyot snorts in protest, and Prattles immediately finds a basket of carrots. Leaving the bewildered horses in the kitchen, we make our way down narrow wooden steps into a windowless cellar lit only by one candle.

Trauen's hand slips out of mine, and he dashes across the room into the arms of a busty woman rocking in a chair and crocheting a blanket.

It's the stoic maid whose name I still don't know.

"You're here!" I'm the first to speak. "My God, what has happened!" I vainly attempt to force back tears as the fear that I'm trapped in a crumbling godless world overwhelms me, and I barely stifle a sob.

CHAPTER 13

The stern maid frowns at me as though I am an overreacting tween with a sudden influx of hormones. "Hush, now. You'll frighten the child." She tenderly caresses Trauen's wild hair as he stares at my tears, wide eyed.

"Connie rushed here to check on me, the ever dutiful big sister," Dallet says. "The shadow illness has got so bad in some of the poorer villages that they locked down the capital, warning all residents not to leave Magdalin or they'd be shut out."

"On whose authority?" Sir Lightlee raises his voice.

"Please." Dallet begs Sir Lightlee to keep it down.

"The royal council. The fools," Connie spits in a whisper, crocheting faster as an acceptable alternative to loud speech. "It'll only make it spread faster by seeding panic." Trauen watches her flying fingers and the hook so closely, I fear she may poke one of his eyes.

"Why are we whispering?" I ask.

Dallet looks at me. "You were in Jenton's shop."

My face involuntarily puckers at the mention.

"What happened to him?" Garren repeats my earlier question. "Besides the obvious."

"It began shortly after Connie arrived, 'bout a week ago," Dallet says. "A rider notified the town that the City of Stairs was closed to all until further notice. Many in Oodlesville and the surrounding ranches depend on commerce to the great city."

"And they cancelled the harvest festival," Connie interjected. "First time since the good Queen died. It wasn't just the loss of sales. Everyone's spirits were brought down."

"We were told we could still sell to officials at the gates," says Dallet, "but only as the city needed. Many goods were deemed unnecessary, like hide and wool, for example, so certain occupations were hit harder by the news."

Garren shakes his head. He knows better than any what's coming next; he watched the slow decline of Fisherman's Haven after the merpeople shut down the bay.

"People became less productive—" Dallet continues.

"Laid about gossiping and worrying, when they should've been working," Connie says; she completes yet another row in the blanket as though demonstrating productivity. Trauen is sitting on the floor with two of her other hooks, sword fighting with them.

"But work for what, Connie?" Dallet shakes his head. "It's like you said. Folks lost spirit. They were angry, and when some turned gray after the announcement that there would be no festival, they became scared." Dallet takes out a handkerchief, mopping sweat off his bald head. "It was Mailene who called the town together—"

"Awful woman." Connie snips the end of the color she was using and starts the next row, weaving in a new color.

"Somehow she convinced people that the way to stop the spread was to..."—Dallet glances at Connie who is nodding toward Trauen.—"uh, to end those with the shadow illness."

"End?" Sir Lightlee's hazel eyes seem to burn in the candle light.

Garren stiffens.

"Mailene said those turned were the witch's servants. Jenton was her executioner." Dallet slid a finger across his throat.

"And people went along with this?" I say. Trauen's half asleep on the finished end of the crocheted blanket, and I just want to hold him. Protect him.

"People who are ruled by fear will go along with anything they think will keep them safe," Connie says, her already-pink cheeks reddening under her freckles. "Until it's them that's under the blade."

"The first ones to go were no accounts," Dallet says. "Drifters, beggars, an old man with no kin. It almost seemed tidy. A 'mercy' Mailene said. Once their heads rolled, their bodies soon disappeared. No evidence to remind people what they'd done." Dallet balls his fists. "I tried to stop it but was told to stick to kneading dough. I should've been more...done more than talk. I..."

"We all should've done more." Connie presses her lips. "We tried to hide the children that turned. But they broke into the bakery."

"That was before we boarded up the windows and reinforced the doors," Dallet added.

"Tore the little ones right from our arms." Connie shakes a crochet hook. I'm relieved she's not knitting. Connie seems the sort who could easily turn a knitting needle into a weapon.

"Families were distraught," Dallet says. "Soon the graying folks outnumbered us. Instead of being passive and dull, like they was usually, they seemed to retain their anger. They done to Jenton what he'd done to their loved ones. And tied Mailene to a post in the center of town till she became one of them."

"Last time either of us saw her," Connie says. "They'd set her free, but she was a-wandering through the streets mumbling 'off with her head, off with his head' over and over."

My stomach twists at the disturbing fairytale my novel has become. Trauen sleeps soundly with no comprehension of the danger he's in—we're all in. We saw no one in the village, yet should we be discovered by those stricken by the shadow illness, would they be malicious? As the power of the Shadow Witch grows, so does the animosity of those afflicted by her.

No one seems inclined to talk anymore. Sir Lightlee leans against a wall with a cushion behind him, eyes closed. Dallet wanders to the kitchen to calm the horses and remove any objects they could potentially knock over. Startled horses would gain unwanted attention. Connie has finished her afghan, spreading it over sleeping Trauen, and starts a fresh project with the remainder of her yarn. Garren is studying from a book filled with medical diagrams. I while away the afternoon writing in a journal I started back in Magdalin. It's just a few loose sheets of rough paper I found in my room paired with a stubby pencil that is in dire need of sharpening.

I lean my head on the cool stone of the cellar wall and tap the end of the pencil against my chin. My eyes close in prayer but my pleas falter against the ceiling. God is not interested in what is happening in the crumbling remains of a foolish fantasy. Yet, a sudden thought strikes me. I sit up and try to capture it before it vanishes. Prior to recording my misadventures in Kalpania, it'd been the longest time since I'd put on paper even the simplest thoughts. I thought my writing days over, but now once again I'm enjoying the release of ideas and feelings as I squeeze the last word onto the final page.

Garren, who leans against the wall not far from me, offers to sharpen my pencil, shaving it with a pocket-sized knife.

"Thank you," I say as he hands it back. "But I'm out of paper."

Garren pulls a book made of unevenly bound pages from his bag and, opening it, tears a few sheets from the back. "I always keep a journal to record procedures and research."

Again I thank him. "You really shouldn't have wasted your paper on me. My journal is just a scribbling of random thoughts."

"May I see?"

I hesitate, tempted to crumple on the spot my latest words. The old anxiety of opening myself up to criticism returns. But I hand my most recent page to Garren and pick at a nail while trying to determine his reaction through a sideways glance.

"Ye write well," he says at last. "Your last thought is inspiring."

To my dismay he begins to read it aloud just as Dallet returns. Connie pauses and looks up from her work.

"Even the presence of shadow creeping over the world is a cause for hope," he reads. "Shadow declares the existence of light, for in utter darkness there is no shadow."

"Well said," Dallet exclaims.

Connie only nods, but I think I detect affirmation in her look. A little bit of pride swells within me to think I wrote something that pleased the reticent woman. It is short lived.

"They are words of naivety. Creating false hope only leads to greater despair." Sir Lightlee's words still the room.

I'm suddenly on my feet without hardly remembering getting up. "You were meant to be a hero. Didn't you say to me once that 'without hope, all would perish'? Wasn't it you who started this whole ridiculous journey with the belief that a child could save the world? Now I think it might have been better if that arrow had found its mark. At least you would have died in optimism instead of wallowing in self-pity."

I turn, taking the steps two at a time before anyone can see the tears that I can no longer hold back. My appearance in the kitchen causes Wyot to give a quick snort. "It's just me," I say in a calming voice. Turning my thoughts away from Sir Lightlee and his criticism, I find some sugar cubes in a dish and give one to Prattles, who nudges me so hard in appreciation that I almost lose my balance. Wyot won't take it when I offer him one, and his head hangs lower than his usual proud stance.

"What's the matter, boy? Don't like it in the kitchen much?" When I start talking to animals, I know stress is getting the better of me.

"He's not himself," Garren speaks softly as he enters the kitchen.

"Is it his leg?"

"No. His leg is fine. And I was speakin' of Liam."

The last person I want to talk about. You can't put your hope in heroes, especially ones you wrote into existence. Of course I can't tell Garren this. "I didn't mean what I said, about wishing he died."

Garren nods, studying me with his dark, serious eyes. A look that again reminds me so much of my brother, who could always read my emotions better than anyone, even Michael. Then one day in a freak accident he was gone. I feel a little comforted that I must have subconsciously created a character like him. There was a boy, a fisherman's son, in my drafts. I don't remember if I gave him a name, but I meant him to become important in later books if I had continued my series.

"Sir Lightlee holds you in high regard. He believes ye are the key to findin' the princess."

I wonder what Sir Lightlee has told Garren about me. Hopefully nothing about me being the new queen. He wasn't there when the mer-queen told Sir Lightlee that my daughter was Princess Taika. Up till now, I'd hoped it was assumed I was a nurse for Trauen.

Wanting to turn the conversation away from myself, I ask, "Did you mean Wyot's leg or Liam's is fine?"

Garren gives a short laugh. "Eh, guess I was unclear. I meant the horse's leg is fine, but was talking about Liam when I said 'he's not himself.'" Garren's brow creases with puzzlement. "Though in truth, the man and the horse are a mirror of each other. I cannot explain why the horse is acting so dejected when his injury was slight, any more than I can explain how Sir Lightlee's leg has healed so rapidly, yet his spirit's so downcast."

"Perhaps you're just a good doctor, and he's an obstinate man."

"I learned under one of the best, but I am still barely more than an apprentice. But there are stories of our renowned knight recovering from injuries that should have been his death. Though I took them as embellished tales." Garren runs his fingers across the stubble on his chin in deep thought.

I nod, and turn my face toward Prattles and pet his nose to avoid giving myself away by unguarded expression. I *wrote* Sir Lightlee as a hero of almost miraculous endurance and good fortune. In my novel, he was a youthful squire that always managed to avoid the worst injuries and to recover swiftly from those he received. I suppose Liam could thank me as much as Garren for his life.

A movement in the shadows catches my eye—Trauen peeking up the steps—and I use that as an excuse to end our conversation before it becomes any more awkward. Garren is no fool, and he must already be curious about me. I'm desperate to avoid questions I cannot answer and answers I cannot explain.

Back in the cellar, we eat a dinner of rolls and preserves. The rolls were baked several days ago, but still delicious. Dallet is excellent at his craft, though he hasn't dared to bake anything recently for fear of attracting the gray-folk. I avoid making eye contact with

Sir Lightlee, and our meal is quiet other than random childish questions from Trauen.

Because of his earlier nap, it takes me a while to settle Trauen down. But a short story and two songs later, Trauen's eyelids are drooping when I remember I haven't given him his medicine. Glancing around, my bag isn't where I left it.

"Has anyone seen my bag?"

"It's here, m' lady." Sir Lightlee walks down from the kitchen where he evidently took the time to shave his several days' worth of beard. "It was left by the horses." Sir Lightlee gives me a cheerful smile as though I never yelled at him earlier. His countenance is more youthful with the touch of silver that graced his whiskered chin removed, replaced by smooth skin and revealing his deep dimple.

I snatch the bag from him, and before I can question him as to how it wound up in the kitchen, Sir Lightlee and Garren are in conversation. Trauen takes the drops of the concentrated medicine prepared by the merpeople without complaint. He says it's sweet. His cheeks renew their glow, and his chest soon rises and falls in the steady pattern of sleep. But I shake the vial and worry over how the medicine is already half gone.

CHAPTER 14

Back home, the inviting rich aroma of coffee would greet me like a "good morning" in a mug and make waking up worth looking forward to. Horses in the kitchen make me wish my aching back hadn't woken me so early. I narrowly sidestep fresh-dropped road apples as Prattles bats his long lashes over sleepy eyes.

"Good morning to you too, Prattles," I mumble as I squeeze past him while trying to push aside all thoughts of coffee.

Tea isn't even an option since we dare not make a fire in the hearth and draw unwanted attention, so I focus on looking for something to take the edge off my hunger. Wyot, with his head hung low, takes no notice of me as I pull out baskets and open cabinets and peek in ceramic jars. There's an impressive selection of goods: loaves of bread, cheeses, eggs, apples, jams of all kinds, honey, pickles, and something that looks suspiciously like mincemeat. Everyone else is still asleep in the cellar, and it seems rude to dig into anything without Dallet's permission. What was I expecting—to find a box of granola?

Selecting a green apple, I take a bite and slip through a doorway into the main room of the bakery. Morning rays filtering between the slats of the boarded up windows illuminate the room. There's a counter and underneath it a shelf with a locked coin box for *neelings,* an empty glass-paned wooden display case for pastries, and a small chalkboard that says "Today's Special" with smeared chalk below it. A table with a blue checkered cloth rests in the corner between two chairs. A clay vase lies on its side leaving a murky stain on the checkered cloth, its wilted flowers scattered across the floor.

The light coming between the slats dims a moment as though something—or someone—passed in front of it. My heart speeds up, and I step across the room and double check the bolts on the door. The door is solid oak and secured by an iron latch. I peep through a knothole in one of the boards to see if I catch any movement outside. What I manage to glimpse of the dusty street looks about as desolate as it did the day before. Then a dark gray eye stares back through the hole.

Stumbling back, I cover my mouth to stifle a scream. The shadow is gone and light streams through the hole again. Maybe it...he...whoever that was...didn't see me, I reason. I am in a darkened room. Tentatively, I glance through the board again and see nothing but the empty street.

Back through the kitchen, I head down to the cellar, smashing into Sir Lightlee on the steps. We both nearly lose our balance, but he manages to brace us.

"Sorry, sorry." I extricate myself from Sir Lightlee. "I saw an eye."

If they weren't already, everyone is awake. Connie lifts a brow. She slept in the rocker and looks unruffled and well-rested despite it.

"I mean, I think there's someone out there." My breath is coming in quick gasps.

"It mayn't have been—" Sir Lightlee is interrupted by a sharp crack, like wood being split. His jaw tightens.

Garren scrambles to his feet. Sir Lightlee draws his sword and hands me his dagger. "The rest of you, arm yourself by any means," Sir Lightlee commands.

Dallet stumbles around the cellar grabbing random items then setting them aside as useless. Beads of sweat form on his brow. Connie stands from her rocker and pulls wide-eyed Trauen to her side and materializes a short knife from underneath her garments. I don't move—my mouth dry as I tighten my fingers around the dagger's hilt and stare at it as though it might suddenly leap out of my hands. It's not that I've never held a weapon. I'm a decent shot when I've gone with Michael to the range, but I've never pointed a weapon at anything but a paper target. The idea of sticking cold steel into anything other than a whole chicken from the grocery store makes my hands go weak.

"I won't be fighting our own people," Garren blurts out. His curved blade remains sheathed at his side. "I heal, not kill."

Sir Lightlee looks back at him from the top of the stairs. "You slew elves. Were they more evil than any taken by the Shadow Witch?"

"You sound like Mailene."

"To the contrary. She believed the shadow illness made the people no different than the shadow elves. On that we agree, but whereas she saw the people as wicked as the elves, I say, the elves are no less a victim than our people." Sir Lightlee keeps his eyes locked on Garren. The banging and cracking has been joined by the frightened braying of horses. "I am not proposing we be the aggressors. Only to be ready to defend ourselves, or you may have no one left to heal. The time may soon be coming when the Shadow Witch openly marches upon our land."

Sir Lightlee leaps into the kitchen as Wyot gives a shriek. I follow to the top of the steps in a sort of daze. Wyot rears at someone coming in from the main room and knocks him down. A groan emanates from the owner of muddy shoes and thick legs. I can't see the rest of him from where I stand, but it seems likely he hit his head on the counter from where he fell. Sir Lightlee moves past Wyot to the doorway as two men step over their fallen comrade.

"Stand down!" Sir Lightlee commands, his sword at their bellies.

The shadow illness has full hold on these men. It's evident in their blank expressions and colorless faces. One of the men holds an ax, the other a shovel. I jump at a loud crack at the back door. Prattles starts toward me, and Garren's firm hand on my back prevents me from falling down the steps.

"They're trying to break down the back door!" I shout the obvious.

Wyot rears again, hitting his head on a shelf that comes crashing down. He wheels and Sir Lightlee stumbles back into the hearth with a grunt. The two men barrel through the door. One raises his ax. Garren rushes past me, his curved blade drawn. He blocks the man's blow with his sword and gives a hard kick to the knee, which yields with a sickening crack. With a sharp cry, the man crumples and trips the man charging in behind him. They both fall under the violent hooves of Wyot, who is beside himself with fright and rage.

Sir Lightlee regains his footing, and he and Garren brace to meet two...no three more men coming through the door. One of them has a sword, and the others are armed with tools. Sir Lightlee parries and thrust his blade through the first man's belly. Garren narrowly misses being speared by a pitchfork. He grapples with the man. And Sir Lightlee cuts down the third. The back door falls in on pitchfork-man, and Garren is sent tumbling back. Men and women—all gray—pour in both from the back door and front room.

Shouts, groans, Wyot's angry screams—it's dizzying confusion. I've moved to a corner in the kitchen, clinging to Prattles with one hand and the long round dagger with the other. Garren's down on the floor and a hollow-eyed woman with a butcher knife moves over him. Screaming, I fly at her with the dagger. She loosens the grip on the knife and drops it. My dagger is deep in her midsection; black blood oozes onto her yellow apron. Letting go, I stumble back. Garren's back on his feet, sword in hand. Dallet's here now, bringing down a marble rolling pin on someone's head.

Sir Lightlee's dagger...my weapon...is lying on the floor, covered in dark blood but the woman is gone. I stare at it, puzzled. Then a man's body, face crushed by hooves, disappears, and I understand. Watching those with the sickness vanish as though they never were is somehow more chilling than the presence of a dead body. One woman lies seemingly lifeless amongst empty toppled fruit baskets, but the fact she remains tells me she's only unconscious. Her tangled hair is thickly matted with dark blood. My head throbs with questions of who she is and what part she plays in this story. Why should another nameless person in my discarded novel matter? Yet I can't tear my eyes away from her.

A hand grabs me and I scream. I'm pulled back as a man charging me slams into the wall. Dallet clubs him across the face. Connie pulls me toward the cellar, and I stumble down the steps with Dallet and Garren after me. Sir Lightlee stands at the top, blocking the way. Connie wipes the blood off her knife blade with a cloth. Blood stains the cellar floor, but whatever person she disposed of has vanished.

Shaking, I glance around. "Wh-where's Trauen?"

Connie nods upward. A narrow, rectangular window gives a brief view of a perfect blue sky. A tall shelf that till now had been blocking the vent is scooted to the side. Only a child, not much bigger than Trauen, could have fit through such an opening. I don't know if I should be relieved or fearful. What would Trauen do alone?

A deafening stillness alerts me. Sir Lightlee remains at the door with sword drawn, but no one rushes him. No one moves.

"What?" A half formulated question escapes my throat.

Then a voice I recognize. "We outnumber you. Surrender and maybe you'll keep your heads."

"You surrender, and maybe I'll spare yours," Sir Lightlee says in a grim voice. "Though, by the Queen, you do not deserve it for the lives you took."

A harsh laugh. "O great knight, would-be hero of Kalpania, you know you fight a losing battle. Your fate was sealed long ago. The Shadow Witch will have your service."

"And, dear Mailene, you are now her spokesperson? Who once fought against her, even to the slaying of children who posed no threat?"

"The Shadow Witch only wishes an audience with the princess's mother," Mailene replies. If Sir Lightlee's words had any effect on Mailene, I couldn't tell by her tone. Her words *did* have the effect of startling the others in the cellar.

"But the Queen is dead," Dallet whispers to Connie, who shushes him.

"Let me speak with her and you all can go free," Mailene says.

"No—"

"Liam," I interrupt. "I'll hear her out."

Garren glances at me, surprise written on his face.

I look away and tighten my jaw. The shock of the battle is wearing off and being replaced with a simmering anger, like a tea kettle approaching boiling point. The Shadow Witch may have me, but never my daughter.

"I'm here," I say, a new strength in my voice. "I'm ready to face the Shadow Witch."

I nod at Sir Lightlee, and he reluctantly steps down as I move to the bottom of the steps where I can see

Mailene. Funny, she really looks much the same as before—gray hair and a pale face etched with a permanent frown. Only her eyes are empty of feeling, but not much more than they were before.

Mailene smiles in a way that makes her frown seem pleasant by comparison. "No, no," she chides me like a wayward child. "Not an in-person audience. I speak for the Shadow Witch."

Mailene plops herself down at the top of the steps, smoothing her soiled apron with pale, gnarled hands. Black blood oozes from under a torn fingernail. Above her are the ragged skirts and filthy trousers of the army of commoners the Shadow Witch has stolen from my peaceful people of Kalpania. The room is permeated with a strong aroma of garlic being cooked in a rusty iron pan, and my stomach lurches when my brain finally interprets that it's the stench of sweat and blood.

"The Shadow Witch tells me you like stories, Michelle," Mailene says in a conversational voice as though we were old friends meeting for coffee. "Why don't you read for us?"

How does she know my name? I blink back the haze floating across my eyes and refocus my anger. I *will* be strong for Sammie. I set my voice to a firm tone like I would use with Sammie when she's giving me lip. "No more games. What does the Shadow Witch want?"

"Get the book." Mailene's voice loses all friendliness.

At first I think to stare her down, but there's nothing in her eyes *to* stare down. She has no soul left. Just the nothingness left in her by the Shadow Witch. I'm not really talking to Mailene but to the Shadow Witch through her. I recall what Sir Lightlee said about those taken by the Shadow Witch being themselves victims, though there is little sympathy in me for Mailene. She was awful before.

"You want me to read, so you'll know where my daughter is. I won't do it. I won't help you find her."

Mailene cackles. "The Shadow Witch wants *you* to know where your daughter is. She knows Princess Taika is in the Tangled Woods. The princess's powers prevent her from entering in the woods after her. But the Shadow Witch doesn't want *her*. She only wants what *you* want. She wants your daughter out of Kalpania. You must find her and take her back to your world."

I feel like the eyes of everyone in that cellar are burning holes in the back of my head. Isn't that what Queen Nateliah of the merpeople accused me of? Taking away their princess? But Sammie isn't the princess...is she? My mind is reeling. "I-I can't. I don't know how to get home." My voice sounds small.

"That's simple. Your daughter wrote herself into our world. She can write herself out." Mailene stands and dusts her dress off, which only accomplishes smearing more blood across her apron, and she escorts herself and the rest of the shadow people out of the bakery.

Slowly, I take deep breaths. At last, I turn and face Sir Lightlee and the others in the room. All I can do is cry.

CHAPTER 15

Sir Lightlee stands nearby, a look of consternation on his face. Connie walks over and wraps her arms about me. Never did I expect such an act of compassion from the stern woman, and I'm only beginning to understand that, like all of Kalpania, there is a greater depth to her than my initial impressions. For a moment, I allow myself the leisure of a long suppressed cry.

Pulling away and wiping my face, I imagine I look the furthest thing from a queen.

"Liam," Garren breaks the awkward silence, "the Queen is long dead. Ye were there."

"I was mistaken," Sir Lightlee answers.

Garren crosses his arms, eyes alive with suspicion. "Ye were sole witness of the Queen's demise and now say that ye were 'mistaken'?" He looks at me. "Where would ye take the princess? What world? Who are ye really? Her mother, I think not."

"I never claimed to be the Queen or Princess Taika's mother."

"Garren," Sir Lightlee interjects, "there are things about our world of which many are ignorant, but this is neither the time nor place for this discussion."

"Indeed," Connie says, who has been throwing items in a basket while we talked. She hands it to Dallet, who is staring at me with a rather dumbfounded look.

We cautiously make our way upstairs and out the back door. The shadow villagers are mostly gone, though a few still mill about aimlessly. They pay no attention to us, and Oodlesville is quickly returning to the desolate place it was when we arrived. Sir Lightlee has led Wyot out of the kitchen, but Prattles is nowhere to be found, having bolted at some point out the open back door.

"Where do you suppose Trauen is hiding?" The worry in my heart causes my voice to waver.

"Wherever he's gone, Prattles will have found him," Dallet says. "That pony is as good as a hound, ma'am."

"Well, where has the pony gone?" I snap.

"After finding the boy, he likely carried him back to Dallet's stable, my lady," Sir Lightlee says. "It was from Dallet I borrowed him."

"Fine. Then let's get on with it. But let me make one thing clear. I'm not 'my lady' or 'ma'am,' and for the last time, I am certainly *not* the Queen of Kalpania."

Connie reaches out and lightly touches my arm, but I wrench it away and stride off in a random direction, before stopping and flapping my arms to my side in exasperation. I don't know where Dallet's stable is. Sir Lightlee leads Wyot past me, his mouth in a firm line, and we follow him down the abandoned streets of Oodlesville. I drop back until I'm walking beside Garren. I feel a need to explain, but he refuses to look at me, and maybe it's just as well because I don't know what I'd say.

At the edge of town, we arrive at a pretty acre or two of land with a quaint dome house, painted red, and a round, green stable with a thatched roof. A white picket fence encloses a section of the property containing a vegetable garden.

"Beets need harvesting," Dallet says.

It looks to me like most of his vegetables are ready for harvesting. The zucchini is getting too big on the vine and soon wouldn't be good for anything but making bread, but maybe that is his intent, or had been before his bakery became a shelter.

"Who eats beets?" Sir Lightlee says.

"I do," I say.

"It's good for your digestive constitution," Garren says. "Myth claims it also improves brain function. Perhaps ye could confirm?" Garren glares at Sir Lightlee.

Sir Lightlee frowns back at him and his fingers close into a fist. For one terrible moment, I think he is going to take a swing at Garren.

"There's Trauen," I say, relieved to divert their attention and more relieved to find Trauen safe.

We've come around to the backside of the property. Trauen is lying on his back in the grass eating a carrot and giggling as Prattles tries to nibble at the long green carrot top that Trauen is waving in his face.

Prattles snorts and looks up. Trauen rolls over and leaps to his feet, running toward me.

I kneel down on one knee, and Trauen wraps his arms around my neck. For the second time in the same day, tears stream down my cheeks. He's safe. I have him in my arms—and for a moment, I imagine I am holding JJ. I pull Trauen back and look at him. His face is smudged with dirt, leaves cling to his mop of hair, and grass stains his trousers and stockings, but he's grinning. His face has a healthy glow, and I detect no gray in his hair. Trauen looks better than I have ever seen him, almost a new person from the one I met that night in Magdalin, and I wonder if it is true that the shadow illness cannot be cured.

Trauen holds up a tiny purple wildflower. "For you, Mama."

My heart beats a pace quicker as I gently take the flower. How have I never noticed how much Trauen and

JJ are alike? He's confused. After all, he lost his mother...

"Do you love me forever and ever?"

"JJ?" My voice hitches in my throat.

Trauen nods. "When me and Taika used to play make-believe, I was JJ and she was Sammie,"—he spins in circles looking up at the sky—"and we lived far away in a little house with no ponies or puppies."

"And what happened?" I whisper, barely audible.

Trauen stops spinning. "The witch stopped us from playing, and Taika runned away, and I got sick."

"You saw the Shadow Witch?"

Trauen shrugs and resumes spinning until he falls down in the grass.

I look behind me to where Sir Lightlee and Garren stand.

"Now do you believe she is the mother of the prince and princess?" Sir Lightlee says to Garren.

"The boy called her 'mama.' Common enough confusion in young children who adopt a new caretaker. I'll need more proof than that." Garren looks at me. "Ye said yourself, ye're not the Queen."

"I'm not, I'm..." I stare at Trauen—JJ—doing somersaults in the grass. "I'm not from here. I came to Kalpania to find my daughter Sammie...JJ, my son, he's..." I point toward Trauen. "I don't understand," I mutter, dropping my arm helplessly to my side.

Connie looks between me and Sir Lightlee. "I think, Sir, it's time you explain what you know." She turns to Dallet. "Your house seems safe for the time being. I'll start the tea if you take care of the horses."

~~~

Sammie pulled herself up and along a branch barely wider than her own body. Slippery with wet moss, Sammie had to be careful, her knuckles paling in tight grip of the smaller branches along the way. Finally reaching a broad flat branch, she flopped down, panting. Spottie, waiting on a branch above, swished
~~~

her tail, blinking in bored expression. Tony scrambled up behind Sammie with no trouble. Cha-Chas' rough pads and thick nails gave them good traction. Coming alongside Sammie, he shook the damp from his shaggy fur.

"Seriously." Sammie hugged her knees and shivered.

Tony apologized with a lick to her face with his warm tongue, but Sammie just pushed him away and surveyed her surroundings. Across a great gulf was the center of the Tangled Woods. Orchards, heavy with glowfruit, lit the home of the Cha-Chas like thousands of rainbow lanterns. The beauty of this sight was dulled by the realization that The Branches did not extend across the gulf. Peering over the edge, Sammie saw the dark twisted roots weaving through thick mud and swamps. The Roots—Sammie shuddered. A place of nightmares and home to many shadow creatures.

Flopping to her back, Sammie stared at the thick canopy of leaves above. The Leaves extended across the gulf, but Sammie feared climbing through the thin branches. She had come so far; she could see the Cha-Chas' home but could not reach it. Sammie blinked back tears. The novelty of living in Kalpania was wearing off as the reality of her situation set in. Every muscle ached. Scrapes stung her legs and arms, and her torn, wet sundress clung to her body. Somewhere farther back when she had become too warm, Sammie had left behind the robe given her by the merpeople. Mama was always scolding her for leaving her jackets and sweaters behind at parks and friends' houses.

"Serves me right that I'm cold," Sammie said because that's what Mama would have said. Sammie let the tears fall. Mama wasn't here. Not to scold her for being forgetful, or to comfort her by taking her own jacket off and wrapping it around Sammie's cold shoulders.

Tony barked.

"I'm tired," Sammie said. Yet she sat up. The sun was setting, and Sammie didn't like the idea of being within view of The Roots after dark. What if the creatures below climbed up?

Tony shook his head.

"I don't got magic," Sammie answered.

Tony's tongue lolled out of his mouth in a doggish grin.

"Tony Cheesecracker, you silly dog, I'm not the princess. How 'bout you tell me something useful, like how do the Cha-Chas get over there? The ones that can't fly?"

Tony wagged his tail.

"Why didn't you say so before?" Sammie stood up. Of course there was another way.

Sammie had forgotten all about Mrs. Weaverwhipple. Once Sammie had found one of Mrs. Weaverwhipple's children in Mama's strawberry plants. He was so young and small that Sammie had to use a magnifying glass to get a good look at him. That's when Sammie became sure there must be a way to get into Kalpania, though she never found out how the fuzzy little fellow ended up in Mama's strawberries. The Weaverwhipples were always misplacing children. They had so many.

Sammie followed Tony along the wide branch, trying not to look down at The Roots. Spottie followed lazily behind. Around the next bend of branches, a great web came into view covered in droplets that reflected a myriad of glittering colors from the glowing rainbow fruit across the gulf.

Sammie gasped. "It's so beautiful!"

Tony barked in agreement, though Spottie didn't seem impressed. She was nosing around in Sammie's bag.

"I'm hungry too," Sammie said. "We'll eat soon." Sammie was hopeful.

Something tickled Sammie's shoulder. "Oh, hello."

Sammie carefully allowed the little fuzzy guy to crawl onto her hand. He was no bigger than her pinky nail, which was still larger than the Weaverwhipple she found in Mama's strawberries. "Is your mama home?"

The Weaverwhipple wiggled his two antennae in affirmation before hopping off to a nearby leaf. Sammie didn't need to go much farther before she spotted many more Weaverwhipple children swinging and playing all around the branches and through the leaves—some tiny, others bigger than Sammie's head, all covered in fuzzy hair and in nearly every color. Sammie squatted down to pet a cat-sized Weaverwhipple that had crawled over to her shoe. Her pale blue-green hairs were silky to Sammie's touch, and like all Weaverwhipples, she had six hairy legs growing out of a tiny thorax set between her head and much larger abdomen. With the three eyes in front, she looked at Sammie while two compound eyes, one on each side of her head, kept watch about her. Sammie knew it was a "she" because of the large abdomen for laying eggs when she grew up, which wouldn't be for a long time because Weaverwhipples lived for hundreds of years, so growing up took a good deal more time than it did for little girls.

Sammie came to a great trunk rising out of the branch on which she stood. She plucked a thick web, and like the string of a giant guitar, it hummed through the branches above. A dark red Weaverwhipple as big as Tony came swinging down on a web, stopping at eye-level with Sammie. Sammie took a quick step back and did a curtsy, like she imagined polite girls did in old-fashioned books, only they probably didn't trip on their feet and nearly fall.

Mr. Weaverwhipple peered at her sternly, his red hairs shivering in the breeze. Of all the Weaverwhipples, he was the only one that frightened

Sammie—just a little. He had to be stern because he had many eggs to guard high above.

"Sorry to bother you, but I need Mrs. Weaverwhipple's help."

Mr. Weaverwhipple disappeared into the canopy of leaves above as quickly as he had come.

Tony gave two sharp barks.

Sammie spun around and caught Spottie about to pounce on the nearest Weaverwhipple child. "Don't you dare!" Sammie reprimanded. "They are not spiders. Spiders are nasty, naked things that bite. Weaverwhipples aren't like that at all."

Spottie grumbled and lay down.

"Don't you know, if it wasn't for the Weaverwhipples, all sorts of gross bugs might crawl out of The Roots?"

At that moment, a gentle humming came from the huge web spun across the gulf. The sun was now fully set and the purple moonlight danced across the web as Mrs. Weaverwhipple plucked the vibrant strings. Shining droplets flew off the strings in beautiful cadence. Sammie smiled at the thought of bugs and shadow creatures being rained upon as Mrs. Weaverwhipple played her song. Serves them right, Sammie thought.

Sammie didn't know the tune Mrs. Weaverwhipple played, but it reminded her of the lullabies Mama used to play for JJ when he was a baby. The soft melody filled the air and flooded Sammie with the sadness of happy memories of long ago. Mrs. Weaverwhipple's golden hairs glistened along her enormous body in swaying rhythm. Sammie sat down, putting an arm around Tony and leaning into his thick fur. Her eyelids fluttered until she closed them, relaxing into the simple tune.

Sammie had the feeling that Mama was carrying her in her arms and laying her in bed after a long car ride, only her bed swayed like a great basket. Blinking,

Sammie saw a shimmering golden sky above her, but was vaguely conscious that it was the belly of Mrs. Weaverwhipple. Sammie rolled over feeling safe, tucked between Tony and Spottie in a silky bed, and too sleepy to be afraid of the giant gulf they were suspended over as Mrs. Weaverwhipple carried them to the other side.

CHAPTER 16

The words fade away, and I set the book down on the table. I reflexively reach out and touch the delicate teacup containing water and Trauen's purple wildflower. Sir Lightlee sits across from me with Connie and Dallet to my right and Garren on my left. With the exception of Connie, no one has touched their tea or bread. On a sofa in the adjoining room, Trauen naps covered in the afghan Connie made. Jam smears his face and his chubby hand still grips the crust of his unfinished bread.

We keep the curtains drawn and only a single oil lamp lights the room to minimize attracting attention, although for the time being we've determined there is little to fear from the shadow people. The Shadow Witch waits for me to make the next move.

Weaverwhipple? A shiver runs down my spine. Sammie has created enormous spider-like creatures in my world just to spite me. We were *supposed* to be doing a study on insects. Sammie had a complete meltdown when I asked her to look at her library books and write three or four sentences about any insect of her choice. JJ was happily coloring a picture of a bumble bee.

"I want to do a black widow," Sammie said. I had no idea why. Sammie was terrified of spiders.

Patiently, I reviewed the characteristics of insects. "Now why aren't spiders insects?" I asked.

"I don't know." Sammie shrugged.

My patience was waning fast. "How many legs do spiders have?"

Sammie mumbled, "Eight," as she grabbed her books and huffed off to the picnic table outside. I would rather she write at the table indoors, but I didn't want to push things when I'd thought I'd won the battle. I couldn't have been more wrong.

Sammie came back with a whole page describing what a spider insect would look like, including illustrations.

"This is pure fantasy, Sammie!"

"But this is what a weaverwhipple looks like. They aren't really spiders—"

"You have to do your report on a *real* insect."

"Weaverwhipples are real! I saw one in the strawberries."

"Enough!" I snatched Sammie's paper and tore it in half. "School isn't the time for make-believe."

"I *hate* school!" Sammie fled the room, slamming a door.

I drum my fingers on top of the little book. The golden title, *The Shadow Witch*, seems to glow in the candlelight. *Another score for Sammie*, I think wryly. Her weaverwhipples did in fact meet the standards to be classified as an insect, and in at least one world, they are not fantasy.

Two creases form between Garren's brow. "So this...Sammie, is Princess Taika, and she is going to the midst of the Tangled Woods. Why?"

"I think, to get a cure for JJ, uh, Trauen," I answer.

Garren raises an eyebrow at Sir Lightlee.

Sir Lightlee clears his throat and licks his lips. Everyone looks at him expectantly.

"Well, Sir?" Connie prompts.

"Our world, our history, all had its beginning in another." Sir Lightlee looks up at me. "Our Queen is from this other world. And she created ours."

I stare back at Sir Lightlee. *How does he know this?*

Garren puts a hand to his head. "Our history goes back thousands of years. Michelle, I don't suppose ye claim such an age?"

"I-I'm thirty-six."

"It doesn't work like that." Sir Lightlee scoots back his chair and stands.

"Please enlighten us," Garren says. "I'm sure it'll make as much sense as anything ye've claimed so far."

"Give him a chance to speak." Dallet speaks more forcefully than I've ever heard from him before. Connie nods in agreement.

"Michelle imagined a world and thus ours was born." Sir Lightlee continues to stand as though addressing a larger audience. "Time in our world is not synchronized to hers. Our history, though indeed thousands of years, was born in only moments of her time. And our future is likewise in her hands."

Sir Lightlee looks down a moment then draws back his shoulders. His eyes pierce me. "I watched our Queen fall. She abandoned our future. Abandoned hope. Abandoned us."

"You were...just a story." I'm staring at my hands. Not daring to make eye contact with anyone. Connie reaches out and puts a hand on my own.

"How do ye *know* this?" Garren asks my inner question, but his tone sounds less than satisfied with an explanation I know to be true.

Sir Lightlee sits back down and takes a long draught of his tea, nearly emptying the cup. Then stares at it longingly as if wishing it were something stronger. "I understood it the day the princess became an enchantress. The day she sought to rebuild where the Queen left off."

Garren opens his mouth, but I cut him off. "It's true," I say. "Sammie found my journals and was writing in them." I look up at Sir Lightlee and then let my gaze fall on each of the others in turn. "But I swear, I did not know any of this...that you...this world was real. And I am sorry."

~~~

Sir Lightlee's melancholy plucking of the lute mingles with the evening call of a mockingbird as I watch Trauen's chest rise and fall. His medicine is dangerously low, considering how far we have to travel, and I still don't understand how he's gone through it so fast. I gently brush away the hair that falls across his forehead. His cheeks have a healthy glow, but I wonder what will happen to JJ if the medicine fails. Trauen is somehow connected to him; maybe they are one and the same. I don't understand it any more than I understand how Sammie is Princess Taika or I'm the Queen.

We made camp under the sheltering branches of a juniper before the shadow of the towering White Mountains. Sir Lightlee preferred to make his bed in the open to keep watch. We're on a hill, and the countryside sprawls before us, but Oodlesville, tucked away in its cozy valley, is no longer visible.

Stretching, I join Prattles where he's tied under a nearby tree. He nuzzles me, and I pet his nose, giving him a sugar cube taken from Dallet's kitchen. I admit I'm going to miss him. Taking horses into the Tangled Woods isn't advisable. Even the branches wide enough for a horse to tread would be dangerous. According to Sir Lightlee, Sammie's unilopes are the only hooved creatures nimble enough to leap among The Branches. I'm not looking forward to venturing into Sammie's wild-wooded creation. Just standing on a ladder to rescue JJ stuck in an ordinary tree made me nervous.

Removing Prattles' saddle, I rub him down. The sun has set, but there's still a pink glow in the west, and I almost imagine I can see the distant blue haze of the
~~~

Unending Sea. I close my eyes and listen to the wind blow across the long grass and through the junipers, merging in rhythm to the strings of the lute. Involuntarily, my body gives a shudder. I took a brief nap at Dallet's place while waiting for Trauen to finish his breakfast before we packed up and headed toward the hills. Now, the dream comes back to me—a voice crying over the waves like the wind moaning over the grass. It's Michael's voice calling to me. I shake my head as though to free it of disconsolate thoughts.

"Liam," I call back, interrupting his chords. "Should we let the horses go back to Dallet's now or in the morning?"

We don't want to take them into the pass because of the giants, who would make a soup of them if they could.

Sir Lightlee had already removed Wyot's saddle, but I walk over to the horse to offer him the last sugar cube. His head hangs low, and he barely flinches as I approach. What happened to the proud horse that used to terrify me? "Can animals get the shadow illness?"

Sir Lightlee's lute falls silent.

I tentatively touch the horse's mane. Despite the dimming light, I can clearly see his once jet black mane has dull gray strands. Not the vibrant gray of Prattles, the spotted pony, but a sickly color, like a dirty mop. I pull away my hand. "Liam?"

I turn around to find him standing behind me, a hard look in his eyes. "I suspected as much," he says. "I waited only for physical proof."

Sir Lightlee's baritone voice is flat and too calm. Only now do I realize that his sword is drawn.

"What are you..."

Sir Lightlee moves toward Wyot.

"No!" I scream. I run at him, trying to grab his arm. He pulls away, and I stumble backward and fall into Wyot. The horse gives only a resigned snort and takes two steps aside, but otherwise does not react to our sudden scuffle. I stand in front of the horse, facing Sir Lightlee.

"You can't kill your horse," I say, panting.

Sir Lightlee's lips are drawn tight. "I'd rather him dead than the Shadow Witch have him," he says through his teeth. There is a tremble in his voice that reaches his hands.

Holding his gaze, I step forward and grab the hilt of his sword. "To kill him would be to admit there's no hope. No rescue for those afflicted."

"There is none."

I glance toward the juniper where Trauen sleeps. "There must be. I have to believe it. You said the future was in my hands. I won't abandon Kalpania. I will pen its future."

Sir Lightlee yanks free of my hands, but sheaths his sword. "Send the horses home." He turns and walks away.

Heart still racing, I untether the horses, but Wyot won't budge. The horse has lost not only his fire, but even the will to live. After a moment's thought, I link Wyot's harness to Prattles. "Go on," I tell Prattles and give him a slap on his rear. He starts off at a slow trot, tugging Wyot into a stumbling gait after him.

When they disappear around a bend, I head back in the dark toward the outline of Trauen's juniper but then pause at Sir Lightlee's camp. He's back at his slow plucking, but this time he sings in a voice that sends a cold chill down my spine.

"Spring's new buds will fall to Autumn
Vibrant life to gasping breath
Summer merely warm distraction
Ere Winter's chill grips all in death.

"Every life is but a shadow
Once it's born, it fades away
Hope but lingers in dusk's dim glow
As the Night consumes the Day."

"Well, that's...cheerful," I say. "Maybe you should come up with a new verse."

Sir Lightlee ignores me. And my conscience pricks at my heart because I think I see a tear slide down his face in the flicker of his lantern. But then it is dark.

CHAPTER 17

In the morning, packing camp is a somber affair. The mood feels like the day I packed up my life and moved halfway across the country, away from family and friends to Michael's new duty station. Only this time it's to venture from my carefully mapped out world of Kalpania into the giant tangled trees created from a nine-year-old's daydreams. Sir Lightlee hasn't spoken a word since last night, and I'm in no mind to break the silence. We have become forced traveling companions bonded by two goals—to find Sammie and obtain the glowfruit necessary to slow Trauen's illness.

I roll my extra pair of linens inside my blanket roll, noting with satisfaction that for once it's not speckled in rainbow sand—an unintentional souvenir picked up at the Shimmering Shores. Thankfully, Connie graciously offered to give my tunic and suede leggings a good scrub while we were at Dallet's place. As for the thin under linens, they have the advantage of drying quickly, allowing for quick scrubs anytime a creek is available. I let them dry overnight while wearing the extra set as sleepwear. Still, despite the linen barrier to soak up sweat before it reaches my outer clothes and an alum mineral stone I picked up in Fisherman's Haven for "deodorant," I crave clean modern clothes and amenities. My world back home is feeling more like a dream with each passing day in Kalpania.

Looking up, I pause to watch Trauen. He's squatting on the ground softly talking to a band of ants trailing across the dirt. He blocks their path with a stick or rock and claps his hands when the ants reroute around it.

"JJ," I call, curious if he would respond to that name and relieved when he doesn't. That Trauen pretends to be JJ isn't proof that he *is* JJ anymore than Sammie pretending to be a princess makes her one. Then again, JJ rarely responds to his name when he's immersed in playing, so that isn't hard evidence either.

Trauen picks up a leaf, smiling at an ant wandering around trying to find its way off. I discover myself smiling with him. How had I forgotten that learning isn't all about worksheets and schedules?

"You can walk up-slide-down," he says excitedly to the ant as it crawls on the underside of the leaf.

My smile fades. JJ always says "up-slide-down" no matter how many times I correct him. My throat feels suddenly thick, and I swallow hard. Whether Trauen is JJ or not, their fates are somehow connected. Sammie isn't my only child in danger. "Trauen, please take your medicine," I choke out, fighting against emotions threatening to overwhelm me. "We have to leave."

Trauen sets the leaf down. "You can go home now, ant." He runs over to my arms, grinning. I try to clean the dirt off his face with my handkerchief but give up and administer his medicine. Just looking at him, I would think he was healed, but I've already seen how quickly the shadow illness takes hold without the juice of the glowfruit. Holding the translucent vial in the sunlight, I estimate there is only a week's worth left. Not enough.

"We have no time to waste," Sir Lightlee says, hiking his pack on his back and walking past me without a glance.

I strap Trauen's bedroll onto his back and take up my own, as well as my pack and leather pouch. Trauen runs up and grabs Sir Lightlee's hand, and I keep a few paces behind, not wanting to make conversation after last night. I'm not sure if Liam's angry with me or grieving over his horse, but either way, it seems best to give him some space. Eventually, it becomes unhealthy to spend too much time with characters from a book, and I'm pretty sure I've long passed that point. I miss Garren's steady presence and good sense, but he has his other countrymen to think of. A physician has no time for side quests.

Sir Lightlee keeps a steady pace that has Trauen practically at a run, but he slows when our path steepens. His armor was left behind with Dallet. He's wearing trousers and an overcoat, but thankfully that ridiculous feather in his beret was lost at some point. His sword is at his side, and I still have the dagger since the fight in the kitchen. We planned to take only what was necessary since we're traveling on foot, but he stubbornly brought along his lute, which hangs in its own bag beside his pack. I shake my head. Does he think he's going to tame the giants with a song? Speed and quiet is what's needed to get through the pass undetected. I gave the giants poor vision, so we have that going for us. Not much else.

The pass between the mountains is a broad valley, with a river winding throughout, but we avoid it. Instead, we take a narrow trail that switchbacks around the mountain and amidst trees and rocks. Smoke rises in tall plumes at one of the river bends, and Trauen points at it excitedly.

"Is that the giants' fire!"

"Shhh, yes," I say.

"I see one! I see a giant." Trauen nearly slips off the trail.

"Shhh!" Sir Lightlee answers, "Indeed it is, so walk quietly."

From up here the giants might be only men and their hovels of regular size, until you compare them to the trees near the river, which in fact are huge sycamores, and realize the giants' true size.

"Will we meet a giant?" Trauen asks in a loud whisper.

"Hopefully not," Sir Lightlee says.

"But I want—"

"Shhh!" Sir Lightlee and I shush him simultaneously. We look at each other, and Liam shakes his head as I roll my eyes. If it weren't for the danger, it would be almost humorous. Naturally, the boy wants to meet a giant with no concept of what that means.

"So what *are* the chances of meeting a giant up here?" I whisper, not because I'm worried the giants in the valley below might hear us, but rather crossing paths with one nearby.

"They traverse the mountainside to hunt or trap on occasion. We must be prepared to hide, but our likelihood of escape is small," Sir Lightlee says.

"Their vision is poor. If we see them first and hide before we are spotted—"

"It won't matter if they have a wolf with them."

"A wolf? What?" I grab Trauen's hand and try to hurry him along faster. "Put down the pinecones please, Trauen."

Trauen reluctantly drops his handful, all but one. "Just the big one, okay?"

"Fine," I answer him, then turn to Sir Lightlee. "But the giants don't keep pets."

Sir Lightlee pauses, scanning the next bend of the trail ahead before continuing. "They began breeding wolves a while back for hunting. A giant subspecies."

Giant wolves? I groan. That would be Sammie's doing. Wolves are her favorite animal—that is when it's not bears or foxes. It seems to change frequently, and like everything when it comes to Sammie, I can't keep up with her.

The trail levels in a nice spot with pines, rather than the steep inclines we had been hiking around. The river is out of view, and the giants feel far away. I breathe a little easier. We could be strolling along the mountains of California. When was the last time we left the city and took a hike as a family? Why did we have nothing better to do than to stick to rigid schedules? My thoughts drift back to Trauen's ants. Instead of staring at books and writing papers, we could've searched for insects in nature.

Sir Lightlee takes advantage of the mostly level ground to set Trauen down. He'd been piggy backing behind Liam's pack for the last uphill stretch. The man's stamina is impressive. Stubbornness has its benefits, I suppose. Trauen falls back to me and holds my hand, but it isn't long before I feel like I'm dragging a dead weight.

"C'mon," I say, "You need to pick up your feet."

"Can't," Trauen mumbles.

He's been a trooper, really. This hike is asking a lot of a five-year-old boy. It's asking a lot for a grown woman. I long to take off my boots and rub my feet.

"Any chance we can take a short break?" I call to Sir Lightlee as I plop down on a large rock. I've forgotten to worry about giants. We're nowhere near their settlements. "It's almost noon, and Trauen and I are both beat."

Sir Lightlee stares back at me with a wrinkle in his brow as he always does when I use slang. "Beat what?"

"Tired. We're *exhausted*," I say with more annoyance in my voice than is warranted. After all, it isn't his fault I gave everyone in Kalpania a vocabulary barely more modern than the King James Bible minus the "thees" and "thous."

"I feel this place is too open," Sir Lightlee begins as he tracks back toward us.

"What do you mean? We're surrounded by pines."

Sir Lightlee shakes his head. "We should at least move off the trail if we are to remain in one place.

I nod my assent, and we climb a little ways until we come to a huge outcropping of granite boulders surrounded by a thick stand of aspens already in golden autumn array. Gratefully, I shrug off my pack and pass out lunch. Sir Lightlee shakes his head at my offer of food and only sips from his canteen, his eyes constantly shifting, watching our surroundings.

We eat with only the sounds of nature—the rush of the wind in the trees and calling of birds. The air is cool and pungent with pine and a hint of moisture. Clouds billow in the west.

"I hope it doesn't rain," I say as a gust litters leaves across our laps.

Sir Lightlee hops up to fetch his beret that blew off his head while I calm Trauen, who is whining about a leaf stuck to his half-eaten apple.

I look up and notice the silver highlights in Sir Lightlee's hair before he shoves on his beret. I've noticed gray in his hair before, which is not unheard of for a man in his thirties, except that at other times, he seemed to have none. I pick at a chipped fingernail, wondering if the answer to Trauen's fast waning medicine isn't right before me. It would explain Sir Lightlee's mood swings. A tightening in my chest squeezes my heart into a loud rhythm. Sir Lightlee has been nothing if not loyal. How can I accuse him?

Turning of the hair seems to be the first physical sign of the shadow illness. It's the first thing I notice when Trauen hasn't had his medicine in a while. It was the first signal that Wyot's loss of spirit was due to more than an injury. If Sir Lightlee truly has the shadow illness, how long has it been? I remember he often kept his coif on his head even after removing his helmet for the night. Going back even farther in my mind, there was the time in the garden of Magdalin that he refused to remove his helmet at all. And the whole reason we took Trauen on this journey was because the palace supply of medicine was stolen. Now, as I watch Sir Lightlee fidget with his beret, my thoughts keep whispering, *Stolen by whom?*

I make a noise of clearing my throat. "Li—"

Sir Lightlee holds up his hand. "Back," he mouths, waving his hand toward the boulders. He leaps to his feet, still waving at us to move back.

I grab Trauen's hand, hushing him. Reaching the granite wall of the boulder, I realize that what I had taken to be one boulder is two large boulders crammed against each other, yet there is a crack about eye-level with Trauen that descends down between the two. Gritting my teeth, I slip down feet first and Trauen scrambles after me. I have to crouch to keep from whacking my head on the rock above. I can't tell how far back the crevice goes, and I hope there's no need to find out. Peeking out, I can't see Sir Lightlee at all. He's no longer at the spot we made lunch.

My whole body feels itchy as I try not to imagine any creepy crawlies in this damp spot. I'm pretty sure my hand already brushed against a web.

"Trauen, don't wander back there," I say.

My ears strain, expecting to hear an outcry from Sir Lightlee or the booming roar of a giant, but there's only silence that stretches for so long that I worry all the more. I've determined to crawl out and see what's become of Sir Lightlee, but as I turn to tell Trauen to stay put, I discover he's gone.

"Trauen!" I call in a harsh whisper.

I hesitate at the idea of crawling any farther back into the rock; I'm not even sure I'd fit. Boots appear near my head. Sir Lightlee reaches down a hand, and I take it long enough to scramble out of the hole.

"Trauen, he's missing."

Sir Lightlee smiles faintly and points up. Trauen waves to me from atop the boulder a good twenty feet up.

"Trauen!" Then remembering that giants could be about, I lower my voice and rasp, "Be careful."

Trauen leaps across the boulders like a mountain goat and my heart leaps with him. He disappears. In what seems forever, but is really only moments, Trauen reemerges from the crevice.

"I found a way up." He beams with pride.

"You shouldn't run off. And you could've fallen," I say, causing Trauen's face to fall.

"You are most skilled," Sir Lightlee says, returning the smile to Trauen's face. "But we must be cautious. Stay hidden next time till I signal all is clear."

Trauen nods seriously. Sir Lightlee boosts Trauen back onto his back, and heads for the trail.

I stumble after them, picking the leaves out of my hair. "Where'd you go?" I pant as I catch up. "What was that all about?"

"Nothing, only a bear," Sir Lightlee answers.

"Only?"

"I want to see a bear," Trauen interjects from Sir Lightlee's back.

"He is lazy and fat, readying for the coming winter." Sir Lightlee says. "We will leave him alone to his foraging."

I follow, peering around me. Having only been thinking of giants, I hadn't concerned myself with what other creatures might be in these mountains. I wasn't even sure what sort of wildlife I wrote to be in them. This was once the stomping grounds of the wood elves, who acted as rangers and protectors of the hills against the giants, but Sir Lightlee's assured me that when they turned to shadow, the giants drove them all to the North Woods. The breeding and training of giant hunting wolves proved to be a match that even the swift elves couldn't compete against.

Back on the path, Sir Lightlee sets Trauen down and distracts him from the monotony of our trek with a story about the time he wrestled an angry bear. Watching them interact, I wonder if I was way off base to suppose that Sir Lightlee would have stolen medicine from a sick boy.

CHAPTER 18

Day seems to fall prey to twilight early, but I surmise it's largely due to the mountains hiding the sun prematurely. Not that I'm complaining. The sooner the sun sets, the sooner we stop to make camp. Trauen has already fallen asleep on Sir Lightlee's shoulder. I help transfer him to his bedroll. He really should take his medicine but I'm reluctant to wake him. Shaking the vial, I wonder if it wouldn't be best to spread the dosage out and save it unless I see his hair turning. Watching Sir Lightlee from the corner of my eye, I stow the medicine in an inside pocket of my cloak instead of my pouch. If Sir Lightlee is stealing it, he'll have to search me, and I'm a light sleeper.

Using fallen branches, Sir Lightlee helps me construct a lean-to against the trees over Trauen. I spread pine needles and leaves across the top, hoping our makeshift shelter will at least keep the damp off of us. Sir Lightlee waves me off as he selects a spot for his own, insisting that I see to myself and Trauen. I put our only extra blanket on Trauen and plop down beside him and pull off my boots. Usually, I sleep in my linens, which are more modest than most people's PJs, but in the cool mountain air and the danger of lighting a fire with giants in the region, I want every layer of warmth available, so I remain fully clothed.

Taking out my comb, I attempt to yank it through my matted hair while watching Sir Lightlee put the finishing touches on his lean-to that somehow was put up faster without my help. Camping was never my thing. I huff, tempted to give up on my hair, but knowing that if I don't smooth it out, I'll only have a worse mess to deal with later. The last time I washed it was at Dallet's using egg to clean it and cooled tea for a rinse. For once I'm thankful for my annoying little sister's "crunchy" leaning lifestyle lectures. I was too fearful of the effects harsh lye soap would have on my hair and had used nothing but water before then. My "breakfast on my head" as I used to teasingly call my sister's method made my hair less greasy and more manageable, that is until leaves and twigs infested it.

Finally satisfied that my hair is tangle-free, I braid it tightly before lying down and trying to find a lump free spot under the lean-to. I snuggle close to Trauen for warmth, and fall asleep counting how many days I've been in Kalpania...*thirteen, no fourteen days...has it really been two weeks?*

~~~

My eyes pop open. *Was that a snort?* I reflexively reach for Trauen and can feel his steady breathing. Slowly, so as not to alert what I fear is a bear outside our lean-to, I reach for my dagger, then freeze as the night is pierced with a howl so close that it leaves my ears ringing. An enormous snout shoves its way into our lean-to sniffing and drooling and knocking down half of the branches as I scream stupidly. Trauen groans, and I grip my dagger ready to do battle with the monster when it suddenly withdraws. Trauen is awake and rubbing his eyes.

"Don't move. Be quiet," I whisper. Maybe the beast won't notice Trauen if I distract him. The dagger in one hand and a branch in another, I scramble out of the
~~~

lean-to ready to face one of my biggest fears—a huge dog. And not just any dog, but an unnaturally large wolf.

Despite my warning, Trauen scrambles up and peers out. The giant wolf hovers over Sir Lightlee who has taken out his lute and begins plucking a vibrant melody! The beast drops to his haunches and raises his nose in another wild howl. Sir Lightlee nods for us to leave, and I hesitate a moment before grabbing Trauen's hand and dragging him away while trying to shush his demands to "pet the big dog." Liam's baritone voice chimes in with his lute, and as if on cue, the wolf's howls rise an octave. The strange duet is soon joined by another chorus of howls, more distant but drawing closer with every new line. We stumble in the dark in the opposite direction of the wild ensemble.

I'm desperate to put distance between us and the pack of wolves soon to descend on Sir Lightlee, but with every step my heart accuses me for abandoning him. But it isn't remorse slowing our flight, but a night so black that I can barely make out the trees and nearly gouge out an eye on a protruding branch. Trauen trips, crying out and nearly bringing me down with him. I help him up, trying to reassure and hurry him at the same time. As we move more carefully with only the faint light of a thin purple moon to guide us, Liam's voice is carried by the wind in mournful farewell:

> "O, invisible hand
> That driveth the leaves
> Bendeth the grass
> But breaketh the trees.

> "Ushers in rain
> To dry it up again
> Where hast thou gone
> And where hast thou been?"

The answer, I think, as I grip Trauen's hand, we'll never hear as Sir Lightlee's song fades from earshot. Soon after, the howls also have died down, and I throw all my concentration on the ever steepening mountainside in an effort to push out gruesome images of the beasts feasting on the knight's body. The terrain directs us naturally downward. This time, I'm the one who slips on loose leaves, and I rest my hand against a tree, panting. Without the imminent danger of wolves breathing down upon us, I have time to reflect on our position. What would Trauen and I do without a guide and zero supplies?

"I'm tired," Trauen complains as he attempts to lie down at the tree's base.

"Not here," I whisper, afraid of my voice carrying. "Come on. Just a little farther." I coax Trauen to his feet as he grumbles and whines, and am thankful for the darkness so he can't see the tears coursing down my face. We trek on for what feels like an endless night, not knowing where we are going or when it's safe to stop. What if the wolves track our scent when they are finished with...I shake my head, not wanting to complete that thought.

The ground has evened out and maybe we've found a path. I boost Trauen on my back and soon hear his soft snores against my shoulder. Every muscle in my body has reached the end of my endurance, yet somehow I stumble numbly along, my lungs burning. A small clearing opens before us, and as though with welcoming arms, an immense tree stands in its midst. Five great branches spread out from its middle forming a cradle in its center. I wake Trauen and boost him up and manage to scramble into the tree after him.

With my back secured against a broad limb and Trauen cradled in my arms, I give myself over to the emotions I'd kept at bay. My body shakes as tears mingle into Trauen's hair, and I swallow the thick feeling in my throat. *Liam*...I shut my eyes against the night, but his face lifted in song is burned into my mind. Because of him, we're safe, for now. My sleep deprived mind finds comfort in being off the ground and hidden from view, refusing to acknowledge that we aren't nearly high enough to be out of danger from the massive wolves.

~~~

My eyes open to a face...no, not a face, an enormous gnarled nose and two huge pink eyes as big as dinner plates. I start, giving a terrified yelp, kept from falling due only to being well secured between the branches. Trauen is gone, and my chest fills with grief and rage; I force myself to turn back to the hideous face.

"Where is he? Where's my boy, you stupid creature!" I try to scramble to my feet in the tree, but my left leg is asleep.

The monster smiles, exposing pointy incisors. I hate myself for creating such insufferable, stereotypical monsters. Of course, they eat human flesh. I might as well have killed Trauen myself, and I pour out my fury at my own shortcomings as an author on this thing before me.

"You know I can just write you out of existence? I'll create the most horrible ending to your pitiful life. You should never have been created in the first pla—eeeyee, help!"

The giant grabs me between pinched fingers, holding me out like a dirty washrag and carrying me across the meadow toward its stone house as I fling my legs and arms around wildly like a toddler pitching a fit. Of course, I managed to find shelter within a few hundred yards—and a few giant footsteps—away from the brute's home.

The beast of a giant pulls open the massive wooden front door to its ugly abode. It looks more like rocks piled by a child and topped with mud-plastered branches than something designed with intelligence. Grass grows on the roof, and when the creature drops
~~~

me like a ragdoll on its dirt floor, I lie stunned for a moment staring at the roots dangling from the ceiling like haphazard cobwebs. Actually, I think there are cobwebs woven into the roots, evidenced by several good-sized spiders.

I close my eyes paralyzed by fear, only to open them again when I feel hot steam on my face. A long tongue dangles above me as a blob of drool lands on my face, but my eyes transfix on monstrous canine teeth. My arm reflexively blocks my face as the wolf's nose nudges me.

"Leave it," a deep female voice commands.

The bear-sized wolf backs away and crouches in a dark corner.

I sit up slowly, watching the giant, that I now realize is a she-giant by her rumpled dress with flowers on it as big as my face. She clumps around her kitchen, transferring a huge steaming pan from a great hearth to a wooden table tall enough for me to walk under if I duck.

My eyes dart back toward the wolf when a wild giggle arrests my attention. Trauen leaps atop the back of the wolf and hugs it behind the neck. The wolf rolls to its side, knocking Trauen off and exposing a belly that must have only recently weaned pups. Trauen crawls over the wolf, rubbing her belly as the beast thumps her tail loudly across the floor.

"Trauen!" I cough up his name in astonishment.

The wolf licks the boy across the face, leaving his hair plastered to one side of his forehead. Trauen stops playing with the wolf only long enough to wave.

A note twangs warping higher. My head swivels to see Sir Lightlee sitting in an enormous wooden rocking chair tuning his lute.

"Perhaps a seat might be more comfortable than the floor," he says dryly, but a smile plays on the corner of his mouth. Sir Lightlee points to what I at first mistook for a table, but now realize is meant to be a footrest.

"Make yerself at home, breakfast is almost ready," the woman giant says as she rummages through a basket.

Moving in a daze, I pull myself up onto the wooden footrest, keeping a careful watch on Trauen and the wolf. "What, exactly, *is* breakfast?" I whisper hoarsely to Sir Lightlee.

Sir Lightlee plucks another string, turning another peg. Plucking it a second time, he seems satisfied with the sound and moves to a new string.

"Trauen, why don't you leave the wolf alone and come sit by me?"

Trauen shakes his head and lies down with his head against the wolf's side.

"Her name is Mildred," Sir Lightlee says. "Gertie assures me she's good with young ones." He strums across all his strings, listening for a moment, and then tweaks one more.

"Gertie? Who's Gertie?"

"Our hostess," Sir Lightlee answers.

"Liam! We are in a *giant's* house. *We* are probably breakfast. And Trauen a snack for the wolf! Of course it *likes* children."

"Be not dismayed. Gertie is a fine cook. She'll only make the best pies out of you."

"Are you bewitched!"

Sir Lightlee bursts into a hearty laugh. Something I had not heard from him in a long time. "I feared the same last night when her pack of wolves caught me. It turns out that Gertie has sworn off human flesh."

"We all have," Gertie interjects. "Well...most of us. I wouldn't a-wander too close to Robbie's place."

My eyes switch from her to Sir Lightlee, who is grinning, not sure if I believe what I'm hearing. "You know, I actually thought you...and all this time...I slept in a tree!" I can feel my face flushing. I'm not about to tell him I cried over him.

"Apologies, my lady, if I had known your whereabouts."

"Oh stop, please." I lower my voice. "Can we be *sure* she isn't lying to pacify us until she's ready for us?"

"Breakfast!" Gertie calls.

The wolf lopes over and is given a dead hare under the table. Watching her, I'm not sure I can stomach breakfast.

Sir Lightlee shrugs, setting his lute down. "I wager we'll find out. We are at her mercy."

Trauen runs over, and Gertie picks him up, talking to him like a baby and setting him on the tabletop. She hands him what to her must be only a teacup but is as large as a mixing bowl to the boy. Sir Lightlee climbs down from the rocking chair and walks to the table.

He submits to Gertie picking him up as well, though she puts him on a giant stool and pats him on the head. I bite my tongue, literally, in an effort not to cry out when I'm likewise hoisted to the opposite stool. Gertie smiles at me with her pointed incisors and pats my cheek. I suppose to her, we all seem like children. She scoots before us each a bowl of what I'm relieved to find is only warm oatmeal with berries and cream, and not the unsavory things I had been imagining. We are all given large wooden spoons of varying sizes. Mine is marked with the number one-half.

"It's a measuring spoon," I say, more to myself than Sir Lightlee, who gives me an amused wink as he sips out of his spoon.

Gertie noisily slurps at her own oatmeal in the most disgusting fashion, and I swallow my distaste with the relief she's eating that and not us.

"So...Gertie?" I'm uncomfortable at bringing up the subject, but I must know. "What caused you...um...the giants to stop, you know..."

"Eatin' people?" she says without missing a beat, and not seeming in the least offended.

"Yes."

"Well, it all began after the shadow illness. Wood elves was our main food, ya know. But when they became shadow elves, they wasn't too good tastin'. Gone bland, even with salt added." She pauses as though expecting us to sympathize. "Well, we ain't good at hunting wild things, them being too quick and quiet. And with the shadow elves sabotaging our traps, and raiding farms being a bit of distance to travel. We was in quite a plight."

I nod, hoping my face looks compassionate and not disgusted.

"But then, that's when we learned about breeding huntin' wolves."

"Yeah, but..." I'm not sure if I should ask, in case it had never occurred to the giants to use the wolves to catch humans.

Gertie laughs. "Yer a-wandering why we don't use the wolves to hunt you folk?"

Sir Lightlee smiles. "I asked the same question last night."

"And?" I prompt.

"Because," Gertie answers. "We lost a taste for human flesh. We even grew a liking for gardening. I think it's on account of the shadow illness."

"What do you mean?"

"It don't touch us 'cause we changed our ways."

"None of you have gotten sick?"

"They don't get it," Sir Lightlee confirms, excitement edging his voice.

"Because they stopped eating people? That doesn't make any sense. The wood elves didn't eat people. They were good, and they've all turned—"

"I know, I know," Sir Lightlee interrupts. He leans toward me. "It's her."

"Who?"

"Your daughter, the princess. Taika. Sammie. Whatever you want to call her," Sir Lightlee says. "I think she changed them."

"She rewrote their story," I say, catching on to Sir Lightlee's meaning.

A look of discomfort passes across Sir Lightlee's face at my mention of "story."

"She changed our *world*," Sir Lightlee says.

"The glowfruit was her addition," I muse. "It slows the illness. So, you think maybe Sammie can...end it?"

"Maybe," Sir Lightlee says. "And perhaps that's why the Shadow Witch wants you to take her home."

CHAPTER 19

Trauen laughs as Mildred leaps ahead of us with him on her back.

"Hang on," I call out, though I doubt he hears me. He's too engrossed in the novelty of riding a wolf, which still hasn't worn off over the last couple of days. "I don't like it," I mumble.

"It was good of Gertie to let us borrow her wolf," Sir Lightlee says. "We've made better time."

"I know. It just makes me nervous, that's all," I answer back. "Anyway, I was really talking to myself."

Sir Lightlee just raises a brow and continues on in silence. It feels dismissive, and I'm already exhausted and stressed from two full days of hiking since we left Gertie's cabin. Sir Lightlee has been quieter than usual, and I haven't felt much like talking either. Our conversations have been reduced to necessary communications only. Now, I'm just feeling argumentative.

"I'm sure *you're* relieved to not have to tote Trauen on your back, but that doesn't mean I have to trust a wolf."

"I am uncertain why you are angry with me," Sir Lightlee says.

"I'm not, it's just..." I pause, trying to organize my jumbled emotions. I'd been feeling irritable toward Sir Lightlee ever since Gertie's. "I thought I'd lost Trauen to a giant and that you were eaten by wolves. And then you acted like it was all a joke."

"Far be it," Sir Lightlee says, "My gaiety was an expression of relief. For I had thought I met my end in the most unknightly of ways. Without a battle, or armor, or my...my steed."

"Unknightly?" My pitch rises in surprise. "You were willing to sacrifice yourself for Trauen and me. I don't know of anything more knightly than that."

"That is high praise indeed, from the Queen."

I glance at him, for at first I think he's being sarcastic, but I see a tinge of color spread across his face and realize he is sincere.

I sigh. "I'm not really a queen, you know. I'm an ordinary person in my world."

Sir Lightlee looks at me. "But not to ours."

"How do you know about my world? I mean, I know you heard me tell the mer-queen I was not from this world, but how did you know I wrote yours into existence?"

Sir Lightlee adjusts his beret as we walk, never seeming satisfied with how it rests on his head. He intently stares off in the distance for so long that I think he either didn't hear my question or forgot about it.

"I did not at first realize we were a...story in your world," Sir Lightlee says, breaking the silence.

Our path has become steep and rocky, and he offers me his hand to help me up over a group of boulders, but I shake my head and scramble up on my own. Trauen and the wolf are farther ahead than I'm comfortable with, but I ignore the urge to call after him.

"I only knew," Sir Lightlee continues when we're on more level footing, "that the Queen created the world, I supposed through enchantment."

My forehead furrows. "But the Queen of Kalpania was only a fictitious character. She wasn't supposed to be me."

Sir Lightlee raises his eyebrows. "Indeed. You did not pour yourself into her?"

"Well...maybe a little." I blush. "I might have imagined myself as the Queen. But you didn't recognize me when I first got here."

"No, though perhaps I should have," Sir Lightlee says. "I saw the resemblance, but believed at first your tale that you were her cousin—for I thought you dead."

We walk without speaking for a while, and I think on what Sir Lightlee has told me. When I wrote, I entered the story only in my mind. Now I am here physically, and it follows that I would look as I really am, rather than as I fancied in my imagination. I wonder if this explains why Trauen resembles JJ, but not perfectly. JJ is not here physically, but he's here somehow within Trauen? What about Sammie? From what I've read in the Shadow Witch's book, she *is* here physically. I don't understand how it works, and I doubt Sir Lightlee does either.

"So when exactly did you realize the truth about your world?" I voice my thoughts breaking the afternoon stillness. "Back at Dallet's, you said you understood it when the princess tried to rebuild."

"There have been differences in our world. Like you saw with the giants," Sir Lightlee says, looking ahead and not at me. "I'd connected them to the princess. Then I knew you to be the Queen when the mer-queen revealed you were Taika's mother."

"But you're dodging my question. None of that explains how you knew your world was a story. If you know something you're not telling me; if you know how I can get home but don't want to say because you think I'll just abandon this world—"

"Would you not?" Sir Lightlee turns his hazel eyes suddenly upon me. "We are only a story to you. A story!"

"You were once...but that was before." I clench and unclench my hands then try to shove them in my pockets, forgetting my tunic has no pockets. Why do people make clothing without pockets? I have only the inner pocket in my cloak where I've hidden Trauen's medicine. My hand goes to it and an unwanted suspicion nags my mind.

"But to answer your question," Sir Lightlee continues more subdued. "I do not know the way to your home, for I know not how you came here."

"Can I trust you?" I say.

"You doubt my loyalty?" Sir Lightlee's voice hardens.

"Take off your hat."

"Excuse me?"

"You heard me," I say.

Sir Lightlee looks away, and at first I think he'll refuse my request. Slowly, he removes the beret. His dark hair is peppered with grays, more than the few I saw the other day.

"You have the shadow illness," I whisper. "You have for a while, haven't you, Liam?"

Sir Lightlee licks his lips. "Since..." He sighs. "Before you arrived."

"You've been stealing Trauen's medicine," I say coldly. "How could you? You were the reason the supplies were stolen from the palace to begin with!"

"No!" Sir Lightlee almost shouts. He takes a deep breath. "Not for myself. There were others in Magdalin. It wasn't right for the palace to hoard it all. I defied the royal council. But I did not know our supply would be cut off by a landslide along the bay road. I never intended to put Prince Trauen in harm."

"But you *did* steal his medicine in the vial." I continue to stare accusingly at him. I'm not about to let him pass off his theft as a noble deed.

"What would become of Trauen if I cannot help him?" Sir Lightlee says. "And all of Kalpania if their greatest knight is found even to be ill, much less fall to the shadow illness?"

"You think you're all that? You self-conceited—"

"They've depended on me since *you* abandoned us! If my loyalty to Kalpania and in *your* service is self-conceit, then so be it!" Sir Lightlee marches away from me, calling out, "Trauen!" He whistles. "Mildred! Come."

I shade my eyes with my hand from the lowering sun. I don't see them ahead on the path anywhere. Honestly, I can barely make out the path. Where they wandered off is anyone's guess. I jog to catch up with Sir Lightlee but avoid eye contact.

"Great. The boy's lost and alone with a wolf. Hope the beast doesn't get hungry," I say.

Mildred, with Trauen still clinging to her thick wolfish mane, tops the ridge above us. Sir Lightlee holds up his hand in their direction as if to say, "See, they're fine." We climb up to them in stiff silence. Trauen slides off Mildred and grabs Sir Lightlee and me each by the hand.

"Come, see!" Trauen says, pulling on us.

We pass through the last of the tall pines onto a broad clifftop, and what lies before me causes me to suck in a breath. *Sammie, what have you done?* Is all I can think.

The cliff we're atop drops off into unseen depths. The canyon below is a twisted mass of enormous branches—countless trees grown into one. Trunks, immense as buildings, plunge into the dark depths below, while branches, some as broad as streets, twist and wind, making innumerable paths across the canyon's unseen end. A few of the branches grow into the cliff's side, making it a simple matter of stepping off the solid earth onto the tangled maze. Far above a thick canopy of leaves filter the sunlight, keeping the Tangled Woods cool and dim.

I glance at Sir Lightlee, and he seems as rooted in place as the trees.

"You've been here before, right?" I ask. "To get glowfruit?"

Sir Lightlee slowly shakes his head; he seems likewise astounded by the scene before us. "That's not normally within my duties. Adventurous merchants..." Sir Lightlee adjusts his beret and pulls his overcoat around him. "I know not how far to the center. We have little time before nightfall." That said, he grabs Trauen tightly by one hand and steps off onto the nearest branch.

Mildred gives a short howl in farewell, before turning towards home. I don't blame her.

Uneasily, I transfer my weight from the ground to the branch, and trying my best to not look down, I walk gingerly across. I've nearly caught up with Sir Lightlee and Trauen when I slip on a mossy place, landing on my rear with a cry. I scramble to my feet quickly before Sir Lightlee can even think of helping me up.

"I'm fine," I say as he turns. "The moss is slippery."

He nods. "Do you need—"

"Nope. I have this. You just keep Trauen from tumbling down to only Sammie knows where."

"I see you've decided to trust me again. Or are you only humoring me for the moment?" The rebuke and hurt in Sir Lightlee's eyes pains me.

I pull my cloak around me in the coolness of the woods and look down. Had I not only just praised him for his willingness to sacrifice himself before accusing him of self-conceit? "You are courageous, and I know you mean well, but you also lied." I look up. "Why didn't you just tell me you were sick?"

Now Sir Lightlee is the one to look away. He rubs his face with his hands, and I can't help but notice his fast growing stubble is white.

"Liam? Are you okay?" I walk over to him, I'm actually worried now. "I mean it."

He turns and looks at me, and his eyes are glossy. "I...I don't know. She's trying to take me."

"The Shadow Witch?"

Sir Lightlee nods.

"Fight it," I tell him. "You have to. I wrote you to be the hero."

"Then why..." Sir Lightlee's voice drifts off.

"Why what?"

He turns away and stares at Trauen, who is squatting on the branch and playing with a beetle crawling in the moss. "We are wasting time." He lifts Trauen by the arm and walks ahead.

I stare after him a moment before following, wishing I could shake the dread filling my soul.

CHAPTER 20

Sammie walked through the orchard of glowfruit, purple juice running down her chin as she took a bite of the fruit she picked earlier. Tony Cheesecracker had already gulped down a blue one. Even finicky Spottie had taken a few delicate bites of the fruit before deciding it was more fun to bat it around with her paw. A mouse-sized Weaverwhipple child perched on Sammie's shoulder. Sammie had already discovered Weaverwhipples weren't interested at all in glowfruit. They preferred bugs, which was fine by Sammie. The fewer the better.

"Only JJ." Sammie spoke her thought aloud. "He thinks bugs are cool." Sammie wrinkled her nose remembering the time JJ dumped a collection of beetles on her bed. It had been an accident, but Sammie had still been mad. Sammie wasn't mad anymore. She missed JJ.

Sammie tossed the core of her fruit aside. Its seed would grow into another glowfruit tree. The grove of trees didn't grow in perfect straight lines like those at the cherry orchard Mama had once taken them to. No, the glowfruit orchard was wild, and grew however it wanted, and Sammie liked it that way.

Spottie and Tony were chasing each other around the trees now, playing a game that had no rules. Tony would turn invisible just before Spottie caught him while Spottie would hide up in a tree until he reappeared and try to pounce him. Sammie ran after them laughing, recovered from her tiredness after her good night's rest in Mrs. Weaverwhipple's basket and her breakfast of glowfruit.

Sammie fell into the grass, exhausted for the moment. The small Weaverwhipple hopped off her, probably afraid of being squished.

"Okay, guys," Sammie said as she got up, "we need to find the other Cha-Chas."

Tony barked and led the way. Soon they came to the center of the orchard. Here the glowfruit trees grew in a large circle around a clearing, and in the center was the mother glowfruit tree. Its branches stretched over the clearing forming a leafy roof. This was the Cha-Chas' home when they weren't out busy exploring and playing in the Tangled Woods.

There were many Cha-Chas at home, although certainly not all of them. Big ones, small ones, shaggy ones, ones with short fur, and some Cha-Chas even had wings.

Sammie called out to one she recognized. "Picklefoot!"

Picklefoot flew over, and landed at Sammie's feet wagging his thin pointed tail and folding his white feathered wings behind him. Sammie rubbed his shiny black fur. He was a medium-sized Cha-Cha with a boxy head and deep bark. He leaped up on Sammie and licked her face. Sammie pushed him down, and the dog's stomach rumbled, followed by a distinct odor that made Spottie growl and Tony shake his head.

"Eww, Picklefoot!" Sammie waved a hand in front of her face. "Go make gas somewhere else."

Picklefoot put his ears back and whined an apology.

"Fine. You can stay," Sammie said. "But only if you help us find Peanut Butter and Jelly Sandwich the Third.

Picklefoot gave a deep rumbling woof.

Sammie glanced from Picklefoot to Tony. "What? Are you sure?"

Picklefoot whined and Tony barked.

"Absolutely, we have to rescue him," Sammie said, her face serious. "Call all the Cha-Chas. We need to have a meeting and form search parties."

~~~

Trauen has settled down and is almost asleep. I had read the last portion about Sammie aloud. I don't know if he connected it to his sister, Taika, or not, but he seemed comforted by it. I tuck the blanket gently around him and kiss him on the forehead.

"Goodnight, Mama," he says with a yawn. "I love you."

"I love you, too."

"Forever?"

"And ever," I answer.

"Will Daddy ever come home?" Trauen says.

"I'm not..." My thoughts wander to what the mer-queen said about the King. How does she know he won't come back? "Soon. Go to sleep."

Trauen closes his eyes, and I glance over at Sir Lightlee, one side of his face illuminated by the small fire in the alcove where we've taken refuge for the night. I ponder Trauen's question. If I'm the Queen of Kalpania, what does that make Michael? I'd given up writing shortly before Sammie was born. I was too embarrassed to ever let Michael read more than a few snippets, especially after all the rejections I'd received from agents and publishers over the previous years. During his first deployment, I'd been so depressed that I trashed everything—deleted documents off my computer, took a literal hammer to a thumb drive— everything except my handwritten journals. I'd collected
~~~

them since a child and simply couldn't bring myself to throw them out. Instead, I buried them in my closet.

"What do you know about Trauen's father, the King?" I'm sure Sir Lightlee overheard my conversation with Trauen.

"He left to fight a war overseas against Valdisar—"

"Yes, I know that. I wrote Valdisar to be..."—I blush a little at this—"to be the stronghold of the enemy, but...do you even know what the war is about?" I suddenly feel terrible that this world is in a senseless war, and maybe that's why my novels failed—why this world is failing—no one knew what they were fighting for.

"I mean," I clarify, "I never developed that part of the story, and Kalpania didn't have a king."

It feels weird talking about my book series to a character of my novel, and judging by the expression on Sir Lightlee's face flickering in the firelight, it isn't too comfortable for him either.

"We have been at war to some extent with Valdisar for as far back as our *history* goes," Sir Lightlee says. "Has it occurred to you that perhaps you set in motion things that are very much real? Maybe Kalpania is a story in your world, but is a factual place in...in this." Sir Lightlee lifts his hand toward the night sky. "That our world is a rightful world—however it may have begun. That we are deserving of life. Of existence."

"You...this world...it's all grown beyond anything I ever imagined," I admit.

"But to answer your question, I never met the King," Sir Lightlee says. "I was...indisposed at the time of your marriage, and when I returned, he was gone to war, and you were believed to be dead."

"When was this?"

"I was gone out of Kalpania almost a decade. I returned a year ago and met Princess Taika for the first time."

I stare into the dying fire, adding a few more twigs and dried moss and watching as it briefly flares back to life. Later, I would have to ask Sammie how long ago she discovered my journals. I suspect it coincides with Sir Lightlee's return.

"Let the fire die," Sir Lightlee says. "I'll watch it till it does. You should rest."

The fire is burning a small impression into the hardwood floor of the branch we shelter in, and though the wood seems fire resistant, neither of us care to risk setting the Tangled Woods on fire.

"Oh, here." I hold out the vial of medicine to Sir Lightlee.

His eyes dart to the vial and back to me. "It's Trauen's. I can't—"

"I've already given Trauen some. There's only a few drops left. Take it."

"Then I can't take it," Sir Lightlee tries to shove my hand away.

"I was wrong to say you were conceited." I press the vial into his hand. "But you are proud and stubborn. Anyway, you were right about one thing."

Sir Lightlee closes his fingers over the vial. "And that is?"

"We need you."

CHAPTER 21

The coolness of the morning has given way to warm humidity. Though Kalpania is nearing autumn, The Branches of the Tangled Woods is like a greenhouse; the same canopy of leaves keeping the sun off of us traps heat and moisture. I doubt that even in the dead of winter it ever gets more than mildly chilly. I've rolled my cloak up and shoved it in my bedroll on my back—which, by the way, is soaked in sweat. If we were just taking a relaxing stroll, it might actually be enjoyable, but hiking hours on end with bedding and packs, not to mention practically dragging a tired five-year-old boy, is beyond exhausting.

"C'mon, Trauen, you've got to pick up your feet."

The boy just groans.

Sir Lightlee stops and looks back at us, mopping his brow. "I can carry Trauen for—"

"You can barely carry yourself," I snap. I'm worried more than ever about Sir Lightlee. His hair has gone shockingly white, and his face is more careworn than I've ever seen it. If we had only met today, I'd have thought him fifty.

Trauen doesn't look much better. His hair too, is mostly white and his hands feel clammy. I touch his forehead. The coolness of his skin concerns me even more than his hair. He's not even sweating.

Sir Lightlee sits on a large knot protruding from the branch path we're walking on. I lean against a trunk across from him and slide my pack off my back for a moment's respite. Trauen finds a bed of moss and lies on it and almost immediately passes out.

"Are you hungry?" I ask, fishing around my pack for something edible. "I think it's past noon." It's hard to tell what time it is in the woods, so I'm solely going on my stomach.

Sir Lightlee shakes his head. "We need to keep going."

I find a carrot and bite into it. "You need to rest and eat. Trauen's already asleep. We can spare a moment's break."

Sir Lightlee resignedly shrugs off his pack. "The Trees have deceived us. I fear we are walking in circles and getting no closer to the center of the woods."

It seems that way to me too. We have a compass and though our goal was to head east as much as the winding branches allowed, more often than not, our path took us another direction.

"Sammie always had an impractical imagination," I say. "The Tangled Woods is a bigger mess than her bedroom, but it's not like the trees are intentionally thwarting us."

"I wouldn't be so sure about that," Sir Lightlee answers. "These woods are imbued with the princess's magic, and as with the glowfruit and the giants—things she touches are resistant to the shadow illness."

"That's a good thing, right?"

"I have the shadow illness, Michelle." Sir Lightlee's hazel eyes burn with desperation. "The Tangled Woods traps all shadow creatures in The Roots. It's a place of nightmares. The Trees are trying to pull me down. The greater the Shadow Witch's hold on me, the greater the Trees' resistance."

"Because they think you are the enemy," I say softly, finally beginning to understand. "But that means Trauen—"

I turn to where he's lying on the moss...where he was lying.

"Trauen!" I spring to my feet and run to the edge of our branch and look over.

Sir Lightlee moves to my side; he points. "There!"

Trauen, still asleep on moss, has been moved multiple branches down from us. The branch he's on is winding and turning ever downward.

Sir Lightlee leaps from our branch to another below us and runs along it in Trauen's direction, jumping again to a new branch. I take a deep breath, and drop to the lower branch with an "oomph" and scramble after him, desperation squeezing my heart.

"Trauen!" I call out again, hoping he wakes.

Tears stream down my face, blurring my vision. I wipe them with my sleeve and follow along a broad branch that heads downward. Trauen's branch is now twisting to the left away from Sir Lightlee, leaving Liam stranded by a gulf. He swivels on his heels and makes a wild leap to another branch that he nearly misses because it moves. I turn left and down toward Trauen. I scramble out onto a branch that is barely three feet wide, praying I don't slip, and now I am directly above him. It's about a ten foot drop, but the branch Trauen's on is broad. Turning to my belly, I dangle my legs over...and let go.

I actually land on my feet, only to slip on the damp moss and almost squish Trauen. Sputtering, I spit moss and lichen out of my mouth and cough. "Trauen!" I crawl over to him and shake him.

He groans, and his eyes flutter open for a moment. Then he closes them and turns over.

"Trauen, wake up." I pull him into my arms. "Liam, I have him!"

"Michelle!" Sir Lightlee is running along a branch that is writhing like an angry serpent. It suddenly plummets downward like a dropping elevator, and Sir Lightlee makes an insane leap to another branch, running along it without losing momentum then jumping to another. He's nearly reached us, only about twenty feet distance, when the branch he's on jerks wildly. Sir Lightlee loses his balance and falls with a heavy thud onto a branch below us. He lies there unmoving, as the branch carries him down and away, lost to sight in the abyss below.

"Liam!" My shout turns into a scream as our branch likewise plummets into the deep.

<div align="center">~~~</div>

My eyes blink open. I must have passed out momentarily, but I'm still clinging tightly to Trauen. "Trauen, wake up." I slap his face gently. "C'mon, Trauen."

Trauen rubs his eyes, and I brush the hair from his face, peering at him in the dim light and waiting for my eyes to adjust. He stares at me looking confused, but I'm relieved to see that his eyes have not turned to that dead fish gray typical of those overcome by the shadow illness. I hug him, sobbing.

"Ow!" Trauen protests.

"I'm sorry, Trauen." I'm probably squeezing out whatever life he has left in him. "Are you okay?"

He looks around in a daze. "I don't like it here. It's cold."

The branch we are on is half submerged in opaque water. A head pops out of the water—a huge catfish that opens his wide mouth before submerging again. It occurs to me that Sammie used to be terrified of large fish when she was little, and I remember what Sir Lightlee said about this being a place of nightmares. How bad can a nine-year-old's nightmares be?

"Where are we," Trauen says.

"The Roots," I whisper, before I catch myself. "Don't worry. We just need to find a way up, and then we won't be far from your sister."

I don't know where Sir Lightlee fell, but if he lived, he'll have to fend for himself. I have to get Trauen out of this place. Our branch runs up at an impossible angle to climb, but there is a building-sized trunk ahead of us with a branch that winds around it that doesn't look too steep. How deep is the water? Reluctantly, I test it with my leg and find a squishy bottom.

"Okay, Trauen, climb on my back. We're going for a walk."

Trauen makes a face, but climbs on piggyback style without fussing. Sliding both legs into the water, I allow our weight to settle. The murky swamp goes above my knees and is quickly soaking my leather leggings. The water's not that deep, but my legs are half submerged in mud, making walking a slow squashy affair. Every step stirs up putrid smells of rotting fish in stagnant brine.

"Trauen, hold my shoulders. I can't breathe," I say, trying to pry his death grip off my neck.

"This place is stinky," Trauen says. "I don't want to breathe."

"Me either, but I kinda need to."

My eyes dart around our surroundings, looking for dry footing anywhere. Sometimes our progress speeds up when we hit a section of shallow water with rocky footing, only a few steps later to be unexpectedly plunged to my waist in a deep bog. Periodically, great roots protrude from the swamp like giant knees. I use these as markers to judge how far we've gone. The giant trunk ahead is farther than I estimated. I take a breather at one knobby root, leaning against it. Trauen climbs off my back and sits atop its knee like he's riding a horse. Something bubbles from the water, and I really hope it's just another fish.

Trauen points to something between two tree trunks opposite to the one we're headed toward. "What's that?"

"It's just a large rock," I say.

"Rocks can move?"

"No. What?" I turn and squint at it.

The "rock" rises, sprouting six legs, and crawls out from between the trunks. It has eyes at the end of two long stalks, and one huge claw that's holding a pulpy mass.

"I think...we should go." I encourage Trauen to climb back onto me.

I force my legs to wade through the muck faster, glancing back at the huge crab. The creature is as big as my SUV and has little difficulty crawling through the swamp on its long legs. It's close enough now to make out what's in its claw. Two hooves dangle from one end as the crab pauses to pick at the bloody mass where a unilope's head and shoulders used to be, and uses its smaller claw to bring chunks of meat to its mouth. A bad taste rises in my mouth. We're almost to the trunk...

The trunk has a mass of roots around it that have built up a sort of hill at its base. I'm relieved to be out of the water, but that feeling is short lived. The wide branch twisting around the trunk is not part of the tree itself, but a vine, and it's steep and thorny. It would be an exhausting climb and one I'm not sure Trauen can make—but he has too.

"Cliccccckkkk!"

I swing around. The crab is near enough for me to see that its pupils are long slits set in deep blue and looking right at us. It clicks again, and drops its mangled dinner, opening its large claw and stepping sideways in our direction.

There's no time to climb. I grab Trauen's hand and drag him around the tree's base, looking for a place to hide. Trauen stumbles over a root, falling and scuffing his chin. The crab has reached the base of the island; its blue eyes follow our movement.

"Trauen, get up." I help him to his feet and put him between me and the crab.

I look behind me. The crab clicks and places a crooked leg on the island.

My breath comes in short gasps. My eyes dart around, and I spot a rotten hollow in the trunk. "Inside, hurry." I shove Trauen and scramble in after him as the crab clatters behind us.

The hollow is narrow and dark. "Go, go." I push against Trauen's back and stifle a scream as something tugs at my tunic. The crab's big claw tries to wedge its way in after us. We crouch at the back, and Trauen whimpers.

"Shhh, it's okay," I whisper, pulling him tightly to myself.

The claw stops short of our position, unable to go any farther. It opens and closes a few times, and I get ready to kick it, but then it's withdrawn. Trauen is breathing heavily, while I'm holding my breath and squeezing his hand too hard. The crab continues to scuttle about the tree, using its smaller claw to pick at something around the base. It seems to have forgotten our presence, but we are effectively trapped.

I shift uncomfortably in the mud. I don't think there's a single inch of me that isn't covered in muck. Trauen's teeth chatter. It's too dark to see if his skin is turning ashen, but he is feeling colder to my touch by the minute. This place can't be good for him. I've lost my cloak along with my pack in the fall.

"Trauen," I whisper, hugging him tight, trying to give him what little warmth I may have. "Hold on, okay."

I look up, and the hollow goes on into the darkness above us, but there's no way out except the way we came in. I'm thankful that Sammie thinks bats are cute, so I can hopefully check that off the list of horrors that might be found here. My mind starts a mental list of things she's afraid of—*large fish, crabs...snakes? No, she likes reptiles, thank heavens.*

Trauen whimpers pointing to the back wall. He wiggles out of my arms, scooting away.

I'd been leaning against the wall until now, but at his reaction, I shuffle forward and look behind me. The wood is pockmarked with a honeycomb of holes as if it had been attacked by an angry woodpecker. Something is wriggling in one of the holes above my head. I scoot back a little more. The writhing thing falls out landing near my knee—an enormous pale worm. I jerk back and smash the thing with my boot, only for another worm to plop on top of my boot. I'm trying to shake it off when Trauen cries out.

More things are wriggling and falling from the holes—centipedes, black beetles, huge ants. The long, crooked legs of a spider emerge, followed by a huge black abdomen. Its slow descent on a thick web reveals the red hourglass signature of a black widow. Then the clattering feet of roaches, dozens of roaches crawling out of the holes and running down the wall. One lifts its wings and flies toward my face.

I scream, waving my hand. Trauen is already crawling on his hands and knees toward the exit. *Nope, nope, nope.* Being skewered by a giant crab is preferable to this. *I'm going to kill Sammie!*

Trauen and I tumble out of the hollow at the same time, both of us gasping and panting. I'm madly brushing off my clothes and hair with my hands, trying to rid myself of the creepy-crawling feeling. Trauen is crying. I pull him into my arms brushing his white hair and speaking to him in a low voice to calm him.

Holding Trauen tightly, I swivel my head, but the monster crab must have moved on. Trauen is still shaking, or maybe I am, it's hard to say. Out of the darkness of the hollow, I'm able to examine Trauen. Not only has his hair turned white, but his lashes as well. Tears streaking down his grimy face reveal his skin is pallid. His lips are turning black. He's not shaking anymore, but instead has gone limp and this worries me far more. His skin is cool, no cold. Much too cold.

"Trauen, listen to me. You have to fight!"

I pull open one of his eyes. It's still full of color. Full of life.

Trauen stirs and wraps his arms around me, and I hug him back fiercely as though I could somehow impart my own health to him. If only.

And as I stare across the dull bog of The Roots, the shadows shift and grow—whispering and snickering and swirling like a dark tornado, whipping my hair around with a cruel, mocking wind.

CHAPTER 22

I put my arm to my forehead, trying to block some of the wind and water being thrust at us by whatever this new manifestation is. The swirling shadow unwinds itself and forms a circle of over twenty shadow creatures around us. Their wings beat furiously, whirring like angry wasps. Then the air stills as they land and fold their wings behind them.

The ghastly creatures are unlike any shadow beings I've seen before. They are translucent, giving the appearance of dark, gray ghosts, yet somehow they seem solid. I don't think I could go through them any more than I could run through a glass window.

One of them walks forward daintily on muddy slippers and touches my face sending an icy chill into my stomach. "What do you suppose it is, Lulu?" she asks. "A giant?"

I suppose I might be a giant to these creatures that are only three feet tall.

"No, Lola, dummy," says Lulu, putting a hand on her hip. "It's the Enemy the Shadow Witch warned us about."

"Well, she has, like, just an awful sense of style!" Lola says. "Why wouldn't I think she was one of those stupid giants? Just look at her clothes, Lily."

Lily flaps her wings over. "Forget her clothes, her hair is simply dreadful." She plucks a strand from my head.

"Ow," I exclaim.

The fairies all giggle—a high-pitched twittering of obnoxious school girls. I groan. This nightmare isn't of Sammie's creation, but mine. Once they were light fairies—one of my earliest characters when I was only a child not much older than Sammie. I thought I was pretty clever creating transparent fairies made of solid light and snarky attitudes. Now they are shadow fairies, but honestly it didn't make them much worse, just all the more ridiculous.

"And what does the Enemy hold?" Lola asks.

"Oh, nothing," says Lily, "just an almost shadow being. Perhaps, I can help it along." Lily reaches a wand to touch Trauen, who is nearly unconscious in my arms.

I slap her hand. "Get away!"

I stand, holding Trauen and towering over the shadow fairy, but this doesn't intimidate her the way I hoped.

"Take a chill pill," Lily huffs. "Or maybe I'll turn you into something worse than shadow."

Oh, that's right. I gave them my childhood attitude complete with nineties slang.

"I'll do worse to you. Do you know who I really am?"

The light fairies were able to wield a variety of magic spells, for good of course. I'm not sure what the shadow fairies are capable of, and I'd rather not find out, but I'm not about to be intimidated by a creation of my eleven-year-old self. It's humiliating.

"I could end your existence or...change you into ugly hags."

"She can't really do that, like, can she?" Lola whimpers.

"No, duh." Lily rolls her eyes. "She doesn't even have a wand."

Lulu flutters over. "No threats, fairies. The Enemy has a mission to complete." Lulu is the leader, but I'm not expecting her to help me. "She will rid us of the little *princess*." Lulu emphasizes "princess" in a mocking tone, complete with hand motions exaggerating a princess wave.

Why is the Shadow Witch so eager for me to get Sammie out of Kalpania? I'm thinking that Sir Lightlee is right. Sammie must be the key to a cure.

"And as for you." Lulu directs her attention to me. "You can't do anything to us you haven't already done."

What does that mean? "So then, get out of my way," I say. "If you're so eager for me to leave with the princess, tell me how to get out of The Roots."

Lulu shrugs. "Climb. But there's no leaving for him." She points to Trauen. "The Trees won't allow shadow creatures to go free."

"He's not—" I wrinkle my nose as I'm assaulted by the smell of rotten dog food, reminding me of when we used to live downwind of a dog food factory.

"Pee-ew!" The fairies scatter, squealing like frightened little girls.

A boxy black dog lands on the hill, barking at any remaining shadow fairies and flapping white...wings!

I back away, hoping the dog takes no notice of me, when my attention is drawn to a muddy figure splashing through the swamp clinging to another dog that looks like a filthy wet mop.

"Don't worry, Mama, these are Cha-Chas. They're friendly. Just not to shadow fairies."

"Sammie!"

I stumble forward, and pull Sammie into a hug, squishing her against Trauen. Sammie, never much of a hugger, wiggles free.

"Who's the boy?" Sammie asks, looking at him curiously and touching his hair. "He has the shadow illness."

"It's JJ...I mean Prince Trauen, but I think...I don't know. He's connected to JJ. Oh, Sammie, how did you find me? I've been trying to find *you!*"

"Prince Trauen!" Sammie ignores my question. "Oh, no! We need to get him some glowfruit right away!"

"I know, but we're trapped in this awful place—"

"Don't worry, Mama, Mrs. Weaverwhipple brought us down here to look for Peanut Butter and Jelly Sandwich the Third—"

"Sammie, we can't look for a stuffed animal!"

"He's a Cha-Cha! But anyway, Mrs. Weaverwhipple will carry us out. She's not far."

"Sammie, I'm not going anywhere with a giant spider."

"Weaverwhipple."

I take a deep breath. This isn't the time to argue with Sammie, and I don't have a lot of options. "Okay, fine...what is that smell!" The rotten dog food smell overpowers even the bog.

Sammie giggles. "Oh, that's just Picklefoot. He's been gassing. It's kinda his superpower."

"Sammie, that's disgusting. Did you write him that way?" I frown at the winged dog, who is fanning his smell around.

Sammie laughs. "Yeah." She makes her way across a shallow section of the bog and onto a log.

I follow behind her, struggling to balance myself while also carrying Trauen. "We need to have a discussion later about appropriate writing topics."

"*Appropriate* wouldn't have saved you from the shadow fairies." Sammie glances back at me with a mischievous smile. Holding her arms out, she walks nimbly across the log to the next island in the bog with another enormous tree towering above.

I make it there without slipping off, and gently set Trauen down at the base of the tree. Sammie squats beside him, and I pull an eye open. Its faint color is the only sign that he hasn't wholly been taken by the shadow illness.

"He's real bad," Sammie says.

"I think you can cure him," I say.

"I can't," Sammie says, "the glowfruit—"

"I think you can cure Kalpania. You're Princess Taika."

"But I'm not," Sammie says. "Only in make-believe."

"Sammie, listen to me," I say. "This is more than just make-believe. Trauen is JJ and you are Taika, and somehow, I don't know how, but I'm the Queen of Kalpania."

"He doesn't look like JJ, exactly…"

"I know, it's hard to explain, but I have a theory."

A shadow falling across us makes me spin around, and I shove a fist in my mouth to halt a scream.

"Mrs. Weaverwhipple." Sammie curtsies clumsily. "This is my mama."

Mrs. Weaverwhipple hangs above us and waves two long antennae in greeting.

I wave two fingers weakly, breathing deeply to calm my racing heart.

Mrs. Weaverwhipple lowers a webbed basket, and Sammie and the muddy mop I assume is Tony climbs aboard. I place Trauen in the basket, cringing with the expectation of touching sticky webs and am surprised to find it soft to the touch.

"It feels like silk," I say.

Sammie wraps her arms around Trauen. "Mrs. Weaverwhipple makes sticky webs and silky webs. Do you know she can even sew clothes!"

"Well, you could certainly benefit." I take note of Sammie's torn, muddy sundress. "Listen. Get Trauen to the orchard and take care of him. Now that he's safe, I have to find Sir Lightlee."

"Sir Lightlee? He's here!"

"He might be injured. I'll explain later."

"Take Picklefoot," Sammie says. "He can help. He's a good tracker, and he'll keep the shadow fairies away."

I nod, reluctant, but seeing the wisdom.

"Oh, and maybe you can find Peanut Butter too. He's fallen down here somewhere. We've been looking for days—"

"We'll see."

"Mama, I hate it when you say that."

"You need to go, Sammie. I love you. Be careful and wait for me in the orchard."

"I love you too, Mama. I'm sorry about the notebook and losing Peanut Butter..."

"Don't worry about that. Just stay safe."

Mrs. Weaverwhipple draws back up into the trees, the basket swinging below her giant golden abdomen. It hurts to watch them go, but Sammie and Trauen will be safer in the orchard, and I can't leave Sir Lightlee down here after all he's done for us.

"Mrs. Weaverwhipple will meet you again right here," Sammie yells down as the glittering web basket swings out of sight.

Why didn't I say I was sorry too? Because I am sorry. Sorry about being so angry. About yelling at Sammie for things that weren't really her fault. About telling her to stop daydreaming because what I had really meant was to stop dreaming altogether. That's what had happened to me, and I thought I could protect Sammie from the hurt of failure. But there is no time to dwell on my faults because I have to find Sir Lightlee.

I stare around at the swamp, feeling overwhelmed and discouraged. Where am I even supposed to begin? Sir Lightlee could be anywhere. He could be dead. Horrible images of him lying face down in the water disturb my mind.

A wet nose nudges my hand. I withdraw it quickly.

Picklefoot whines. *I help find lost man.*

Did the dog just speak to me? I stare skeptically at the dog, who is wagging his tail so fast that his whole butt is wagging.

I speak. I find lost man. I chase away bad fairies.

"Great, a telepathic dog. What will Sammie think of next?"

I a Cha-Cha.

"Yes, I know. Be a good Cha-Cha and go find Sir Lightlee."

Picklefoot spins in a circle three times before flying over the swamp. That much I envy him as I'm forced to follow, wading in the filth. My toes are cramping from cold, and the soaked leather leggings chafe my thighs.

"Hey, don't go too far. I'm not looking for you if you get lost." Actually, I don't want to be left alone in this place.

I come back. I not leave you.

Picklefoot speaks to my mind from over twenty feet away, but it's like he's right beside me and it startles me. It's like having earbuds in, and I wonder how far away he has to get before I can't "hear" him anymore.

The little light that reaches The Roots is waning fast. I have no way to judge the time of day, and it's felt like the longest twilight. Now I fear it's evening and shudder at the thought of being in The Roots at night. I keep a sharp eye out for any unsavory creatures. The shadow fairies don't worry me as much as giant crabs. I doubt Picklefoot's "superpower" will be as effective on anything more ominous than the silly fairies.

Now that I think about it, I wonder why the fairies are even in Kalpania. I wrote them out of the story after I turned thirteen because I thought them childish. *You can't do anything to us you haven't already done.* I remember the words of Lulu. People in Kalpania become ill when they lose hope. The fairies never had any. I'd already crossed them off. And the same goes for the wood elves. I'd written them into the story to replace the light fairies, but later took them out because they were a copycat of a certain famous author's elves. One of my struggles as a young author had been to create truly unique creatures.

"And now they have become shadow beings," I muse to myself aloud.

I pause to rest on a branch lying above the water. Was this the one I came down on? I can't see Picklefoot. I can hardly see my own hand.

Barking, then, *Come, hurry!*

"Come where? I can't see you!"

I stumble in the dark and fall in a deep bog, sputtering and trying to rid my mouth of the brackish taste. Wading through the water, I see white flashing ahead. *Picklefoot!* His wings are luminous in the dark, glowing with a light of their own.

I climb onto the island lit by Picklefoot's wings.

I find him. The words in my head sound mournful.

"Sir Lightlee?" My heart skips a beat. "Is he okay?"

I find Peanut Butter.

"What?"

Then I see him. A small, curly haired, brown dog lying at Picklefoot's feet. His belly moves in rapid, weak breaths, his fur matted with a dark substance.

"Is that...is that blood?"

Picklefoot whines.

It's a lot of blood and there's a deep gash in his side.

"How is he still alive? And what injured him?"

His superpower healing. Picklefoot nudges Peanut Butter. *He trying to heal himself.*

"Can he?"

Maybe, I not know. But I see man, not far. Has fire.

Sir Lightlee!

"Which way," I ask.

That. Picklefoot points with his nose.

"Take Peanut Butter to where we are to meet Mrs. Weaverwhipple. He's small. You can carry him right?"

Picklefoot nods.

I carefully lift Peanut Butter and lay him across Picklefoot's back. Peanut Butter whimpers, and I may not be a dog lover, but I hate seeing anything suffer.

Picklefoot folds his wings across his back, pinning Peanut Butter to secure him.

I walk, he says.

"Be careful, I'll meet you there with Sir Lightlee."

Picklefoot treads carefully following the shallow areas and high ground, and I turn in the direction he pointed to.

With Picklefoot gone, the swamp again descends into blackness, but it also helps me spot the fire flickering at the base of a tree. I pick up my pace. A man sits against the trunk with his head on his knees.

"Liam!" I call.

He doesn't move. Sleeping? Unconscious? Or...

"LIAM!"

I splash through the water and climb over a log onto the island, tripping on a lute the moment my feet touch the damp ground. The lute is smashed, strings curling in every direction.

"Oh, Liam," I say.

He still hasn't lifted his face off his knees, but a finger twitches across the hilt of the sword in his right hand. The blade is bloodied and...brown fur plastered to the steel.

CHAPTER 23

The words on my tongue are stuck to the roof of my mouth and my knees waver. Neither I nor Sir Lightlee speak or move as though we've both been frozen in time. Nothing but the popping of the fire and scratching of crickets can be heard. A distant frog croaks. I close my eyes and open them slowly as if expecting the scene before me to change—Sir Lightlee to be looking up with a quick smile and words of encouragement, and the blood on the sword to be gone. Maybe he had to defend himself against any number of monsters. Brown fur didn't have to belong to Peanut Butter. Why would I assume that?

"Liam." My voice halts in my throat. "What happened? Your sword..."

"No hope." Sir Lightlee's voice is hollow, and muffled on account of his face still being planted in his knees. "The Cha-Cha thought to bring hope. I put an end to that."

Is this really happening? "Why...why would you..." I swallow, and step around the fire so that I stand right in front of him. "Look at me, Liam. Tell me you did not mean to harm the dog."

Sir Lightlee looks up. Even the heat of the fire can't warm the pallor of his face. But it's his eyes that nearly evoke a scream from my lips yet simultaneously freeze it in my throat. I've seen some terrible eyes since I've been in Kalpania—eyes hollow with despair or empty of imagination and glazed over like dead fish—but nothing prepared me for what I see now.

Sir Lightlee stands slowly. "You, look at me," he says.

But I could do nothing else, though I want to tear my eyes away, for where his eyes should have been are empty sockets of endless depth that draw my soul into them like two black holes wherein not even light can escape.

"Look at me," he says, "and see your handiwork, the pinnacle of your creative endeavors."

No! I scream, only I don't think I actually say it aloud, the world is darkening around me. *I didn't create this, but the Shadow Witch!*

I am the Shadow Knight. His voice is in my head, or I'm in his. *And I am your faithful servant. The one you made to be the hero of the story, but you betrayed me as you did so many others.*

I want to scream, pull away, but I've been sucked into those eyes. I can't even tell if my feet are still on the ground. Am I standing or have I fallen? I have no sense of direction, or instinct of where my arms and legs are. My body is absent of all feeling, except this horrible wrenching in my gut, and I can see nothing, and hear nothing save the voice of the Shadow Knight. Am I still in The Roots?

You are in the nothingness that you subjected the light fairies and wood elves to when you wrote them out of Kalpania. The nothingness that is the souls of all shadow beings where is no light, no hope, no future.

Let me go! Oh, God, help!

The Shadow Knight laughs. Aloud I think, but it's hard to tell. Not the musical laugh of Sir Lightlee, my friend, but a grating noise, like an inharmonious strum of a bass guitar.

There's no god in this world except you. No faith. You are alone.

I left God out of my world for fear that it might turn away some readers and am now reaping its fruition. But I'm not alone. I may have excluded God in my creative endeavors, but He hasn't forsaken me. That much my heart tells me.

I'm not alone. I'm NOT ALONE!

I'm back in The Roots. The Shadow Knight stands before me, empty eyed, and a malicious grimace on his face. I avert my eyes from where his should be. A tear trickles down, tickling my face and landing in the corner of my lip.

"I'm sorry," I whisper. "I'm sorry I wrote you out of the story." *How long has he known? Has he known all along?* He long accused me of abandoning Kalpania and ever an accusing glint lit his eyes since he learned who I am.

"You did more than write me out," the Shadow Knight snarls. "Do you remember what you did? Look at me."

The Shadow Knight reaches his left hand up, for his right still clutches his bloodied blade, and tears his shirt, exposing his chest and a mangled hole in its center. One of his left ribs is snapped off and missing, and behind the mutilated muscles, half a discolored heart beats slowly next to a gray lung.

My face is soaked; tears slide around my mouth and drip off my chin. I sob audibly and lick my lips tasting bitter salt. I hadn't forgotten. How could I forget the day that Bradley broke up with me, and my teenage heart thought it was the end of the world? After a sleepless night of sobbing, I sat up at three a.m. and wrote a tragic end to young Squire Lightlee—speared in the chest, jousting with a knight in a foolish contest to win the Queen's heart. Of course, I had the Queen weep appropriately over him, knighting him post mortem, and giving him an honorable burial. The half of the heart torn from his chest was cremated and placed in a locket that the Queen wore about her heart always.

So now I ask the question that I should have thought to ask long ago, but with all the unbelievable things that have taken place in the last two and a half weeks, it never occurred to me that Sir Lightlee should not be alive. "How...but you live...were alive before, before you became this?"

"I was brought back from the shadows by Princess Taika."—Am I imagining it or did his voice soften?—"She gave me a new name, Liam..." His voice fades, then hardens again, spitting. "But she could not heal my heart, and I have ever carried and hidden this gaping wound you gave me."

"But you said she was the cure."

"There is no cure, for the Shadow Witch is the god of this world." He raises his sword to my belly. "Take me out of The Roots, to your daughter. I will send the both of you...*home.*"

If ever there was a way to say "home" in a manner that is terrifying, it is the way the Shadow Knight spews it from his lips like over-bitter coffee. I spin on my heels and plunge into the bog. I hear a splash behind me and know he's following. I scramble on a log and make my way along it as hurriedly as I can in the dark. I come to the end and only inky blackness lies before me. Chancing a glance back, I see the Shadow Knight hobbling across the log. Sir Lightlee must have injured his leg in the fall. A surge of hope—*The Shadow Knight isn't invincible!*

Taking a deep breath, I leap off the log, going over my head in chilling water. My legs kick wildly, scraping against a submerged branch, and as my head emerges, I gasp for air and sputter from the shock of the cold water. My boots weigh me down, and I almost go under again as water douses my face from a nearby splash. I feel a tug at my shoulder that threatens to pull me down, and my breaths come fast as fear squeezes my throat. I kick hard and elicit a grunt as my boot makes contact with something firm. Then I break free and swim until it is shallow enough to walk again. Behind me, somewhere in the dark, the Shadow Knight growls in pain and anger as he struggles in the pool.

Good, I think. He can't swim well with a disabled leg. But as I stumble away, my heart grieves for the friend I lost, and it's like a piece of me is being left behind. I created him, and then destroyed him in an unheroic death to get back at a stupid crush. But Sir Lightlee was never really Bradley. He was an idealized version of foolish teenage dreams of what the perfect man would be, and even he couldn't live up to my fantasies. In the latest version of my series before I abandoned them, the Queen kept Lightlee's heart around her neck to remind her that she could put her faith in no one.

Deep clay oozes into my boots with every step, and I pant with the effort it takes to free each step from the sucking mud. Wading through the swamp water was better than this. My right leg pulls completely free of its boot, and failing to keep my balance, I fall to my hands and knees. Grunting, I pull my boot free and shove my mud-covered foot back in. Have I lost the Shadow Knight? I'm not going to wait around to find out. Adrenaline alone, I think, must be driving me forward as I stumble along holding my side that's cramping from exertion.

I hit more solid ground and pick up speed only to run dab smack into one of the huge trunks that are as dark as the night around me. For a moment, I lie stunned, holding a hand to my head. I'm angry enough to scream if I wasn't terrified of the Shadow Knight hearing me. I can't keep going on blindly like this, I don't know if I'm anywhere near the meeting place with Mrs. Weaverwhipple, and for all I know, I'm running in the wrong direction. My sole consolation is that the Shadow Knight has got to be having a harder time of it with his bad leg. Figuring my best bet is to wait here till morning light, I curl into a ball at the base of the tree, a miserable wretch stained by mud and tears and regrets.

I had guarded my heart, until I met Michael, and once again fell head-over-heels, to once again be disappointed, though I'd never spoken it aloud—always feeling that he put his military career above me as I muddled my way through motherhood alone with two young children. And had I ever been any fairer to Michael than I had to Sir Lightlee, laying the burden of my insecurities as an author and an individual on him? And Sammie? Poisoning her mind against dreaming of anything at all because mine weren't realized?

God. I silently call to Him. The One I should have depended on from the beginning. The All-Sufficient-One in whom my worth is found—not in my failed writing career, not in marriage or in motherhood, not in the perfect homeschool or my daughter's successes. Those were all unfair burdens I placed on myself and others. My hope is in the One who could not fail me, the Friend that sticks closer than a brother even when I had forgotten Him in every aspect of my life. *Why art thou cast down, O my soul? And why art thou disquieted in me? Hope thou in God: for I shall yet praise Him.*

And staring into the darkness of the swamp, I see a light, blinking and growing until they form two perfect white angel's wings. When my weary mind finally comprehends what I'm seeing, I almost laugh out loud. My "angel" is Picklefoot, and never am I so glad to see a smelly dog. He lands near me, and I could almost hug him...almost.

Then a basket sways down from above, and I gratefully climb into it between Picklefoot and Peanut Butter, who is still alive and even lifts his head to whimper at me. Then we are drawn up and away. *Thank you, Jesus, for Sammie's imagination...*

CHAPTER 24

The earthy smell of rich soil reminds me of gardening with Sammie and JJ when they were little before we became too busy with school for such real-life learning experiences as watching things grow. I open my eyes, squinting as scattered sunlight flitters across the bending grass and into my eyes. Rolling to my back, I look up into a canopy of green against a clear blue sky, and dancing in the wind are Christmas bulbs? I shut my eyes tightly. I must be waking from a weird dream, and I don't want to because everything hurts, but the neighbor's annoying dog won't stop barking. Something warm and damp runs across my face.

"Ahh!" I sit up too fast and the blood rushes from my head, making me dizzy. A square-faced black dog barks. "Hush. Sit," I say, but not too harshly because I probably owe him my life.

I sitting already.

"Okay, just…" I pause to scratch a rash on my face from lying in grass. "Where am I?"

My home. Picklefoot grins, if a dog is capable of such a thing.

Something soft nudges my arm. *Peanut Butter!* Even I can't help but pick up the small, curly-haired dog and hold him in my arms. His side, though still matted with blood, looks completely healed. Peanut Butter wags his stubby tail.

I stumble to my feet, still holding Peanut Butter, and look around. What I had mistaken for Christmas bulbs in my sleepy state must be glowfruit, and my stomach grumbles, reminding me I haven't eaten anything since yesterday before we fell into The Roots. *Trauen!*

"Picklefoot, take me to Sammie and Trauen. Where do you think they'll be?"

Picklefoot barks and half romps, half flies off.

I pluck a low-hanging red fruit that looks somewhat like a giant cherry and hurry after him against my protesting sore muscles. The glowfruit is delicious though maybe a little oversweet. Right now, my mind is too full of other things to contemplate what it tastes like, nor do I give a thought to my unwashed hands or the dried mud that covers me from head to foot.

We arrive at the grove's center, which is full of more doglike Cha-Chas than my former self would have been comfortable with. Having survived the horrors of The Roots, overly silly dogs imagined by a nine-year-old don't faze me. A shaggy white dog that I almost don't recognize as Tony, the mud somehow cleaned off him, comes running toward me barking.

Tony stops short of me, and he and Picklefoot bump noses and seem to be communicating. They both bound off, then Picklefoot circles back toward me saying, *Follow.*

I set off after them, gripping Peanut Butter tightly in my arms. I'm not sure why I don't sct him down. He started this adventure in that fading world called "home," and it's as if I fear that by releasing him, I will lose touch with reality itself. I draw him close to my chest, my fingers subconsciously petting his soft curls until they come to the rough spot where blood still mats the fur. A lump rises in my throat, and I blink away images of Sir Lightlee's blood-slicked sword.

We walk toward the base of the enormous tree that shelters the field in its canopy of leaves—the glowfruit mother tree. I reach out and run my hand along its smooth mahogany bark and look up as its leaves rustle high above in the breeze. Every leaf is a different shade of green from almost yellow to nearly black. Following Tony and Picklefoot around the trunk that's nearly as big around as my entire house, we eventually come to a place where two large roots protrude from the base and into the ground to make what amounts to a small, roofless room.

Sammie sits crossed legged twirling a leaf in her hand, pausing only to wipe her nose across her arm. Next to her Trauen sits against the tree, staring blankly and not acknowledging my approach. Sammie looks up, tears streaking across the mud on her face.

Sammie leaps up and grips me in a hug. "Oh, Mama," she says in a voice halted with sobs and muffled between my shirt and Peanut Butter's fur. "I didn't...get here fast enough...glowfruit wasn't helping...couldn't save...him."

I tighten my arms around Sammie, my eyes transfixed on Trauen. Under his shock of white hair, his eyes stare blankly, looking at neither me nor Sammie. I unwind myself from Sammie's arms, passing Peanut Butter into them.

I crouch beside Trauen, brushing the hair from his forehead. In a voice barely above a whisper I say, "Trauen...look at me."

Lifting his hand, I hold it in mine. It's as cold as ice, but I don't let go even though a chill runs through my body from my head to toes. I force myself to look into his dead gray eyes.

"JJ," I say. "It's Mama." I kiss his hand and my tears mingle between our fingers. "Talk to me."

My eyes fall on a leaf on the ground, one of those from the glowfruit tree. It's shaped like a heart. I pick it up with one hand, remembering last Mother's Day.

Sammie and JJ made a handmade card, drawing a big tree with heart-shaped leaves and bright fruit in every color from their crayon box. I fall back, sitting against the mother tree and pull the limp Trauen in my arms, sobbing.

Sammie sets Peanut Butter down. "Look, it's Peanut Butter. Mama found him."

Peanut Butter squeezes between me and Trauen, whining softly. I'm suddenly enveloped in warmth like hot cider on a cold day. I blink in surprise through my tears. Peanut Butter is licking Trauen, and I think his cheeks are beginning to glow.

"Look!" I say.

"Peanut Butter's sending hugs!" Sammie's eyes brighten. "His superpower is healing!"

Hope surges within me, but also doubt. "Can he...you think he can heal the shadow illness though?"

"I think, maybe," Sammie says. "JJ always feels better when Peanut Butter gives him Daddy's hugs. That's why I wanted to find him."

"Can he give him our hugs, too?"

"I'm sure he can," Sammie says. "Look at Trauen's hair!"

Sure enough, starting at the roots, it begins to turn back to its natural color until not a white strand can be found. Trauen pulls Peanut Butter into his arms and hugs him tightly. His skin is glowing with a healthy color. He looks at Sammie, and then turns to me and smiles.

"Mama!" His eyes sparkle with renewed life. "You found Taika!"

Sammie giggles. "He thinks I'm the princess, too!"

I laugh. "Because you are, Sammie, you are!"

~~~

I splash my face in the natural hot spring that feeds the glowfruit orchard. The water is warm, but not too warm, and bubbles gently up from the ground forming a crystal clear pool between the rocks. I bathed in my
~~~

linens earlier and let them air dry on my body throughout the afternoon, while my thoroughly scrubbed outerwear dried on the branches of a glowfruit tree. I feel the tunic and leggings with my hands and satisfied that they are dry, I dress.

The quiet of the late afternoon is broken with shouting and barking. I glimpse Sammie and Trauen running between the trees chasing Tony and Peanut Butter and the other Cha-Chas in a game of tag. My smile seems to leech all the tiredness out of my body, and I forget for a moment that I still have no clue how to get us back home.

This my home. You want live with me?

I jump, startled. "Picklefoot, don't do that!" I'll never get used to a dog reading my thoughts and randomly inserting his own.

I sorry. Picklefoot materializes in front of me with confused wrinkles in his forehead.

I sigh, and kneel on one knee. Tentatively, I pat his head. "Just warn me first. Let me know you're there before you speak to me."

Like this? Picklefoot gives a deep, throaty bark, and I snatch my hand back.

"No! More like, just stand where I can see you and don't sneak up on me." I rise to my feet. "In fact, I'd prefer you to stay visible at all times."

Picklefoot wags his tail and flaps his wings in affirmation.

I shove on my boots, lacing them. Over a lunch of glowfruit, Sammie had explained to me that the reason I could hear Picklefoot's thoughts, but not any of the other Cha-Chas', was because he chose me to be his person. Peanut Butter chose JJ, and Tony Cheesecracker, Sammie. I wrinkle my nose and gag, backing away from Picklefoot.

Sorry, he says.

Apparently, I don't get a choice in the matter, and I'm stuck with an animal companion whose superpower is farting. Besides becoming invisible, all Cha-Chas have a superpower, Sammie tells me, but Peanut Butter and Jelly Sandwich the Third has the rarest power—healing. Tony's superpower is the ability to understand and communicate with all other animals, which is how he made friends with Spottie.

I had the pleasure of meeting Spottie my first day in the orchard, nearly choking to death on a glowfruit when she pounced my boots from behind a bush. After three days stranded here, I may choke if I have to eat one more of the sugary fruits, but the rest has been good for Trauen, who's acting more like the energetic boy I remember...but I'm remembering JJ. I silently whisper a prayer that JJ is well and safe, and cling to the hope that Trauen's well-being is proof.

I unhook my side pouch off a tree—at least I had not lost that in the fall. *The Shadow Witch* topples out to the ground with a thud. I pick the book up, thoughtfully. Mailene said that Sammie could write herself out. *Why not?* If we are living in a story, why can't we change it? My heart quickens. It's so simple; the answer's been in front of me the whole time. I just need—fishing through my pouch—"Where is it? Please let it be here," I mumble. *Yes!* I pull out the short pencil. I can end this nightmare...get us home...

"Daa—ng!" I barely revise my curse in time as Sammie and Trauen skip over to me. My pencil leaves no mark on the pages of *The Shadow Witch*.

"What's wrong, Mama?" Sammie says, scrutinizing my face. Sammie always has an eerie way of knowing something's bothering me no matter how hard I tried to fake otherwise.

"Nothing...Sammie, can you write in this book? Write us home?"

Sammie takes the book from my hand, turning to its cover. "This is the Shadow Witch's book. You can't write in it. We need the other one."

"The one the Shadow Witch holds?"

Sammie nods her head.

Naturally. I roll my eyes. Leaning against a tree trunk, I rub a hand across my face. "So...basically what you're saying is that we can't get home without going to the Shadow Witch?"

"She's the bad guy," Sammie says as if that explains everything.

Trauen's eyes are growing wide.

"Sammie! We have no supplies. No guide. I don't even know how to find her. And even if we could, she's not going to help us!"

Trauen grasps my hand with his. JJ never likes it when Sammie and I argue.

I close my eyes for a moment then level my voice. "You brought us to Kalpania somehow. Can't you just get us out the same way?"

"I-I don't know how I got here. I wrote in the book and then I was here." Sammie crosses her arms. "How did *you* get here, Mama?"

"I don't know." Exasperation is etching its way back into my voice. This conversation is going nowhere. Typical.

Peanut Butter runs up to Trauen wagging his stubby tail. Trauen laughs running off with the dog, his face a-glow with joy and health.

"Why doesn't Peanut Butter heal everyone?"

Sammie walks across a log balancing herself with her arms sticking out. She pauses long enough to say, "It's not that easy. Peanut Butter is only one Cha-Cha, and Kalpania is big."

I sigh and pick up the Shadow Witch's book that Sammie left lying on the ground. "Sir...the Shadow Knight,"—I don't want to acknowledge that monster is Sir Lightlee—"tried to kill Peanut Butter."

Sammie slips off the log. She looks up at me, eyes wide. "The Shadow Knight? He's back?"

"What do you mean 'back'?" I say.

"Mama! What happened to Sir Lightlee? He didn't—" Sammie's eyes are brimming with tears. "That's why he didn't come back with you. I just thought he was...I forgot because of Trauen...how could you?" Sammie stomps a foot.

"How could I what? It wasn't my fault. What do you mean 'he's back'? He was the Shadow Knight before?"

"Well, you killed him." Sammie flops onto the ground, wrapping her arms around her knees. "You killed him again." She wipes her arm across her face and sobs into her knees.

It all makes sense now. Everyone I disposed of in my story—the light fairies, the wood elves—turned to shadow. Sir Lightlee would have been like them until Sammie resurrected him.

I sit down beside her and wrap one arm around her. "I'm sorry, Sammie. I am truly, incredibly sorry. But..."

Sammie looks up, brushing tears and hair from her face.

"Why didn't you fix his heart when you brought Sir Lightlee back?" I ask.

Fresh tears streak down Sammie's face. "I-I didn't want him to be too perfect. He's 'posed to get his heart back when he defeats the Shadow Witch."

"She has it?"

Sammie nods. "She took the locket from the Queen when she killed her."

I frown. I thought *I* was the Queen. How connected are our counterparts? Every time I think I've finally figured it out...

Sammie leaps to her feet. "Mama, we *got* to help him."

"How?" I stand slowly. "He already tried to kill Peanut Butter. It's too dangerous."

"We can't beat the Shadow Witch without him. Anyway, we need her book to get home."

"Why?" I say, looking down at *The Shadow Witch* that I still grip in one hand. "Why do we need her book? How do you know?"

"I...sorta wrote it that way."

"What way?"

"Two books—one that shows and one that tells. This book shows what's happened. The other one tells what's gonna happen if you write in it."

I contemplate that for a moment. Pretty clever for a nine-year-old, really. A chilling thought strikes me. "Wait...then can't the Shadow Witch write any future she wants?"

"Oh, no!" Sammie says. "The Shadow Witch can't write stories. She destroys them."

"And you know this because?"

Sammie stares at her feet, making S's in the dirt with one foot.

"Sammie!"

She looks up, biting her lip. "Because I made her." Sammie's face flushes.

"You?" Now it's my turn for my face to become hot. "Why would you do that?"

"Well," Sammie says in that how-do-you-not-know-this tone. "Every story's got to have a bad guy."

CHAPTER 25

The Shadow Knight stood alone in the Great Mesa Desert, his cloak waving in the breeze. He pulled his hood over his head, his gaze wandering across the bleak landscape devoid of any color. The gray sands were dotted with darker gray shrubs and rocks that cast deep black shadows. If he still had the ability to squint, he would have under the bright sky that was a blinding silver-white haze in the afternoon sun. Instead, the empty holes that served as eyes sucked in every bit of light, burning as though he had coals shoved in his sockets. The Shadow Knight wished for night, but even the dim starlight was almost unbearable.

The Shadow Knight dispassionately punched a thick barrel cactus and slowly pulled out the long spines embedded deep into his hand. Black blood beaded across his gray skin, sliding between his fingers and dripping onto the sand. The added pain didn't anger him, but rather the inability for it to reduce the pain in his eyes and head...and heart. Furiously, he hacked the cactus to bits with his sword; a large chunk flew into a shrub, frightening away a gray squirrel. The Shadow Knight would have liked to kill it, but it dashed quickly into a burrow. Anger. Fear. Hate. These were the only emotions he could feel anymore, but it was better than feeling nothing at all—than the emptiness left behind when the Shadow Witch took his soul.

The Shadow Knight yanked his sword out of the mutilated barrel cactus, determined to stay angry, for it was the only thing left that made him still feel alive, and he feared becoming a dull, witless pawn of the Shadow Witch even more than he hated and feared her. He served her now again, as he knew he eventually would, but maybe before the world ended, he would kill her. But even as he thought it, he shook his head. That was Sir Lightlee's death throes still echoing in his mind. It was hopeless because hope did not exist. The Shadow Knight sheathed his sword and limped to a large rock, where he huddled in its minimal shade to wait.

He faced the east, the direction the Tangled Woods lay, and smiled grimly. He knew from the mind of the Shadow Witch that they were watching him, the Queen and her daughter—reading from the Shadow Witch's book in the near future. "You won't succeed, Michelle, for you know not your true enemy."

~~~

The pages are blank as I hover over Sammie's shoulder as she reads aloud *The Shadow Witch* to me. Sammie explained to me that the book shows you what you were looking for, and what I had been seeking, I found. But Sammie is seeking Sir Lightlee, and to her alone the book reveals the recent past.

Sammie slams the book shut. "They know we're looking for him."

With pursed lips, I nod. I knew that the Shadow Witch would know the moment we opened the book. I hadn't realized the Shadow Knight would also know, but it makes sense. The Shadow Witch's mind is connected to those struck with the shadow illness. "She's using him—all of them—to destroy Kalpania. But why?"
~~~

Sammie traces the gold lettering on the cover of the book. "Because she has no imagination."

I take the book from Sammie and place it into my side pouch. "What is her goal?"

Sammie stands and shrugs. "To destroy Kalpania."

What am I expecting? A nine-year-old to have a well-thought out motive for her villain? "Okay, so now what? How did he get out of The Roots anyway?"

Sammie glances at Tony and nods. "Her power is growing. Tony says that Spottie saw a shadow fairy in The Branches when she was hunting."

Trauen comes running over. "Look, look!"

He's wearing a pale blue tunic with deeper blue trousers. The material almost appears luminescent.

"Where did you get that outfit?" I ask.

"Come, see." Trauen spins and runs off with Sammie right behind.

I try to keep up with a fast walk, but give up and jog after them. I slow down when we get to the edge of the orchard near the gulf. Sammie excitedly holds up a pale salmon-colored dress made of the same material. Mrs. Weaverwhipple hovers above her. I swallow my revulsion for the giant arachnid-like insect and approach as near as I can tolerate. Mrs. Weaverwhipple waves her antennae at me, and then produces another outfit for me. Taking a deep breath, I walk over.

"Th-thank you," I breathe, and look into the nearest of her five eyes. Unblinking, she searches me with an ancient wisdom and my spirit calms. The fear dissipates as she communicates to me through emotions without any words at all. I take the silky tunic and leggings from her. "Thank you." This time I mean it, and I can't wait to get out of my crusty old clothes. The fabric is amazingly soft to the touch and a beautiful shade of pale green.

Sammie comes running back from changing, spinning in her dress. Soon both her and Trauen are spinning in circles until they fall down giggling.

Mrs. Weaverwhipple waves her antennae again, and one of her great hairy legs produces a dark green silken backpack. Despite the delicate softness of the fabric, it's woven in a way that I'm sure it will hold any burden I place in it. Once again, I'm overwhelmed by emotions, but ones of urgency. Without words, and in a way I can't explain, I simply know what it is that Mrs. Weaverwhipple is communicating. The new clothes and backpack are in preparation for our journey, and she will take us to the location where the Tangled Woods meets with the Great Mesa Desert. The world is dying, and if we can't save it, even the Tangled Woods will fall to the Shadow Witch. It's already begun.

~~~

The red sands of the Great Mesa Desert shimmer under the rising sun. At this altitude the high desert is still chilly in the early morning, and I pull my hood over my head. During her brief farewell, Mrs. Weaverwhipple expressed that the garments she made for us would protect against both the cold nights and heat of the day. The light material and long sleeves would reflect the sun's rays to keep our skin cool, yet be sufficient to keep off the worst of the night's chill.

Taking a hand from both Trauen and Sammie in each of mine, our backs to the Tangled Woods, we step forward from the shade of the last branch and into the desert. Even the children seem subdued by the vast landscape, barren, save for prickly cacti and a few shrubs. I had half-expected it to be gray as seen by the Shadow Knight, but to our eyes the desert is vibrant with color. The blue-green shrubs stand stark against the red sands, and a towering purple cactus is highlighted by the deep blue sky, a sky more blue than any I'd ever seen on Earth. Not even the Shadow Witch could reach it, only change the perception of it by those overcome with the shadow illness.

Trauen points excitedly at something. "A fox!"
~~~

At first I don't see the animal until it scurries across the sand and chatters at us from a shrub.

"That's not a fox, silly," Sammie says. "It's a squirrel."

"It's red like a fox," Trauen argues. "And it's too big."

"Mama, tell him it's a squirrel," Sammie says.

"Shhh," I hush them.

Something, dark as the smoke from a recently doused fire, streaks across the sky and fills me with foreboding. It lands atop an outcropping of jagged boulders and stretches its long neck and turns its head to one side to view us. My heart stills at the sight—a great phoenix, the desert bird adopted as a symbol for Magdalin for its beauty and intelligence, but no longer as I had imagined it. Instead of a bird made of pure flames, this creature is of billowing smoke. The phoenix lifts its head and shrieks at a pitch that causes Sammie and Trauen to cover their ears and scream. I want to do the same, but I grab their arms and drag them into a run.

A shadow flies across the ground as the phoenix circles above us, shrieking again. Trauen stumbles, and Sammie's scream turns into a cough as the creature makes a low pass. Smoke burns our eyes and fills our lungs. With effort, I drag Trauen into a bramble of tall cacti. Sammie crawls under it behind him as far as she can without being stabbed and poked by spines, and I use my body as a door to block the entrance.

"Ouch," Sammie yells.

Trauen whimpers, and we all start coughing again as the phoenix lands before us, smoke billowing off of his body as he fans it with his wings in our direction. I glance around looking for anything to use as a weapon. Gingerly, I pick up a prickly fruit that's fallen to the ground. Ignoring the fine spines in my fingers, I throw it at him. It passes through him into the sand untouched. It doesn't matter that the creature can't physically touch us. We're going to die from smoke inhalation.

"Mama." Sammie coughs. "I can't breathe."

"Stay low to the ground," I answer.

Trauen's already lying on the ground and looks as though he's passed out.

In the midst of the phoenix's ear-shattering screech is another sound, if possible, even more horrible. A rumbling roar causes the sand to shift, increasing in pitch until it resembles the scream of a terrified woman. The phoenix's body blurs; it seems confused, unable to hold form. Then it mushrooms out, like an exploding bomb, and dissipates into the wind. The smoke begins to clear, and I breathe easier.

"Trauen." I shake him.

He moans, coughing. But the fresh breeze on his face revives him.

"Are you okay, Sammie?" I ask.

"Yeah, I think, but what is that?" She points.

Our rescuer appears in the clearing haze not ten feet away—a powerful lithe cat-body with a woman's head.

"Sphinx," I whisper. "Sammie, stay behind me."

I'm not sure what the sphinx's intent toward us will be. I didn't create them to be benevolent creatures.

She takes a few steps forward and bows, her raven locks falling around her face. "Welcome, O, Queen and young Princess." Her voice in contrast to her terrifying scream is low and almost purrs.

A thunder of hooves churns up the desert sand behind the sphinx. Then a great centaur stands by her side. He flicks his black tail across his deep chestnut equine body. His hair, as dark and coarse as his tail, falls messy around a muscular brown human chest. The sphinx and the centaur make a formidable display standing side-by-side.

"Oh, I know what that is," Sammie blurts out as if we are playing charades. "A centaur!"

"It's a horse-man," says Trauen hoarsely, mostly recovered yet understandably grouchy.

"That's what a centaur is," Sammie answers.

The centaur also bows. "I am Kostas, my Queen, and this"—he waves toward the sphinx—"is Asenath. We can carry thee a day's journey."

I look between the two, a little astonished. Sphinxes and centaurs are natural enemies for starters, and neither are terribly friendly to strangers. "You will help us?"

"Thou art our Queen," the centaur answers.

"Any foe to the Shadow Witch." The sphinx spits on the ground. "Is a friend to us."

"Time delays not for our tarrying," the centaur urges. "Thy friend awaits thee, and the fate of our world as well."

"I-I'm sorry. What do you want of us?" I'm bewildered and not sure what he expects of me...and what friend?

"Trauen!" I say in a warning tone. He has walked over to the centaur and looks about ready to touch him. To my surprise the centaur reaches down with his human arms and lifts Trauen to his back. Sammie immediately follows Trauen's example and is lifted onto his back as well.

"Asenath has agreed to carry thee," the centaur says. He motions toward the sphinx.

Riding Wyot made me nervous enough. The idea of being upon a lion-woman makes my knees knock, but I would rather not offend her. Neither a centaur nor sphinx would normally carry humans as a burden.

Asenath crouches, allowing me to climb onto her back; standing she is nearly as tall as the centaur.

"I thought sphinxes had wings," Sammie says.

"Greek sphinxes, not Egyptian ones." I hope the question didn't offend Asenath, but she seems as disinterested in our conversation as a regular cat would be.

"Excuse me," I ask, "but how did you know I am the Queen?"

"Thy friend has spread abroad the news," Kostas answers. "Now we run."

And before I can ask this friend's name, I am nearly jolted off of Asenath as she leaps forward.

She turns her head to the side. "Thou mustn't fall. Hold on however thou art able."

I don't know how she expects me to hold on. I don't wish to pull her human-like hair, so I try to steady myself by clinging to the fur above her powerful shoulders before her body merges into human form. But for the smoothness of her movements as she pads effortlessly across the sand, I don't think I could have remained seated without falling. Thankfully, the pace is more of a trot than full-blown running.

The children seem to be enjoying themselves behind Kostas, chatting and asking random questions that he patiently answers no matter how silly. He teaches them about the desert creatures, and how to find water, and which plants are edible, and how to tell which way is north, south, east, or west. Regret floods me when I think of the opportunity for conversations that were missed because I couldn't conceive of learning beyond a pencil and piece of paper.

Kostas lets us break every so often to rest and snack on our glowfruit. He introduces root vegetables and prickly pear and desert chives to our meals, and I'm grateful for the added variety. During lunch, Asenath goes off to hunt for her food, and Kostas urges her to eat her raw and messy meal out of our presence.

Kostas stands rather than sits under the meager shade offered by the gnarled juniper. I bite into a spicy-sweet root that tastes like a carrot crossed with a radish, while watching Trauen and Sammie engage in playing an imaginary game with the hard juniper berries. Though the bitter berries are inedible fresh off the tree, Kostas tells the children they're useful for spices in recipes and have medicinal properties.

"And is good for gin also," adds Asenath returning from her hunt.

Kostas folds his arms. "If thou use it for medicine, and waste it not in riotous parties."

Asenath stretches her long body in a cat-like fashion before lying down. "I use it for medicine..."—she smiles, showing her long fangs and even her human features appear suddenly feline—"and parties."

"You spoke of the fate of the world," I say to Kostas to intercept their argument.

Kostas's disapproving frown directed at Asenath turns more downward before he addresses me. "The shadow elves have marched upon Kalpania. Word is they have overtaken the City of Stairs, and that without resistance."

"Magdalin is conquered?" I swallow my shock. The city was designed to withstand months of siege. It should not have been easily overcome.

"Let them march upon my people, and see how they fare," Asenath says.

Kostas stomps a rear leg and swishes his tail. "Be not so eager to shed blood. It may come upon us soon enough."

Asenath growls. "Then let it come and be done with. May my claws send many an elf into oblivion before I die."

"Please, the children," I say. Sammie and Trauen have fallen silent, eyes wide with curiosity.

"Why hide from their ears what soon they shall see with their eyes?" Asenath answers.

Even Kostas nods. "In these dark days, it is best they be prepared."

"But not unnecessarily frightened," I say.

"I'm not scared," Sammie says.

Trauen leaps to his feet. "Me either. I can fight." He kicks the tree with a foot and winces.

Asenath purrs in amused approval. "The prince has the blood of the sun. Unfortunate, he will not live to see his full strength tested."

"Asenath!" I say.

Kostas snorts, and to my relief commands us to proceed with our journey.

We don't see any more shadow phoenixes, but as the sun lowers, Asenath and Kostas become more alert and bid the children to be quiet. The phoenixes, once creatures of the day, I'm told are most active between dusk and dawn. We top a slight rise, and spread before our view is the heart of Kalpania. We are at the western edge of the Great Mesa Desert atop the Ruby Cliffs, and the farms of Kalpania below appear as a green and brown patchwork quilt. The sun sets over the distant blue haze of the Unending Sea, turning the cliffs below deep red, hence their name. Far to the south, the peaks of the White Mountains rising above the red desert landscape complete the enchanting scene, and I wish I could capture it with my eyes. Were I a painter, I would memorialize it on canvas when I return home.

Our guides make for an outcropping of boulders surrounded by shrubby mesquite trees near the cliff's edge.

"We can take thee this far, and no farther," Kostas says. "We have our own peoples to care for, but thy friend may guide thee from hence."

"Is there water?" I lick my wind-chapped lips.

I'd lost our canteens in the fall into The Roots, so we were down to just one that Sammie brought with her from Fisherman's Haven. Thankfully, Kostas carried a large leather waterskin, so we had enough to go around, but I'd love a deep draught of cool water, and not the lukewarm water heated by the sun.

"A well can be found amongst the boulders," Asenath says.

"It was dug long ago," Kostas adds, "and taps into a deep underground stream. It runs low in autumn, but when the snow melts come spring, a waterfall spurts forth from the midst of the Ruby Cliffs. 'Tis a beautiful sight."

"Would be better yet," Asenath says, "if it would remain in the desert where it is useful than spill to the valley below."

Kostas glares at her, but lets the argument go.

We say our farewells and thanks, and then walk toward the clearing in the rocks. Only a glimmer of sunlight remains above the horizon and the night air has already turned chilly, but a great bonfire blazes ahead.

Rounding a boulder, I'm startled by a friendly nicker—and what should I see but Prattles shaking his shaggy mane, and Garren standing suddenly to his feet?

CHAPTER 26

Garren's bushy eyebrows seem ready to fly off his face. "Michelle?" His eyes widen the more when his gaze strays to Trauen then over to Sammie.

"Garren," I say with equal surprise. Apparently, this is the time for us all to state each other's names.

Sammie and Trauen, of course, are engrossed in rubbing Prattles' nose, who cheerfully accepts the extra attention.

"What are you doing here?" I ask. "You were the friend Kostas spoke of?"

"The centaur? He brought you? But where's Sir Lightlee?

My throat tightens. "He is...can I sit?"

Garren holds out his hand toward a flat rock, and I sit, after which he reseats himself. "I was acquainted with Kostas's people during a particularly bad outbreak of a foot disease unique to equine. He owed me a favor, and so promised to search for Sir Lightlee."

"If Kostas and Asenath hadn't found us when they did...well, we owe them, and you, our lives." I glance around the blackening night at the thought of the shadow phoenix. The warmth of the fire feels good in the fast dropping temps, yet a shiver prickles across the back of my neck, but not from cold. "The phoenixes. Won't this fire draw them to us?"

Garren shakes his head. "They're creatures of darkness and smoke. Fire no longer draws them, but repels them."

"Are there any left that are still free of the Shadow Witch?"

"Not that I know of." His eyes follow Sammie and Trauen chasing each other around the bonfire, sword fighting with sticks.

"You'd think they'd be worn out," I say. "I sure am."

Garren gives a faint smile. "Children are more resilient than often given credit. I see ye found your...your daughter?"

I nod. "Sammie, come meet"—I glance sideways at Garren—"my friend." I hope Garren still considers me a friend, considering his coolness toward me ever since Sir Lightlee declared me to be the Queen.

Sammie skips over followed by Trauen. Sammie smiles and does another one of her silly curtsies. "Hello, Mr. Garren. How is your cousin?"

Garren sucks in a quick breath. "Ye're the little girl that Yernar told me of. The one tryin' to get a boat?"

"I didn't get one, but the merpeople took me on an orca."

"I like the merpeople," Trauen cuts in. "I rode a whale!"

"It's called an orca," Sammie says.

I think he's about fed up with Sammie correcting him. He turns to me. "Tell, Taika, that I rode a whale."

"Yes, I saw." I deflect the question. "Both of you get into your bedrolls." Another amazing amenity given to us by Mrs. Weaverwhipple are these tightly wound cocoon-like blankets that are softer and more comfortable than any sleeping bag. We slept on them our last night in the Tangled Woods.

The children lay their bedrolls out across the sand and I tuck them in. Garren walks over and hands a canteen of water to Sammie, who guzzles it in greedy gulps.

"Thank you," she says, smiling.

Garren responds with a smile of his own and passes the canteen to Trauen. Once the children are tucked in, I return back to the rock where Garren sits resting his chin on a fist, a pensive frown on his face and dark look in his eyes. My stomach knots at the thought of telling him the truth about Sir Lightlee...the truth about me, and what I did to him.

"Garren," I say to get his attention. "About..."

Garren looks up and his eyes cut into me. "Did ye know I've met Princess Taika in the palace? Twice."

I shake my head.

"Meeting a princess is not something ye quickly forget. This child"—he waves towards Sammie settling in her bedroll—"she is like the princess, but not the princess."

Different, yet the same—like Trauen and JJ. "I'm not sure how to explain it—"

"Explain what is your intent. To usurp the throne? To replace Princess Taika with your daughter?"

"Garren, listen—"

He stands to his feet and points a finger in my face. "Explain how ye fooled Sir Lightlee...and where, might I add, is he?"

"If you don't believe I'm the Queen, why did you tell Kostas that I was?"

"I..." Garren glances away. "I hoped rather than believed. It's spreading faster."

"The shadow illness? I...I heard Magdalin was taken."

"Without a fight." Garren sighs. "Instead of trapping the illness without as was their intent, they trapped it within. When I arrived, Magdalin was in the control of the shadow people, and they preventing those that were well from leaving. I..." Garren's voice breaks. "I could hear their cries at the gate and could do nothing. Nothing! And I a physician." Garren sits back down with a slump, the fire gone out of him. "Now even the merpeople are reporting cases. I spread the news of the Queen's 'miraculous' return because hope was the only medicine I had."

I sit tentatively on the rock, leaving a good space between us. "I want to help. You don't have to believe I'm the Queen, but believe that."

Garren's lips tighten, his eyes still distrusting.

"What brought you here?" I ask.

"I found my friend Johann and returned with him to Dallet's. Connie was gathering a small group of survivors to lead to the mountains for refuge. Dallet was..." Garren swallows. "Gone. And then I saw Wyot wandering listlessly beside Prattles. Upon seeing me, he became suddenly violent. I set him free, and on a whim followed him till I lost him in the desert."

"You thought he would lead you to Sir Lightlee?"

"Wyot's bond with him is strong. I knew Sir Lightlee must be in danger." Garren's voice halts. "Perhaps beyond help. Has he contracted the illness?" His eyes plead with me.

I turn my head away not wanting to meet them. "He...has become the Shadow Knight." And though my voice is a faint whisper, it seems to carry in the still night air.

When Garren doesn't respond, I turn back to him. "Ye...ye lie," he says, but his voice lacks confidence.

I look at my hands in my lap. "I wish I was." Wiping my eyes, I look back up. "Sir Lightlee didn't contract the shadow illness. He's had it all along. Since before we met."

Garren stands, giving a slight shake of the head. His hands clench in fists, and he paces a few feet from me, cursing under his breath and sounding every bit more like a sailor from Fisherman's Haven than the calm physician I've known. When he turns around, the fire lights half his face, and he looks young and vulnerable and so much like my brother did the day I lost him.

"I should have known something wasn't..." Garren's voice trails off. He walks over to the fire and pokes it, adding another chunk of mesquite wood.

"It's not your fault," I say.

"What good is a physician that can't heal? Can't even see that his patient is sick?"

Garren kneels by the fire on one knee, and I come over by him and sit down crossed legged. I want to offer him words of comfort but they're stuck in my throat. Anything I could say would seem shallow anyway. Instead, I study the back of his head that's turned away from me for any sign of the shadow illness. His black curls seem untouched by gray, but his broad shoulders slump in defeat.

"The Shadow Knight stood by the Shadow Witch when she slew our Queen." Garren speaks slowly, his voice monotone. "Sir Lightlee couldn't save the Queen, but fought the Shadow Knight from sundown till sunrise. Sir Lightlee sustained major injuries, but in the end defeated the Shadow Knight, although the Shadow Witch escaped during the night." Garren turns toward me and his voice becomes hard. "Or so the story goes. But now ye tell me my friend was the Shadow Knight all along. And how can ye be the Queen if she died?"

What can I tell him? I still don't understand the connection between this world and mine. At my silence, Garren grunts and grabs the canteens. "Going to refill the water." And he disappears beyond the boulders and shrubs.

A slight breeze rustles the mesquite trees, and I pull on the hood of my tunic. I'm preparing my bed near the children when Sammie says, "Mama."

"You should be asleep," I say.

"I know, but can you first pray for Sir Lightlee?"

"I...I don't think God cares about a make-believe world. It's a silly little thing."

"Well, but God is big, so it won't be hard for Him. Besides, you said to pray when we're scared, and I'm scared for Sir Lightlee."

I scoot over by Sammie and take her hand. Her childlike logic, or maybe it's faith, amazes me. In the back of my mind I'd always thought a great God couldn't be bothered by our small concerns, but the truth was I never invited Him into my little troubles until they had grown beyond what I could handle. Perhaps there was the real issue; I thought I could handle my own problems. So I pray. I ask Him to keep us safe and help us find our way home, to watch over Daddy wherever he is, to stop the Shadow Witch from destroying us, to help Sir Lightlee, and, yes, even to save Kalpania. When I'm done, Sammie is breathing deeply, and I kiss her forehead and then Trauen's. When I look up, Garren is staring at me with a quizzical crease across his forehead, and I wonder how long he's been standing there. He turns away quickly and makes his bed on the opposite side of camp.

<div align="center">~~~</div>

A mouthwatering aroma of meat and rosemary arouses me from a deep sleep. I sit up and brush the hair from my face. Sammie and Trauen are playing a game of tag around Prattles. Any other horse and I'd be worried it would be startled and kick, but Prattles calmly nibbles around a shrub.

"Here." Garren hands me a wooden plate with the meat of some critter that I decide not to inspect too closely as to what it might have been while still alive.

"You went...hunting?" I say. The meat's gamey and tough with an excessive amount of crushed rosemary rubbed on it, but not all that bad otherwise, or else I'm just really hungry.

Garren shrugs. "Was up early. Couldn't sleep. Thought the children and ye could use a proper breakfast."

"Oh." I stretch and start rolling the beds up because I can't think of anything to say.

Garren quietly starts helping me pack camp. "The children look well," he says after a while as he secures the pack to Prattles. "Trauen...I saw no sign of illness, yet he tells me he ran out of medicine."

I glance at Trauen's glowing face and smile. "He's been cured."

"But how?" Garren doesn't argue with my statement. "He should be...well, I wouldn't've believed it if I'd not seen him with my own eyes."

I pet Prattles on the nose and brush the hair from his eyes. I've actually missed the shaggy pony. "Puppy hugs." I laugh at Garren's expression.

"I'm not sure I really know," I say, "but I think..." What could I tell Garren? Everything Sammie had changed in my dying world had become resistant to the shadow illness. The giants, the Tangled Woods, glowfruit, the Cha-Chas. Sure, Peanut Butter and Jelly Sandwich had healed Trauen, but I think there was more to it. It wasn't just Peanut Butter, but Sammie and me there with him. "It was hope," I say, "and love, and the faith of a child. You said it yourself. Hope is medicine."

Garren opens his mouth then closes it, shaking his head. "I can take you to the mountains to the refugee camp."

"You go," I say. "We're staying here."

"What?" Garren looks up.

"It's time that I accept the Shadow Witch's invitation. She's the key to getting me and my children home."

"Ye can't," Garren says. "It's dangerous. She has an army of shadow elves at her disposal, and she's a witch."

"You're a physician," I say, "if you have an infection, you don't just treat the symptoms, you have to root out the cause. You didn't leave the arrow in Sir Lightlee. The Shadow Witch is the arrowhead, and I'm the surgeon. I know you think I'm crazy, but I wrote this world into existence, and I'm not going to let some witch kill it."

Garren blinks at me as though at a loss for words. I think better of telling him that Sammie created the Shadow Witch.

"There's nowhere safe left in Kalpania," I add. "You know it's just a matter of time before everyone has the shadow illness, but there is a cure. We can save this world, maybe even Sir Lightlee. Look at Trauen." I point to Trauen, who just climbed to the top of a high rock and is doing a victory dance. The old me would have cautioned him to be careful or told him to get down. "To live is to take chances. I'm done hiding."

Garren turns from me and starts removing Prattles' pack.

"What are you doing?" I ask.

"Ye may be delusional, but if ye're staying then so am I. How will ye find the Shadow Witch? Her castle is hidden."

"We find the Shadow Knight. We find Sir Lightlee."

CHAPTER 27

"We found him, Sir." A shadow elf, gnarled and naked save for a loincloth, clambered into the cave, his skin plastered with dried peeling clay to protect it from the blistering sun.

The Shadow Knight brushed past him. "Out of my cave before you fill it with your stench."

The elf cowered back, licking his lips and looking greedily at the Shadow Knight's canteen. "Our water runs low. 'Bring the horse,' you said, and we can refill."

The Shadow Knight growled in revulsion at the idea of the elf's filthy canteen touching the cave's spring. He pulled his hood low over his brow before stepping into the sunlight into a dry wash. "First, I tend the horse."

Outside a second elf held the halter of a large, gray stallion. Wyot. Deep in some part of the Shadow Knight his heart mourned, remembering the former beauty of the animal. "Set him free," he commanded.

The horse stepped toward him, and the Shadow Knight reached out a hand and touched his nose. For a moment he let it linger there. Then he removed the halter and tossed it to the ground. The horse pawed the sand, flies buzzing around an open wound in his foreleg; dark blood trickled down to his hoof.

"Why has he this wound?" The Shadow Knight poured a little water to clean it, and stripping cloth from his inner shirt, he bound it around the leg. Having received no answer, he looked back to the elf that had held the halter. "I said, how has my horse received this wound?"

The elf shrugged. "It was an old injury. Must have reopened."

In one fluid motion the Shadow Knight drew his sword and beheaded the elf. His body crumpled to the ground, but soon vanished. Only the black blood-stained sediment evidenced where he once stood. Turning, the Shadow Knight spied the other elf creeping back toward the cave. In great strides, he overtook him.

"The journey was long. We were thirsty. It was only a small wound," the elf babbled.

The Shadow Knight ran his sword through the elf, pinning him to the cracked ground. "The ground is also thirsty."

Turning from the hissing cry of the elf, the Shadow Knight led Wyot to the spring within the cave. He would retrieve his sword when the elf's body no longer defiled it. Then once the night offered relief from the sun's blinding rays, he would find Michelle. She sought him, but he would come to her. The shadow phoenixes disclosed her location, and soon he would lead her to the Shadow Witch. It was time for their world to end, and with it, his pain.

~ ~ ~

"Sir Lightlee was a warrior, but never cruel," Garren comments as Sammie closes the book. "It cannot be him."

Sammie looks back at Garren. "He was the Shadow Knight before."

Garren glances at me. "How do ye know that, child?"

His voice isn't unkind but verges on patronizing, but Sammie doesn't seem to notice, or maybe she's used to being doubted and not taken seriously. I make a mental note to not be dismissive toward children simply because they are children.

"Well." Sammie hops to her feet as she always does when she's about to go into a long story. "Sir Lightlee was killed in a joust and half his heart was torn from his chest. That's how he became the Shadow Knight, but because the Queen still had half his heart; he couldn't really die, because his heart was enchanted, and even the Shadow Witch can't figure out how to undo it. And Princess Taika found the Shadow Knight in the North Woods and used her powers to bring Sir Lightlee back."

As Garren listens to Sammie's tale, his face goes from skepticism to incredulity. "I see, but what ye are describing is medically impossible." Garren's voice is that of a doctor trying to reason with a difficult patient.

"But not *magically* impossible." Sammie grins and twirls her dress before running off to play with Trauen.

"Michelle—"

I raise a hand. "I know what you're going to say, Garren. Not long ago I would've agreed with you. You did hear about the joust?" I throw this out there as a guess.

"I've heard a lot of rumors about Sir Lightlee that I don't give credit to. People exaggerate when it comes to heroes. I've only known him for a year, but nothing about him leads me to believe he's immortal."

Garren sighs and leaves to tend to Prattles, I think mostly as an excuse to end our discussion. The rest of the day he engages the children in identifying various wildlife and shows them his sketches, which are quite good, but he barely speaks to me. It's a long day, and I'm restless, but I'm going to go along with the Shadow Knight's plan to find us and take us to the Shadow Witch. If nothing else, Sir Lightlee was always a good guide. I try to disguise my nervousness, but despite the autumn wind bringing in cooler temps than yesterday, I'm sweating and hope I don't stink.

We're out of options. It's either face the Shadow Witch or we may never get home. I try to drill Sammie about the Shadow Witch, so I know what to expect, but get only unhelpful answers like she has "no imagination," wants to "destroy Kalpania" and apparently stories in general, and "hates wasting time" and "people who are late." All in all, the Shadow Witch is evidently boring and punctual—real villain material. Reminds me of the college professor I had for English Lit before I dropped out.

Part of me wants to believe that a villain created by a nine-year-old will be a pushover. That I can march into her castle with my "mom voice" and make demands, but the three weeks I've spent in Kalpania tell a different story. The hopeless condition of those with the shadow illness, The Roots, and more than anything the moments I spent with the Shadow Knight show that the nightmares of a child could scare any adult. And one thing I've discovered is that anything I or Sammie has written, no matter how poorly, takes on a life of its own in Kalpania.

For dinner Garren prepares a soup made of wild rosemary and onions and the dried meat he brought with him. It's not half bad, but I'm finding it difficult to eat more than a few bites. My stomach seems to be doing cartwheels. Sammie and Trauen down theirs faster than most anything I've served at home. I notice Sammie doesn't compare Garren's soup to "zombie guts" and spends more time eating than talking for a change. But then they had three weeks of active living to boost their appetites and heaven only knows how Sammie survived on her own.

I put the children to bed even before the sun has fully set. We have no way of knowing when the Shadow Knight will turn up, and I expect our sleep to be interrupted and want the children to get as much rest as they can. They complain, of course, but are asleep in no time. Even Garren looks like he's fallen asleep. He wanted to watch for the Shadow Knight, but I insisted that I couldn't sleep anyway. The Shadow Knight wasn't likely to show up until well after sundown, I reasoned. I promised to wake him at the slightest noise.

I stand by Prattles for company and pet his nose. He nudges me and rubs his nose up and down my shirt. Searching the pack, I find a brush and run it through his mane to get out the tangles and keep myself awake. My eyes feel heavy now that the sun is fully set. Despite the restful day, I'm emotionally exhausted.

I run the brush along Prattles back and am considering putting more mesquite on the fire, when the pounding of hooves causes all tiredness to leave my body.

"Garren!" I shout, running toward him when the screams of horses cause me to spin around.

A cloaked figure sits upon a dark horse that rears only feet away from Trauen and Sammie. Prattles stands between the children and rider with his ears laid back. Hooves churn the dust around them. Prattles bites the other horse as it advances and the firelight glints off steel. I dash toward the children as they stumble from their bedrolls. Garren reaches the rider and his blade clashes with the sword of the cloaked knight. I wrap my arms around the children. They're groggy, but I think they're okay.

Garren is thrust to the ground as the stallion wheels.

The Shadow Knight slides off the beast, and his sword glistens. Blood? Whose blood? He runs his blade across one of the bedrolls to clean it before sheathing it.

Wyot stomps his foreleg, black blood oozing through the bandaged injury. The firelight flickers against Wyot's coarse coat and his head bobs toward me, his knotted mane falling across swollen eyes that are all whites and look at nothing. Pus crusts his lashes and runs down his face.

"Stay," Garren commands, scrambling to his feet and moving between us and the Shadow Knight. "Or I'll send you to the abyss."

"The physician cannot heal, so now is willing to kill?" The Shadow Knight removes his hood revealing his pallid face and empty eye sockets. The face once belonging to Sir Lightlee is sunken, almost skeletal, behind his unkempt gray beard. He steps toward us.

Garren yells and shoves his blade into the Shadow Knight's chest. Sammie lets out a startled yelp. The Shadow Knight halts and stumbles back a step, but rather than fall or cry out, he removes his cloak and tosses it across Wyot's bare back. The tip of the blade sticks out his back, and inky blood slides across its edge.

"That was unnecessarily violent," the Shadow Knight says.

Garren's face is a picture of shock. His hands shake, and he clenches his fists to steady them. The Shadow Knight drills his eyeless stare into him, and whatever horrors and lies he's communicating to Garren's mind causes his face to contort until he openly weeps. Garren falls to his knees hiding his face in his hands with great sobs.

"It's a long journey to the Shadow Witch's palace," the Shadow Knight says, turning to me, "the children should ride. I'll not have them slowing our progress. The Shadow Witch expects promptness."

I avoid his face and instead stare at the sword lodged through his torso. "We're not going anywhere with you," I say through clenched teeth. Why had I ever thought this was a good idea? Trauen peers from behind my legs, his hands clinging to my tunic.

"Mama," Sammie whispers, "do what he says. That's why we're here—to find Sir Lightlee."

The Shadow Knight turns toward Sammie's voice, but her bold face holds his dark gaze. I don't know what passes between them, but to my shock it's the Shadow

Knight that turns away. He grabs her roughly and puts her on the horse then turns to me, catching my arm.

"I believe you have my dagger."

I'd hoped he'd forgotten about that. His hands send a cold chill down my arm, and he's close enough for me to smell his sulfuric breath. I carefully avoid his "eyes" as he withdraws the dagger from my belt. Instead, I watch helplessly as he rips Trauen from me.

"Mama!" Trauen cries out, digging his feet into the dirt.

The Shadow Knight lifts him and sets him behind Sammie on the great horse.

"It'll be okay," I overhear Sammie tell Trauen as he hugs her tightly.

Garren has stumbled back to his feet. Turning to him, the Shadow Knight draws the blade from his body without flinching, but his face is a mask of anger. "I can't be killed, my friend. I've already died once. Haven't I, Michelle?" His smile reveals blackened gums. "Has she told you what she's done? What she really is?"

Garren glances at me confused, and I avert my eyes, wondering what the Shadow Knight might have told him.

Prattles suddenly groans, stumbling to his knees and then rolls to his side. Blood pools around him. Now I understand where the blood from the Shadow Knight's blade came from.

"Prattles!" Sammie cries.

Garren moves to Prattles' side. "He's bleeding out fast. I'm not sure I could save him even if I had the proper tools. Ye've condemned him to suffering." Garren directs this last sentence toward the Shadow Knight, although without directly looking at him.

The Shadow Knight tosses Garren's blade at his feet. "Then end it. Or let him suffer."

Garren picks up his sword, but holds it without confidence.

"No!" Trauen slides off Wyot, hitting the ground hard, but gets right back up running toward Garren.

The Shadow Knight grabs him, and Trauen screams and kicks and bites.

"Stop, Trauen, stop," Sammie says. "There's nothing you can do."

I run to Trauen and throw my arms around him, whispering to calm him.

The Shadow Knight drags us apart and plops Trauen back on Wyot and slaps the horse's hindquarters and motions for me to follow as he takes up the rear. Wyot stumbles into a walk with no urgency and his head hangs low. Trauen hiccups in great sobs, clinging to Sammie, who lets go of the horse's mane to wipe her nose, and I reach out to hold her hand. We leave the camp behind and darkness envelops us, and my heart breaks for Garren left to watch yet another creature die that he can't save.

CHAPTER 28

The purple moon casts a mournful light across the sands that mirror the mood of our somber procession across the desert plain. Trauen nods off, and I steady him with a hand, but with the motion of the horse, he slides to the side despite my efforts to balance him. I take him in my arms, but it's not long before I can no longer support his weight. Reluctant to wake him, I sit in a mostly sandy place free of debris and cacti.

The Shadow Knight grunts at me to get up. The darkness and his hood hide his terrible visage—that and my sheer exhaustion give me courage.

"I don't know if you remember how it is for us mortals, but we need rest."

"Please." Sammie has slid off Wyot. "We're really tired."

To my shock, Sammie takes his hand, and the Shadow Knight yanks it away as though her touch burned him.

"A short rest, then we continue." The Shadow Knight turns away and leans against Wyot's side with folded arms.

We have no bedrolls or blankets, so we huddle together in the sand with Trauen snuggled between

Sammie and me, and I wrap my arms around them both, thankful that Mrs. Weaverwhipple's garments keep in our body heat enough that we won't freeze. Sammie faces me and shivers, but her face is bold.

"Mama," she whispers, then yawns.

"What?" I whisper back.

"He's still there...inside the Shadow Knight."

I stare at her. "Sir Lightlee?"

"Yes." She draws closer to Trauen. "He tried to frighten me with his eyes, but I found him. I found Sir Lightlee and told him to not give up."

"I-I'm not sure he can be saved. He's too far gone."

"He's not all shadow," Sammie says. "That's why he can't be killed."

I reach out and hold Sammie's hands. They're surprisingly warmer than my own. "Is that why he doesn't disappear? Sir Lightlee once told me that shadow beings are nothing."

"The other half of his heart is enchanted," Sammie says. "It can't be turned to shadow."

"The ashes in the locket the Shadow Witch carries?"

"Yes." Sammie yawns. "She can't..."—Sammie yawns again.—"can't touch it."

Sammie dozes off, but I glance over to the Shadow Knight still leaning against his horse with his head bowed down, and I hope once again.

~~~

"Up," a voice growls at me, and I'm hauled to my feet by a rough grip on my arm.

I tear my arm free of the Shadow Knight and coax Trauen awake. Sammie's already sitting up blinking through the wild hair fallen in front of her face. She's going to need a haircut when this ordeal is over; I don't think any amount of washing and combing will free those tangles.

After a night of intense cold, we all need to heed nature's call, and we hike about to find some semi-privacy. Walking does little to loosen the stiffness in my
~~~

legs. A faint glow on the horizon casts an eerie light across the red sands, and the deep shadows cast by large cacti gives the desert an alien quality. Is it morning already?

We return to the Shadow Knight waiting by Wyot and tapping his boot on the ground. He hauls the children back onto Wyot and urges the horse to keep a steady pace. The morning glow only highlights the shabbiness of Wyot's gray fur and mane. I wouldn't have recognized the beast apart from the Shadow Knight. His head droops, and he stumbles at unseen obstacles, and the Shadow Knight must constantly prod him. Can the horse see anything at all? The whites of his eyes are all that remain and look grossly infected.

I compare Wyot to the Shadow Knight. Unlike other shadow beings, the Shadow Knight is restless more than listless, an angry set in his jaw. Not the temporary violence expressed by shadow beings under the witch's control, but a deep seated hatred lines his face. Could Sir Lightlee really be in there somewhere behind this mockery he has become? He could have killed Garren, but didn't. And he still cares for his horse...could he still care for us?

The Shadow Knight walks on the other side of Wyot near his head.

I clear my throat. "Why'd you let us sleep so long?" When he doesn't respond, I repeat the question.

"Anxious to meet your nemesis?" he says.

"I know the daylight brings you pain."

"You know nothing of my pain."

I take a deep breath. "Sir Lightlee, I know you're in there somewhere. You came back before. You can resist the Shadow Witch. I know you hate her."

The Shadow Knight stops and waits till Wyot's passed ahead of him, so that he comes around to my side. "Ah, Michelle," he says, "you would try to save me? Once before you encouraged me to fight for you only to die, now would you have me fight for you again?"

"I am sorry," I whisper, not daring to look into his gaze. I stare at my feet and avoid stepping on a small wildflower. "If I could get home, it would be different. I can fix this."

He shakes his head. "You do not know the enemy you face."

"I know Sammie created the Shadow Witch. She's a child with a wild imagination—she didn't mean to hurt anyone, and she meant for you to defeat the witch."

The Shadow Knight's face loses some of the hard lines. "I know. It's not her fault." He grabs me roughly on my shoulder and turns me to face him. "It's not her I blame."

He releases me and strides ahead. I involuntarily shudder.

The steep walls of a butte tower above us, the eastern side glowing red from the rising sun. Our path winds around junipers dotting the hill before the cliff face. I place a hand on Wyot to steady myself. As we draw closer, it's clear that the walls are not as seamless as they at first appeared, but are covered in ridges made by erosion and set with small caves. We head toward a dark western wall, hidden in shadow, and I wonder where we will go from there. Though I created the Great Mesa Desert, Sammie is responsible for the Shadow Witch, and her palace is a mystery to me.

A red pinnacle that had appeared to be part of the wall rises before us, and when we go beyond it, between it and the western wall is a wide crevice that leads to a great double door guarded by six shadow elves with bows. Two elves push open the doors, and the butte looms above us as we enter its bowels.

The dark halls are lit by torches that glow, not with fire, but...I look closer...electric light bulbs! We enter an immense cavern. Natural light from some opening above shines down on a modern-looking wooden door on the far end. It could be the front door of any house in our neighborhood. More shadow elves line the walls like hideous garden statues. The Shadow Knight helps the children dismount, and we leave Wyot swishing his tail in the middle of the cave, and step up to the door. A placemat on its step reads:

Be Quiet
No Animals
Absolutely NO Daydreaming

Sir Lightlee knocks, and the door opens of its own accord. The four of us step inside and it shuts behind us softly. We walk through an entryway of black and white tiles reminiscent of a chess board and into a wide room. I suck in a quick breath. It's as though we stepped into a modern living room: large, carpeted, and well furnished. The Shadow Knight points to a plushy couch where we sit, and I sink so deep that I think it will be difficult to get back up. Electric lamps light the room with a dreary amber glow and a fan spins slowly above us.

But before us is one thing you would not find in a typical living room—a great stone throne. Between us and it is a low wooden table, the sort you might put beautiful books on, but it is bare. Craning my neck, there are, in fact, no books visible anywhere. Another room to our right is behind bars like a prison. Within is a row of school desks, the old-fashioned kind, all of one piece and made of wood, except these are painted bright white. An analogue clock on a windowless wall displays the time...or would if the numbers weren't all jumbled and the second hand ticking backward.

I lean over to Sammie. "How does the Shadow Witch have electricity?"

"Solar panels on top of the butt," Sammie says.

Trauen giggles.

"It's pronounced 'butte,'" I say.

"Oh." Sammie sounds disappointed.

"Quiet, her Majesty enters," the Shadow Knight says from behind us. "All rise."

As I feared, this proves difficult as my feet don't even reach the floor. We scramble up less than gracefully. Trauen tumbles to the floor first.

The Shadow Witch enters through a door on our left that I hadn't noticed till this moment. Whatever I had been expecting, this was not it. I had supposed her to be the same sickly ashen gray as her shadow beings or perhaps green with a wart on her nose, considering Sammie created her. Instead, the Shadow Witch has a long flowing maxi dress—gray, of course—but her arms, face, and hair are like a film negative, complete with her hair and eyes having that creepy white glow to them. She is a complete inversion of a human, and it comes to mind that about a year or so ago, Sammie had become fascinated with my old 35mm camera and photography for a while.

The Shadow Witch steps up to her stone throne, flouncing her dress dramatically as she sits. Then she motions for us to sit. She taps with her fingernails on a rectangular object that looks suspiciously like a smartphone, and a shadow elf comes through yet a different door to the left, bringing in a tray. A delicious aroma fills the room. The tray is set down on the wooden table, and the elf places one mug before the witch before retreating back to the other room.

"No discussion until after our hot beverage," the Shadow Witch's voice is low and hoarse. She sips from her mug and closes her eyes.

Trauen hops down and picks up a mug.

"You won't like it," Sammie whispers.

"No talking." The Shadow Witch's brow scowls over her glowing eyes.

Trauen takes a sip anyway, burning his mouth and wrinkling his nose. "Ouch! It's gross."

"Silence!" the Shadow Witch says.

Trauen sticks out his bottom lip, plopping onto the floor.

Sammie slides off the couch, picking up a mug and handing it to me.

"Do not spill on the furniture," the witch says.

I realize why the smell is driving me crazy. Coffee! Kalpania has coffee! I savor the earthy flavor. I'd almost forgotten. "Thank you, Sammie," I say.

"Do not speak unless spoken to—"

"Shut up," I say, and Sammie giggles.

The Shadow Witch's eerie eyes almost bug out of her head, and she points a finger at me, but I interrupt whatever she's about to say.

"Let's skip the formalities. Where's the book we need? The one that will take us home."

The Shadow Witch smiles; her teeth are black. She pulls a book from within her dress. It's small; a twin to the one I have. She licks her fingers, thumbing through the pages until she finds the page she wants. She holds out the book. The Shadow Knight steps forward, taking it from her and handing it to me. Does his hand shake, or am I imagining it? I stare down at the blank pages before me.

"Oh, do you need a pen? There's one on the tray," the Shadow Witch says.

I scoot forward on the couch, nearly spilling my coffee. Setting it on the tray, I trade it for a feathered quill pen resting in an inkwell. What do I write? Sammie's tugging at my sleeve.

"What!" I say, not meaning to sound sharp.

"Mama." Sammie's eyes are wide. "Not yet. We have to save Sir Lightlee and stop the Shadow Witch first."

"It's not possible, and you know it." The Shadow Witch frowns at Sammie.

"It is, and you're a liar," Sammie answers.

"Sammie," I say, "we have to go home."

Sammie's eyes fill with tears. "But not before we save Kalpania."

"It's just a story," the Shadow Witch says, "all make-believe. None of this is real, so it doesn't matter."

"Kalpania *is* real!" Sammie rises to her feet, shouting. "It's more real than you. You're nothing."

Trauen whimpers with his hands over his ears.

"Can you all just shut it and let me think!" A blob of ink falls from the quill to the page.

"Please, Mama," Sammie begs. "You know Kalpania is real. She's trying to destroy it."

"No." The Shadow Witch's voice drips with condescension. "Your life back home is real. And real life is hard; you can't always have a happy ending. You can't live in a daydream."

The Shadow Witch's words arrest me. Still carrying the book, I step toward her throne.

"You know I speak truth, Michelle," the witch says. "You said it yourself."

Her face is a negative...of mine! "You..." my hands start to shake.

She smiles at me. "Yes, I am you. You are me."

I throw the book at her, and she shields her face with her arms. The Shadow Knight grabs me from behind and drags me to the room with the desks. I'm shoved back into one, falling over the desk and onto the floor. The desk scoots across the floor with a groan matching my own. I'm lying there in a daze, when the Shadow Knight returns with Sammie and Trauen, one in each arm, dropping them both into the room and slamming the bars closed.

CHAPTER 29

Trauen and Sammie come to my side.

"Are you okay, Mama?" Sammie says.

I sit up holding my back. "I'm fine."

The Shadow Witch walks to the bars, and I stand to meet her. "You have twenty minutes to complete those questions." She points to a desk and then the jumbled clock. "Please don't waste time daydreaming about an escape plan." She turns and walks back to her throne, refilling her mug from the pot on the coffee table along the way.

Still holding my back, I ease myself into the desk chair and pick up the paper. I don't intend to answer any of her questions, but my curiosity is piqued. The questions are written in neat cursive that could have been my own.

I raise a brow. "What do these have to do with anything?" Most of them are random questions about Kalpania's history that I can't answer because it wasn't part of my worldbuilding; the rest are unrelated math equations.

"She likes to ask questions that are *ir...irreverent*," Sammie says. "Just to bore people."

"I think you mean *irrelevant*." I close my eyes a moment and push the paper away. "Sammie, is this really what you think of me? That I'm some kind of witch that gets pleasure out of making you miserable?"

Sammie blinks. "I don't think you're a witch."

I fold my arms and look her in the eye. "The Shadow Witch looks just like me."

"Not just," Sammie says.

"You're prettier." Trauen pats my hand.

"Well…" Sammie puts her arms behind her back. "Sometimes when school is boring or you yell at me, I pretend you're a witch."

I put my head in my hand. "I don't yell."

"But I didn't mean for the Shadow Witch to be you," Sammie says hurriedly. "Sometimes you yell."

"I raise my voice."

"I love you." Trauen gives me a hug.

"I'm sorry," Sammie says.

I look up and there are tears budding in her eyes. I sigh. "I'm sorry too. I know I'm hard on you sometimes. I just want you to succeed in life."

"But only in the things you want me to do," Sammie says. "I want to be a writer like you."

"I was terrible at it," I say.

"I don't think so," Sammie says. "You made Kalpania, and it's beautiful. Why did you stop?"

"I…I guess I didn't think it was good enough." I take a deep breath. "You know what? Let's finish writing Kalpania's story, and you can help me."

Sammie's eyes light up and she smiles. I pull Sammie toward me and wrap my arms around her. "I love you, Sammie," I say. "You too, Trauen." I run my hand across his wild hair.

"I love you, too," Sammie whispers.

"Me too," Trauen says.

"Well, the good news is," I say, "if the Shadow Witch is like me, maybe I can figure out a way to defeat her. To start with"—I look down at the paper—"let's surprise her by actually filling out her 'homework.'"

"Do you know the answers?" Sammie says.

"This is my world...our world; let's do it together." I pull the short pencil from my side pouch. "Okay, Sammie, help me brainstorm an awesome history for Kalpania."

Sammie claps her hands.

"Can I help?" Trauen asks.

"Of course," I give him a hug.

Sammie and Trauen blurt out ideas, and I start scribbling them down as fast as I can. I don't know how much time we have since the clock is unreadable.

"What about the math questions?" Sammie asks.

"We'll do them last if we have time," I say.

Trauen tugs my sleeve. "It's *her*," he whispers.

I look up and lock eyes with the Shadow Witch as she approaches the bars to our prison.

"Time's up," she says.

I stand and walk over to her with a smile of my own. "Why, here you go," I say.

The Shadow Witch snatches the paper through the bars and scowls at it. "Hmm, well...let's see...writing is a bit sloppy...oops, you skipped the long division." She runs her finger along the paper. "These are all very creative answers, Michelle, but school isn't the time for make-believe."

I grab a bar in each hand. "Maybe not your version of school," I say, "but imagination and creativity enhance learning. Sammie's spelling has vastly improved since she started writing stories, and she learned how to identify insects by creating her own, and—"

"Enough!" says the Shadow Witch. "For that, you'll only get one minute to talk to Michael."

"Michael?" I'm taken back.

"Your husband," the Shadow Witch says.

"I know who my husband is," I snap. "He's here?" My mind's spinning. Has Michael somehow been sucked into Kalpania, too?

The Shadow Witch gives a sad sigh. "I'm afraid the King will not be returning. Valdisar has been in my service for a long time. The King's fleet was sunk and the seas claimed him. But I have the power to give you a moment of all that remains of your insubstantial marriage—a long distance communication." The Shadow Witch pulls out her rectangular object and taps it before handing it to me through the bars.

I stare at the object. It's not a smartphone, not exactly. It's a semi-transparent flat block of glass or, in essence, a crystal ball in the shape of a rectangle. At first, it only shimmers, but then I begin to discern a hazy image—waves breaking upon a rock. A disheveled man claws his way out of the water and upon the rock, his hands in bloody ribbons from the barnacles. "Michael!" I gasp.

He lifts his head and looks around as though he heard a voice on the wind.

"Michael, can you hear me?"

"Michelle?" he calls.

Tears spring to my eyes. "Yes, it's me."

Another wave crashes against the rock drenching him. He struggles to his feet and calls out. "Michelle! Where are you? I can't hang on much longer without you."

"I'm coming! I'll be—" The image disappears and the object in my hand changes to an opaque gray. "There soon." I finish in a whisper. My eyes burn with anger and tears run hot down my face. I meet the glowing eyes of the Shadow Witch. "Where is he? What have you done to him?"

She smiles exposing her grotesque teeth and licks her lips. "Don't you always hang up first?" She takes the crystal from me. Her fingers brush against mine, and they're like knobby icicles. "You always have reasons why you're busy or the children need your attention. After he abandoned you, doesn't he deserve the same?"

"He did not abandon me." I want to reach my hands through the bars and strangle her.

"She's a liar, Mama." Sammie breaks into our conversation.

A door slams loudly.

The Shadow Witch reels around. "Who dares slam a door? Make him open and close it ten times quietly."

The Shadow Knight marches from his corner toward the entryway and is met by Garren, weaponless, and followed by two shadow elves. "Your Majesty," one of the elves whines, "he requested permission to turn himself over to you."

"Who is this?" the witch demands.

"Only a humble fisherman from the Haven," Garren says, but he holds his head high.

The Shadow Witch takes a step towards him and frowns. "Why aren't you already my servant?"

Garren looks past her toward me. "Because I serve the Queen of Kalpania!"

"Kalpania has no queen, but a witch." The Shadow Witch waves her hand. "If you will not become my servant, then you will die."

"So be it," Garren says, "but I wish to die by the hand of my friend, Sir Lightlee."

The Shadow Knight turns his head so slightly that I almost miss it.

"There is only the Shadow Knight," the Shadow Witch says, "but I'll grant your request. Take him to the other room; I don't want a stain on the carpet."

The Shadow Knight grabs Garren by the arm and, unlocking the bars, brings him into our room and pushes him against the back wall. Garren faces him with a high chin and looks him directly in the face without flinching. The Shadow Knight draws his sword from the scabbard.

"No!" Sammie cries.

I grab her arm and Trauen's to prevent either of them from rushing in and getting hit by his sword.

The Shadow Knight stands, unmoving, still locked with Garren's gaze, which doesn't waver. Garren's jaw is set, and he pleads with his eyes, but I think not for himself.

"Behead him already," the Shadow Witch says from behind me.

"Sir Lightlee," I say, "you're a hero, not a murderer."

He raises his sword. "I have killed many." His voice is flat and fatalistic. "Our world is a story, and all stories have an end."

"And I abandon Kalpania," I say, "but this doesn't have to be how the story ends."

"We decide that end," Garren says, still holding the Shadow Knight's gaze. "We all die, but I will die as your friend."

"Ignore them," the Shadow Witch interjects. "Why would you listen to one who created you just to kill you? Who broke your heart and abandoned this world to me? I am god now—"

"You are a lie," I answer, and even as I say it, I know the true origin of the Shadow Witch. "Do you hear me, Sir Lightlee. The Shadow Witch is a lie I created when I placed my faith in myself. And when I failed, I gave up hope."

"Hope only delays the inevitable." The Shadow Knight jerks Garren down across one of the desks and rests his sword against Garren's neck, blood beads along the blade. Then he raises it as though judging the distance.

"Don't!" Sammie squeals. She tries to pull free of my grip. "Liam!"

The Shadow Knight inclines his head in Sammie's direction. "Foolish child," he mumbles. "I'm only a knight because a child imagined me to be."

"Don't you remember? You were resurrected by the faith of a child." I raise my voice in confidence. "But she is not the true hope of this world, nor am I. But there is hope. That Hope freed me when you held me in The Roots; you felt it. And He can free you too."

The Shadow Knight's fingers flinch on the hilt. He adjusts his grip.

"Behead. Him. Now!" The Shadow Witch screeches behind me.

The Shadow Knight's hand starts shaking.

Garren slowly sits up, facing the Shadow Knight, and stares into his deep eyes. "Liam, my friend. This is not who ye are."

"I have not a choice." The Shadow Knight's voice wavers.

"You always have a choice." I don't know if my words are penetrating past the Shadow Knight and reaching Sir Lightlee or whether Garren is reaching his mind. I pull Sammie and Trauen close to me.

The Shadow Knight's arm lowers and the sword clatters to the floor.

"What are you doing?" The Shadow Witch marches into the room, scooting aside a desk as she pushes past me.

The Shadow Knight starts to hum. And the Shadow Witch stops in her tracks as though she were gut punched.

Then he burst into full song. It's a harsh noise, not the sweet baritone of Sir Lightlee, but he's singing!

> "Though I may not see tomorrow
> I can do some good today
> Hope is rising in dawn's dim glow
> Darkest Night can't hold back Day."

By the last line, his voice is rich and full. He turns around, and where his eyes had been dark depths, they shine in blinding brightness. The Shadow Witch screams. Rays of light shoot from the Shadow Knight— but I can't call him the Shadow Knight now—rays stream from Sir Lightlee toward the Shadow Witch, like a black hole turned inside outwards and unleashing all the light that had been drawn into its dark depths. The

Shadow Witch cowers, covering her face and trembling. And she vanishes as a shadow dispersed by the sun, and for a moment no one moves or speaks.

"Good-bye." Trauen breaks the silence, and Sammie giggles.

Sammie steps forward and picks up a silver locket off the floor. Sir Lightlee is crouched on his knees with his head down. Sweat beads upon his brow. Sammie opens the locket, and though there is no draft, the ashes swirl through the room toward Sir Lightlee. He takes a deep breath and stands to his feet, opening his eyes— ordinary hazel eyes.

Tears stream down his face, no longer sunken and gray, but full-fleshed and filled with color, and though I can't see it, I know his heart is healed too. Sammie and Trauen rush toward him, hugging him. His dark hair falls disheveled across his forehead as he hugs them back. His beard is wild though no longer white, his face worn yet at peace. He looks very little like a great knight, but somehow very much like a hero. Garren steps forward and places his hand on his shoulder.

Sir Lightlee turns around, and he and Garren clasp hands. Sir Lightlee nods, and they're both smiling but say nothing. I think a handshake and a look is all the two friends need to mend their friendship.

Then they turn toward me. Sir Lightlee holds a hand of Trauen and Sammie in each of his. Garren steps forward and drops to one knee.

"Forgive me, my Queen. For the disrespect I have shown you."

Heat rushes to my cheeks. "Garren, get up. Maybe I'm Queen in Kalpania, but in my world I'm an ordinary person."

Garren stands. "Must be an extraordinary world from which ye come."

"It might seem that way to you. But I promise you'll find many of the same problems in my world."

"As the shadow illness?"

"Yes," I say. "Maybe it's not always outwardly visible, but many in my world have also lost hope. But what made you decide I was the Queen?"

"As I told you before, meeting a princess is not something ye quickly forget...nor meeting a queen," Garren says. "When I faced the Shadow Knight that night at the wellspring, I was faced with my own weaknesses"—Garren glances at Sir Lightlee whose face is grim—"but I also saw that he feared you, feared even this child"—he nods toward Sammie—"and then I knew the Shadow Knight believed what Sir Lightlee told us about you, the truth about our world. And I remembered your words of hope and believed."

I swallow my nervousness at the look of hope in Garren and Sir Lightlee's eyes. They are looking to me to fix their broken world, but I know this is something I can't do. I lock eyes with Sir Lightlee.

"Remember in The Roots when you told me, 'There's no god in this world.'"

Sir Lightlee nods. "You said you were 'not alone.'" His voice rasps with uncertainty as though not used in forever, and I realize this is the first he has spoken since his song. "Tell me," he says, "about this Hope. The One I saw in you."

"There is a God," I say, "and it's not me. I couldn't have created this world by myself. There's an Author in my world too, and I believe He's the true Lord of this country. I just...forgot about Him. I didn't include Him when I wrote, but Kalpania, this incredible place is His creation. I think, He just allowed me to see it—to be a part of it because I needed to grow my faith. Look to Him to heal your world."

Sir Lightlee looks past me. "I think He already has."

I turn and two elves with flawless skin and lush hair lay their weapons at my feet. The only evidence of their once sordid condition is the dirty loincloths.

"Thank you," one speaks, his voice lyrical.

"It is as though we slept," says the other.

"Yippee!" Sammie shouts. She takes Trauen by the hand. "Let's see what Kalpania looks like now!"

247

CHAPTER 30

Before I can stop them, Sammie and Trauen dash out of the Shadow Witch's house.

"There is none that would harm them," one of the elves assures me.

"Michelle."

I turn and Garren holds out a book. I take it from him and flip through the pages, which, not surprisingly, are blank and then examine the cover. It has no title, but looks much like the journal Sammie wrote in that began our adventures. It's the "telling" book as Sammie called it—the one that can get us home. The Shadow Witch must have dropped it. On a whim, I pull out its companion book from my pouch. Its gold lettering displaying the title no longer reads as *The Shadow Witch*. I hold it up to Garren and Sir Lightlee.

"I guess, in this world I'm the story," I say, running my fingers along the embossed lettering that now reads *Michelle*.

A door slams and Sammie comes rushing back, bawling.

"Sammie! What's wrong?"

"Nothing, Mama." She smiles, but fresh tears run down her face and she starts laughing. "Come see!"

I glance back, and Sir Lightlee's brow has a puzzled furrow, but Garren is grinning. Bewildered, I follow Sammie out of the Shadow Witch's house into the cavern where Sir Lightlee had left his horse. Though the stream of light from above the cave is all that lights the room, it feels brighter than before and buzzes with excited voices. Wood elves, greeting each other with pats on the back like long lost friends, fill the room with echoing laughter.

"Mama, Mama!" Trauen skips to me.

A friendly whinny greets me. "Prattles!" The dappled, gray pony trots over, nudging me, but I don't have any sugar or even words. I hug Prattles around the neck, trying not to cry myself and failing. I turn to Garren. "You saved him?"

Garren shakes his head but smiles. "It was beyond my skill. I prayed to the One that I heard ye pray to that night in hopes that He might hear me. I didn't know who He was, but I asked if He would show Himself to me and hear the cries of a lowly fisherman, for I didn't feel I could call myself a physician anymore." Garren chokes up, clearing his throat. Then he breaks into another smile—it seems he can't stop smiling. "Well, the strangest of help came that night. Three dogs, that could only be the elusive Cha-Chas that I believed to be only tall tales, and the smallest of them healed Prattles as though he'd never been injured." Garren grins at Sammie. "It was impossible by all knowledge I possess, but not *magically* impossible."

Sir Lightlee walks over with Wyot behind him tossing a shining black mane around his muscular neck. His fur glistens brilliant red as he prances into the streaming sunlight from above. Then the spirited, yet humbled horse, nudges Prattles and nickers, and Prattles gives a joyful whinny. Sir Lightlee holds out a hand with three lumps of sugar.

"'Tis a small offering," Sir Lightlee says in a husky voice.

Prattles nibbles the sugar from his hand and nudges Sir Lightlee, looking for more. The hardy pony clearly holds no grudges.

"Where'd ye get sugar?" Garren asks.

Sir Lightlee smiles. "The Shadow Witch's drink tray. I don't think she'll mind."

I look down at the books in my hands. Taking the one that says, *Michelle,* I hand it to Sir Lightlee. "I'm not sure what this book might be used for now, but I think you should have it."

Sir Lightlee takes it from me somberly.

"I-I'm sorry about the joust. Are you—?" I tap my hand over my heart.

Sir Lightlee nods. "Good as new. I suppose you will return to your country now?"

"Yes." I look at the journal I still hold. "I will write about Kalpania, about all that's happened here. But its future belongs to you and all the people of Kalpania. You must pen your own story."

"Then we have no Queen?" says Garren.

"You have a Lord, and that is all you need," I say.

"We know little about Him," Sir Lightlee says.

"If you seek Him, you will find Him, if you search with all your heart."

I call Sammie and Trauen over to me and tell them it's time to say "good-bye." While they're giving hugs, I fish out the short pencil from my pouch. I give the journal and pencil to Sir Lightlee and step back.

"It's time for us to finish our story," I say. "Sir Lightlee, will you do the honor of writing us home."

Sir Lightlee writes in the book, and I don't suppose I will ever know what it is he writes, but tears spring to my eyes as I watch him and Garren, Prattles and Wyot, and the wood elves all blur and fade in a collage of colors. And when I can see again clearly, I'm standing in Sammie's bedroom, as messy as ever, and Sammie is smiling at me between tears of her own.

"We're home!" she says, then looks around. "What about Trauen?"

I hadn't even thought about him not returning with us. After all, isn't he JJ? I look at Sammie, whose wide eyes probably mimic my own. "JJ!" I call out and run to his bedroom, expecting to find him asleep.

His bed is rumpled and empty. Sammie runs down the stairs calling JJ's name while I search my bedroom and the upstairs bathroom. Then it occurs to me to check the date and time. My bedroom clock says 10:30 and since my room is lit by warm sunlight, it must be morning. Is it the next morning? Did we pass three weeks in Kalpania in just one night? My cell phone! I'd set it on Sammie's bed right before being transported to Kalpania. Running back to her room, I search her covers and find it buried under a stuffed animal—Tony Cheesecracker of all things. The battery's dead.

I wander back to JJ's room and pick up a black stuffed dog off the floor. "I don't suppose you could tell me where JJ's gone?" Of course, I don't expect him to answer, and I toss the stinky stuffed dog on the bed. Picklefoot's definitely getting thrown in the washing machine at some point.

I kneel by JJ's bed and silently pray for help and guidance. Walking downstairs, I spot Sammie sitting on the couch. The house looks messier than I remember leaving it, and I almost imagine I smell Michael's cologne.

Sammie looks up at me. "Look, I found Peanut Butter and Jelly Sandwich the Third! He was under the couch."

By her omission, I knew she had not found JJ.

"Have you seen my keys?" I ask. With my cell phone dead, and no way to contact anyone, I think the next step is to drive to my mother-in-law's house. *Please let JJ be there,* I pray.

At the squeal of the garage door opening and the rumble of a car pulling in, Sammie and I look at each other and run to the door. We step out into the garage, but the only car is my own SUV, but who's inside? The door swings open and a man steps out with deep shadows under his eyes and an unshaven face.

"Daddy!" Sammie runs to him, almost barreling him over.

Michael! My heart cries. He's home; he's here!

Michael releases Sammie from his bear hug and walks toward me, dazed. I hug him and we both are crying, but I pull away sooner than I want to. "Michael, JJ..." How can I tell him that I lost our son?

"Michelle," he says, his voice a little hoarse. "JJ's at my mom's."

"He is?" I sigh with relief, but my anxiety returns when I see the look on his face. "Is he okay?"

"Yes, yes. He's fine now." Michael's face is an odd mixture of relief, confusion, and anger. "Michelle, where have you been! I-I'd lost hope of finding you or Sammie. I thought—" Michael breaks down sobbing.

It's unusual to see Michael cry. I hold him as his body is racked with sobs, and when he stops kissing me, I ask. "How long have we been gone?"

"Don't you know? It's been twenty-four days since you were reported missing. You didn't answer your phone; my mother found JJ alone and sick; she was frantic; the military sent me home on emergency leave."

"We were in Kalpania!" Sammie blurts out.

"What?" Michael says.

"I'm sorry, I'm so sorry," I say. "Let's go to your mom's and I'll explain on the way."

Michael's eyes dart back and forth from Sammie to me. I'm guessing he's wildly confused between my sudden appearance, and Sammie grinning like we just got back from Disneyland. How on earth am I supposed to explain to him our wild adventures off earth?

I wring my hands as Michael turns the SUV onto the main road. Twenty-four days! According to the journal I've kept that's how long we've been in Kalpania, and now I have a thirty minute drive to try to explain everything. Was it even real? It had to be, right?

Michael glances at me. "Um...what are you wearing, by the way?"

What? I look down and then at Sammie in the backseat. We're still both dressed in the silk clothing from Mrs. Weaverwhipple. At least, I know I'm not crazy. It happened. It really all happened.

I take a deep breath. "Michael, I don't know how to tell you in a way that you'll believe, but Sammie and I were transported to...to another world."

Michael's face is incredulous. He's never going to believe this. I look at the pouch hanging on my side. Even with my scraps of notes I took plus these clothes and Sammie's corroboration, he'll simply think I've lost it. Sammie's already babbling all sorts of unbelievable snippets of her adventure.

"And I found Peanut Butter and Jelly Sandwich the Third." Sammie holds up the brown stuffed dog. "And he made Trauen (that's JJ) all better."

I'm staring at my hands. I want Sammie to just be quiet; she's only going to make it worse.

"When was that?" Michael says.

I look up in surprise. "When was what?"

He licks his lips. "When JJ got better in-in Kalpania?"

I'm surprised he remembers the name. I never mentioned it, and Sammie only said it once. "Uh...a week ago." I open my pouch and flip through my notes, brushing aside fine, glittering sand from one of the pages. "Actually, exactly five days ago. Michael, the light!"

The car squeals to a stop. He almost ran a red light. Michael is usually a cautious driver, and never one to speed or zone out. I stare at him. He looks terrible, and I can only imagine what he's gone through. He looks like he did...

"Michael, I saw you on an ocean rock calling my name. I didn't know if you could hear me."

He turns to me. "It was a dream...but...so real. I had it several times, including this morning...you saw?"

"Daddy, it's green," Sammie says from the backseat.

Michael hits the gas. We're almost there. My heart is pounding.

"Is JJ well?"

Michael nods. "He was brought to the hospital with a fever and in a coma."

I gasp.

"Viral infection," Michael continues. "But the doctors couldn't explain why he was in a coma or why nothing they tried was making him better. Then five days ago his fever broke. By all accounts he was well, yet he was still unconscious."

"Oh, Michael, I'm sorry, I wish I was there."

Michael pulls into his mom's drive next to her Nissan. "Michelle, he woke up this morning, running around the hospital like a kid that hasn't been in bed for twenty-four days. Doctors were astounded. And he babbled nonstop about someplace called Kalpania, and you, and Sammie—and someone named Sir Lightlee." He raises a brow.

That's awkward.

"I came home to get clothes," he finished. "While mom brought JJ home. The doctors want to run more tests later, but somehow I don't think they'll find anything. You really were in another world?"

"Yes. You don't think I'm nuts?"

Michael raises both brows. "If you are, then so is JJ and Sammie. And perhaps me too. I'm just glad you're home."

"JJ!" Sammie hops out of the SUV and runs to JJ who's dressed in jeans and a superhero t-shirt. They grab hands and hop in circles, talking at the same time.

I sigh deeply. "Me too."

EPILOGUE

To dream is to know failure. Every mother wants to protect her child from pain, but one never achieves success without failure, and dreams never come true but through trials of pain. Without vision, hope is dead.

Some think I homeschool to protect my children from the world. Once, that might have been true. Now I homeschool so my children can dream without restrictions—so they can explore the world at their own pace and not be afraid to use the gifts God has given them.

And some days we set aside math and drive to the redwood forest to look for weaverwhipples. Our Creator has made us in His image with a desire to create. Sometimes the real world is hard, but sometimes truth can be found in a daydream.

Once, when I was young, I believed the world was as big as my imagination. Now that I've matured, I know that it is bigger. It is as big as the desires God puts on my heart, and even if I fail in the eyes of others, even if my own dreams are never realized, my hope is found in God and the work to which He has called me.

The End

ACKNOWLEDGMENTS

I want to give a word of thanks to all my early readers, beta readers, and critique partners whose invaluable suggestions and encouragement helped make this book the best version it could be. I want to thank my mother for all the time she invested in homeschooling and her example of patience for which I am still striving to achieve. I would never have had the courage to see this book to print without the support of my husband. And I owe my children thanks for allowing me to borrow from their imaginations, including the names of their stuffed animals. Of course, I want to praise my Lord and Saviour Jesus Christ in whom my hope and worth is found.

ABOUT THE AUTHOR

LEANNA RAPIER is a homeschool mom, blogger, and writer. She runs a homeschooling blog, Navigating Homeschooling, and chronicles her writing journey at leannarapier.com. Leanna grew up in the mountains of southern California where she spent her childhood reading and hoping to find her way to Narnia.

Leanna graduated with a BA in Secondary Education and taught for two years. Afterward, she joined the United States Air Force and studied as a linguist, where she met the love of her life, Stephen Zimmerman. They currently reside in Arizona where she homeschools her four children. Leanna enjoys writing fantasy novels, short stories, and poetry. When not building fantasy worlds or wrangling children, she enjoys reading, fingerstyle guitar, playing RPGs, and walking her three dogs.